An SCU team investigates a string of accidents, only to uncover a deadly and deliberate monster in this novel from *New York Times* bestselling author Kay Hooper.

In Clarity, North Carolina, the residents have fallen victim to an unfortunate series of events. Seemingly random accidents have taken the lives of several citizens in the small mountain town. But these deadly coincidences are anything but. Something is on the hunt in Clarity, and the only clue is a cryptic note given to the victims 24 hours before they meet their ends: "Wait for dark."

Sheriff Mal Gordon knows how to handle his town, but he has no idea how to handle this. Hollis Templeton and her team from the Special Crimes Unit—including her partner and lover, telepath Reese DeMarco—are called in to investigate.

But while the SCU has prepared them for the unknown, the incredible evil stalking Clarity shakes the team to its core when one of their own is targeted. Now Hollis, the "cat with nine lives," finds herself facing death again.

And this time, not even her partner can protect her . . .

continued . . .

Titles by Kay Hooper

WAIT
FOR DARK

KAY HOOPER

BERKLEY
New York

BERKLEY
An imprint of Penguin Random House LLC
375 Hudson Street, New York, New York 10014

Copyright © 2017 by Kay Hooper
Excerpt from *Hold Back the Dark* © 2018 by Kay Hooper
Penguin Random House supports copyright. Copyright fuels creativity, encourages
diverse voices, promotes free speech, and creates a vibrant culture. Thank you for buying
an authorized edition of this book and for complying with copyright laws by not
reproducing, scanning, or distributing any part of it in any form without permission.
You are supporting writers and allowing Penguin Random House to continue to
publish books for every reader.

BERKLEY is a registered trademark and the B colophon is a trademark of
Penguin Random House LLC.

ISBN: 9780515156041

Berkley hardcover edition / March 2017
Berkley premium edition / March 2018

Printed in the United States of America
1   3   5   7   9   10   8   6   4   2

Cover photograph of room with the window open by Vasilyev Alexandr / Shutterstock Images;
Photograph of red shoe by Africa Studio / Shutterstock Images
Cover design by Rita Frangie
Book design by Kristin del Rosario

WAIT
FOR DARK

PROLOGUE

It didn't seem like a big deal when Clara Adams saw, a couple of blocks ahead of her car, what looked like a child playing in the center of the road, almost directly under a streetlight. Dumb, but no big deal, after all.

Idiot kid, playing in the street. Where are the idiot parents?

She put her foot on the brake pedal, already mentally rehearsing what she wanted to say to the kid.

The pedal went all the way to the floor. And the car didn't even slow down.

Clara hadn't been going very fast since the downtown speed limit was only twenty and rose only to thirty-five in the residential areas surrounding downtown. But as she gripped her steering wheel in growing horror, her foot pumping the unresponsive brake pedal, she realized that the car was not only not slowing —it was gaining speed.

She pressed frantically at the car's horn button, but there was no response. Pushed the button for the car's emergency flashers and, again, no response. No way to warn the little boy, whom she could see more clearly now, playing contentedly with a toy dump truck. Even with no one else in sight, she tried to lower the car's window so she could yell a warning at the child. But that didn't work either. Even the steering wheel was fighting her.

As if the car wanted to run over the boy.

The needle on the speedometer inched higher, matching the blue numbers in the digital readout that were inexorably climbing as the car's speed increased.

Clara had no more than seconds to choose between horrible alternatives, and all she knew for sure was that she could not run over a child. So she used all her strength to wrench the resisting steering wheel to the right, trying to aim the car between two others parked at the side of Main Street just before the next intersection. Beyond them was a construction site, as one of the businesses set back from the street was being given a facelift.

A stack of lumber, she thought, was probably the most forgiving barrier she could see.

The car turned—but just enough to avoid the child, shooting past the opening between the two parked cars, crossing into the empty intersection, and then, engine screaming, speed increasing, plowing headfirst into the thick iron post that held the streetlight out over the lanes.

Clara never heard the awful crunch of metal or the screaming engine dying with a sputter. She never heard the car's horn begin to screech, or smelled the gasoline.

Or saw the first flickering flames.

A blessing, most said later, when word got around. That she never saw. Never knew. A true blessing.

THE LITTLE BOY stood up, holding his dump truck, and looked with a singular lack of expression at the wreck no more than fifty yards away from him. Then he turned, still expressionless, and walked away, unnoticed by the people spilling out of restaurants and the businesses that were still open, uninterested in their cries of horror, their frantic shouts for someone to call 911.

He stopped briefly on the sidewalk, an expression of confusion passing suddenly over his face. He heard the shouts and the first sounds of emergency-response people and vehicles, and looked over his shoulder to see flames shooting into the air. It was all he could see, really, because of all the parked cars and all the people.

He wanted to drop his toy and run in that direction along with everyone else, wanted to see what had happened. It looked awfully interesting, and different for Clarity, where nothing ever really happened.

He hesitated only because he had a strong feeling his ma would not be happy about him near a fire.

And now that he thought about it, why *was* he here? Hadn't he gone to bed? It had to be late, or at least it felt late, and he could have *sworn* he had gotten into his pajamas and gone to bed—

"Sean."

He didn't even have a chance to look up before a

large, heavy hand gripped his shoulder. And for an instant, things whirled and flipped inside his head, making him dizzy.

The sounds down the street died into a peaceful silence, and he realized he just wanted to go home. To go home and . . . and slip in through the side yard to the window into the laundry room, the one with the broken lock.

It was the way he always slipped in and out of the house whenever he wanted to break one of his ma's rules or just sneak out to join friends even if he was grounded.

He got grounded a lot.

"Time for bed, Sean."

Yes . . . that was it, that was where he was supposed to be. In bed. He'd leave his dump truck outside near the driveway, where his ma would expect to find it. And then he'd get back into his pajamas and go to bed.

"It's just a dream, Sean. Just a dream. You're fine. You're absolutely fine."

The soothing voice made sense, and Sean accepted the information it offered. He was asleep and dreaming.

He just needed to go get back into bed so when he woke up, he'd know for sure he'd been dreaming.

"I'm fine. I'm absolutely fine," he murmured.

The heavy hand fell away from his shoulder, and eight-year-old Sean Brenner walked away into the unusually cool evening.

He didn't look back.

ONE

"Accident," Deputy Emma Fletcher said, her tone that of someone who had convinced herself of truth.

Sheriff Malachi Gordon frowned at her. "Yeah? And how many years has Brady Nash used his harvester without getting thrown out of a closed cab and into the teeth of the machine?"

Emma winced, even though describing it, she thought, was never going to have the shock value of seeing . . . what was left of a man she had grown up knowing. Spread out behind the machine in a bloody trail of . . . shreds of flesh and jarringly white shards of bone mixed in with the ripped brown stalks and leaves of corn. Like some obscene salad.

Emma fought a sudden urge to gag and silently told herself to stop with the gross mental images.

"Well?" Mal demanded.

Grateful, she dragged her mind back to being a cop. "I don't know. A lot of years. Since I was a kid. I remember seeing him plowing his fields in the spring to plant. Harvesting in the summer and into early fall, sometimes late fall. Plowing everything under after the harvest to get ready for winter. He got older and older, but he never seemed to get any slower." She scowled at him. "Why are you staring at me like that?"

"Just wondering how long it's taken you to convince yourself this was an accident."

"All morning," she confessed.

Mal took a couple of steps back away from the front of the hulking machine until he could look behind it, at the trail of mangled and bloody cornstalks and shreds of human flesh that stretched back for at least a hundred feet.

"No sign it even slowed down."

"I noticed. And he had to have . . . He must have gone into the blades way back there, or else there wouldn't be . . . all the blood and stuff." *Field salad. People salad. Farm salad. Stop it!* She added hurriedly, "And it's a straight path; a car with nobody at the wheel definitely would have wandered left or right. Would a machine like this keep going in a straight line if it wasn't being steered?"

"No idea. I'd assume so, given ground this level."

"Even with the ruts?"

"Especially with the ruts. This machine was designed for planted fields, and they're rutted." Mal shrugged.

Emma cast about for some other question or tidbit of information she might have and came up empty. Too many questions and too little information. It was unusually cool for an August day even in the mountains; she told herself that was the reason why she had jammed both hands into the pockets of her uniform jacket.

"Safety features," Mal muttered. "Brady showed me once when I asked. The controls inside the cab. If the operator has a heart attack or something, that's what he said. A kind of dead man's switch; they tend to be on most dangerous machines. The harvester blades stop turning unless the operator is holding that one lever back—and it won't stay back by itself. They use the same sort of switch on subway trains. And even in gear, the machine doesn't keep moving forward unless the operator has his foot on the pedal."

Emma nodded mutely. That made sense. It made all too much sense.

"So why didn't it stop? It comes to that, how the hell was he thrown out of the cab? Doors are fastened securely, glass is intact. And it *did* come to a stop, here, even though the engine was still running. Even though he couldn't have been inside the cab holding that dead man's switch and with his foot on the pedal all the way down the row since the . . . trail starts way back there."

"I don't know," Emma said. "All . . . this . . . and I'm still trying to figure out why he was even out here last night, nowhere near the barns. That's what his wife said, right? That he went out to check on his milk cows late, before turning in himself, because one was due to calve, and so she went on to bed without him. Woke up hours later, just before dawn, realized Brady wasn't in bed. Not that unusual with a cow calving—until she heard the harvester, looked out her window, and saw it sitting here, headlights and the lights above the cab glaring, engine running. Their dog had been shut in the barn and was barking his head off; Brady wouldn't have left him in there if he wasn't there himself, since the dog sleeps in the house with them. Sue knew something was wrong. Knew it."

"I'm just glad she rousted Hank out of bed to check instead of coming out here herself," Mal said. "Bad enough he had to see this, and call us, and tell Sue—and then come back out and wait until we got here."

He looked over to the split-rail fence, which was more decorative than anything else and bracketed the long dirt driveway up to the farmhouse, noting that Hank Taylor, who was more of a very good friend and partner than an employee to Brady Nash, had his back to the cornfield as he leaned against the fence, gazing off at nothing. The Nashes' border collie, Murphy, sat at his side, ostensibly held by a makeshift twine leash even though the dog showed no sign of wanting to go anywhere—especially toward the harvester and its gruesome trail.

Hank, a widower who lived on an adjacent plot of land with a tidy little house just over the hill, within easy walking distance, had been badly shaken and wasn't the sort of man to try to hide it. He and Brady had been as close as brothers.

Mal walked over to the man and dog by the fence, more out of concern than because he expected to learn anything new.

"Hank?"

"That didn't happen, Mal," Hank said in a queerly conversational tone, still gazing off into the distance.

"We both know it did."

"No, I mean . . . it couldn't have happened. Machines are machines. They work a certain way, the way they're designed to work. They break down or malfunction a certain way. A machine goes wrong, you know why. But this . . ."

"I know."

"Do you?" Hank turned his head to stare at the sheriff, a frown creasing the skin between his oddly glazed eyes. "Do you understand this? Because I don't. It's . . . like something I dreamed. It's like a nightmare I can't wake up from."

"Yeah. Look, Hank, why don't you go on home? We'll have people here for hours yet, maybe coming back over days to study what happened here, and the harvester can't be moved until I give the word. Nothing here can be . . . changed, until I give the word; we'll be putting up *Police Line* tape around the whole area. I know where to find you if anybody else has questions you might be able to help answer."

Hank looked at him a moment longer, still frowning, but then nodded. "Okay. I'll . . . go tell Sue I can keep Murphy with me for a while, since she has her sister now. He's slept at my place before. I . . . don't think he wants to stay around here. The . . . smell. Stronger for him, of course."

"That sounds good, Hank. You go take care of Murphy. And take care of yourself, okay?"

"Sure. Sure, Mal. I'm fine, though. I'm absolutely fine."

Mal stood there for several moments, staring after the tall, lanky man trudging along the fence back toward the house, then slowly returned to the horror in the field and his deputy.

"Is he okay?" Emma asked.

"Are you?"

She drew a short breath and let it out in a rush. "Good point. No, I'm not okay. I'm not even close to being okay, not with stuff like this happening. First that weird car crash, then a grill exploding, and the elevator falling the way it did . . . and now this. Four people dead since the middle of July, all from accidents that shouldn't have happened. That's not normal, not for Clarity. I looked it up. The last accidental death here was from a farmer falling off the roof of his barn. Nearly fifteen years ago."

"Yeah." Mal was still frowning, brooding.

"We've been averaging one body a week, Mal."

"Tell me something I don't know."

Emma cast about mentally once again, then offered a bit uncertainly, "Maybe it isn't Brady. I mean, even if Hank seems sure, how do we even know—"

"His ring."

She blinked, glanced toward the machine, and then looked hastily away. The clearly male hand was oddly unmarked, jutting up from the bloody metal teeth of the machine from a point between elbow and wrist, fingers relaxed but not curled. And he wore a big ring on that hand, his right hand.

Emma wasn't really tempted to get any closer. "I never noticed him wearing anything except his wedding ring," she said.

"Didn't you? He never took it off." Mal brooded, still frowning. "It's his West Point ring."

Emma blinked. "He went to—"

"Yeah. Didn't want to be career military, not in the beginning, just wanted the discipline the school offered. Or needed it. Apparently he was a real hellion as a teenager, and his father gave him a choice between some kind of military training or no bail money or quiet word with the judge the next time he landed in jail for being stupid. He was smart enough for West Point, and that's where he went. Told me he actually enjoyed it, that it suited him. Served the required five years in active duty, then chose a few years in the reserves afterward rather than a military career in peacetime. There was the farm to run, but that wasn't really why he made the choice. He told me once he was almost sorry his age was never right for wartime. Too young for Vietnam; too old for all the Middle East wars since."

"I doubt Sue was sorry," Emma offered. "At least they had a lot of good years together before . . . this."

Mal nodded, still clearly preoccupied.

"What are you thinking?"

He looked at her for a moment as if he didn't see her, and then obviously brought her into focus. "My gut tells me there's something we're not seeing in all this, some kind of connection. And I'm thinking it's time we called in someone who sees a lot more weird crimes than we do."

Startled, Emma said, "Crimes? Aren't they accidents?"

"Any one of them taken alone—possibly excepting this one—I'd probably agree with you, except for one thing they all have in common. Maybe this one too, maybe not. As far as this possible *accident* goes, somebody else could have been in the cab and managed to run Brady over, and if so that makes it murder or manslaughter. Realistically, that's the only way this *could* have happened, given the way the machine operates, with the teeth pulling up, grinding and stripping what's below the machine, not above it. But nobody else was seen, and way out here they should have been. Even at night."

"Fingerprints in the cab?" Emma suggested hopefully.

"We'll print it, but I'm not expecting to find any strange prints in there. With all the crime stuff on TV and movies, only a moron would forget to wear gloves."

"Brady didn't have any enemies that I know of," Emma said.

"Me either. Never heard anything but good of him, and that was my experience with him. I certainly can't think of an enemy pissed enough to consider this as a way of dealing with his grudge or anger. And there's another thing bugging me about this one."

Emma thought she'd had quite enough of inexplicable things but asked anyway. "What?"

"Nobody heard him scream."

Emma swallowed hard, really wishing she hadn't had that sausage biscuit for breakfast, and said reluctantly, "Maybe there was no time. If he went in headfirst . . ."

Scowling now, Mal said, "What it looks like is something impossible. It looks like he was held by that one hand or arm, dangled above the blades—and slowly lowered into them. Literally fed into the machine. Slowly enough that when the blades stopped turning, only that one arm hadn't been forced in."

She eyed the distances involved, then said, "I just don't see how anyone could have done that. There's no room in front of the cab or even a good place to stand, never mind holding a full-grown man out several feet over the blades of a *moving* machine and—and feeding him into them."

"Yeah. And it's not the way the machine works. Or is supposed to work. So did somebody rewire something? Reverse the blades, the engine, something? And say that was done, how did the machine keep on operating with nobody in the seat? Was there more than one person involved? And even so, even if they managed to change the way the harvester operates and somehow feed him into it, how was his arm the only limb or other body part to survive mangling?"

Emma swallowed hard, trying to get horrific images out of her head. "I don't know anything about engines. But it seems to me it wouldn't be easy to . . . change the way they were made to operate."

"No, I don't think it would be. Hank doesn't think it would be, and he knows this machinery. Like I said, on its own, this doesn't make any sense. Along with the other . . . incidents . . . it makes even less sense. None of it makes sense."

Belatedly, Emma remembered something Mal had said. "Except for one thing. You said except for one thing all these accidents have in common. Because it's all been machines?"

"I wouldn't call a plain charcoal grill a machine."

Neither would Emma. "Okay. But you said one thing all the accidents have in common. You know something I don't?"

"You noticed the same thing. They all had cell phones, and none of their cell phones have been found."

"Well . . . except for Karen Underwood and that elevator, all the victims have been pretty much . . . destroyed. So maybe their cell phones were burned or— or shredded."

"Maybe. Maybe destroyed on purpose."

Emma blinked. "Why?"

"To hide something." Mal shoved his hands in the front pockets of his jeans and hunched his wide shoulders. "So I finally did what I should have done from the beginning. I had their cell records pulled and sent to me."

"I haven't seen them."

"No. Came in late yesterday, after your shift. And now I'll have to pull Brady's too. If I find the same thing . . ."

"What? What thing?"

"The afternoon before each of their deaths, Clara Adams, Jeremy Summers, and Karen Underwood all received, exactly at three o'clock, the same text message, each from an unknown number, probably a burner."

"What did the text say?"

"*Wait for dark*. That's all. Just . . . *Wait for dark*."

IT WAS A sort of game.

He hadn't really thought about it in those terms at first. Maybe because the first *accident* had been . . . personal. Some might call it revenge.

He preferred to think of it as justice. And if his thoughts went a little fuzzy when he thought about it at all, well . . . what was there to think about? There were steps he had to follow, a path he had to follow to . . . Well, he wasn't sure where it would lead him eventually.

But he knew he had to follow it, that path. Take each step as it came, each turn, each twist. Listen to the deep, soothing voice in his head that encouraged him when he faltered.

When the fuzziness in his mind cleared just enough to show him things that made him uneasy. Things that frightened him.

The voice was always there. To calm him. To make it all peaceful and certain once again.

Even so, he hadn't expected to feel what he had felt that first time. Watching the car crash and burn, watching the heroic efforts to rescue Clara Adams. Unsuccessful efforts.

The flames, the cries of horror. The shattering glass and smell of melting plastic and rubber. And burning flesh. Wailing sirens.

The fuzziness in his mind had retreated then, but all his attention had been riveted on the wreck. And his own excitement.

It had all been . . . unexpectedly satisfying. Even mes-
merizing. All bright colors and sharp sounds and acrid
smells. Like a dream. Like, he supposed, someone's nightmare.

Even later, when he found out that Clara's heart, apparently a time bomb in her chest from childhood due to
some defect, had stopped beating before her car struck
the pole and burst into flames, it had only diminished his
satisfaction a bit.

She had known what was coming.

She must have known. Because he had been told.

Because he'd had his instructions.

Hacking into her car's electrical system had been easy
for him; electronics were easy. A car, an elevator, a hulking piece of farm equipment. Ironically, the most difficult had been the tricky matter of arranging for a simple
charcoal grill to explode. That had taken ingenuity. That
had, if he was honest, taken more help, more instruction,
than the others.

Still, he trusted that someday his genius would be
appreciated. That was the promise. That he would be
known. That he would be famous.

But he didn't think too much about that. Because the
high he experienced wore off, and even though the fuzziness in his mind returned to soothe him, he hungered
to feel that excitement again. And again. And there was,
really, no end to the *accidents* he could arrange.

"You mustn't rush things."

The hand on his shoulder was large and heavy, and he
didn't look up. But he frowned. "Why not?"

"Everything must happen in its own time. You know that. I explained it to you."

"Yes, but . . . the whole town's shook up now. On edge. Just like you wanted."

"It's enough for now. Enough for right now."

"Why?" He heard the whine in his voice but was powerless to change that, to sound strong and certain. He never could.

"Because of the plan. You remember the plan."

"Yes, but you said I could do *her*. And I haven't yet."

"Soon. All in good time."

"But—"

"All in good time." The heavy hand tightened.

The fuzziness in his mind thickened, until it was like a fog, a chill fog he knew he would never find his way through. Not alone. For an instant he felt frightened, but then that faded, and there was only the peaceful fog, parting to show him the path he had to walk.

"Everything in its own time."

"Yes. Yes, I understand."

His list, *their* list, was a long one.

A list for justice. Because he deserved that much, they both did.

At least that much.

And once everyone knew, once everyone understood, he was certain they would agree with him.

Justice.

And if they didn't agree, well . . . he supposed the path could be a long one. With interesting twists and turns.

After all, they had time.

They had all the time in the world.

AFTER A LONG moment, and hoping it wasn't obvious that the fine hairs on the back of her neck were standing straight out and her skin was covered in gooseflesh, Emma said, "Okay, that's weird. The text is weird. Where did it—they—come from?"

"Like I said. Unknown number, no name. A burner."

"But . . . from *here*?"

"I'm not sure. Those burners can be programmed to show any number located just about anywhere for the source of the call. I haven't asked the cell company to try to give me some kind of triangulation. All I know is that every text message was exactly the same."

"Okay. More than weird. That's . . . I don't know what that is."

"Neither do I. Which is another reason I think it's time to call in outside help."

"You've already called in that expert on farm machinery to look at—this. So he can tell you how this happened?"

"More or less. I can't explain why, but something about this, about the way the blades are positioned, just doesn't look right to me, and how it apparently killed Brady sure as hell doesn't seem right. Hank knows it's wrong, but I'd rather not involve him in this part of the investigation."

"He's been through enough," Emma murmured.

"Agreed. But I don't know enough about farm equipment to know for sure something's wrong. That this death, among all the others, really does stick out as something . . . that doesn't seem possible. The way it apparently happened doesn't seem possible. So I need an expert."

"I hope you warned him," Emma said.

"As much as I could. Actually, I only had to begin talking about a harvester that killed someone; I'm pretty sure his own experience and imagination took it from there."

"Jeez, are there that many farm accidents like this?"

"I doubt like this, but wherever there's big machinery designed to cut and crush and mangle, there are bound to be accidents. He didn't seem all that surprised that a harvester could have killed someone, so maybe it's more common than we know."

"Not a kind of experience I'd want," Emma volunteered. She hadn't wanted all this experience with death, either, but that was the risk she ran in becoming a deputy. Even a deputy in a small town where nothing ever really happened.

Usually.

"No. Me either." Mal brooded, half turned so he could look out over more than half a field of corn still standing.

"Are you going to call in an outside crime scene unit? Since we don't really have one, I mean."

"Too much after the fact for the other . . . incidents. Any evidence would have been burned or else trampled on by us, the rescue unit, bystanders trying to be helpful, and God knows who else. As for this one . . . my bet is anything behind the machine or still inside it won't help us. Maybe his arm will."

Emma blinked. "His arm?"

"I don't see any bruising, but if he died quickly enough there wouldn't be any. Still, a good ME might be able to tell us something we can't see for ourselves."

"We don't really have an ME either," she pointed out.

"Apparently never needed one. None of the local doctors trained in forensics beyond the basics of being able to perform autopsies. And nobody wanted another elected position in Clarity, so they decided against having a coroner as well."

With a slight grimace, Emma said, "I've always been a little surprised we have an elected sheriff rather than an appointed chief of police."

"I'm not. Accountability." Mal's voice was wry. "The mayor and town council wanted to make sure theirs weren't the only elected heads on the chopping block if the citizens got upset enough to feel the need to vote somebody out of office."

"Especially if something like weird accidents that are maybe something else started happening?"

"Something like, yeah. So I've already called the Office of the Chief Medical Examiner in Chapel Hill."

"When'd you do that?"

"While you were waiting with Sue for her sister to come stay with her."

"Okay. Are they sending someone?"

"Apparently, docs trained as medical examiners are part of a network all over the state. More efficient that way, since being an ME in a small town like Clarity wouldn't even be a full-time job. Most of the docs with special training in forensics work in the big hospitals and medical centers, where they get plenty of varied experiences every day, and then get temporarily assigned to law enforcement agencies as needed. We got lucky; the trained doc in Asheville grew up on a big farm and specializes in deaths involving farming and other dangerous machinery."

Emma said, "That sounds fairly grisly. For a job, I mean. When's he due to arrive?"

Mal smiled faintly. "*She* is due to arrive within the next hour. Dr. Jill Easton. With an assistant, she told me, and whatever equipment and tools she believes she'll need based on my description of these . . . events."

"Will they be staying here for very long?" Emma asked tentatively.

"I don't know. I do know I want the doc to look at the other incident reports, especially the photos, in case she sees something we missed. Something only a specialist in forensics might see. And I don't know how long it'll take her—them—to get whatever blood and tissue they need from whatever happened here. Plus, she doubles up: does her own lab work onsite, in the closest clinic or hospital facility. Anything up to DNA testing, but she also sends samples to the state lab for tests and to verify her results. I have no idea how long any of that will take her and her assistant. So I've booked them into Solomon House, no departure date. Downtown might not be the ideal location, but the inn is nicer, and the motel nearest to the hospital is fully booked. Some kind of medical seminar or something."

Emma studied him for a moment, then said, "You're thinking of calling in someone else, aren't you? Not just an ME?"

"I am, yeah."

"So who are you planning to call in?"

"There's an FBI unit I've heard about. Not a lot of information through official channels, but plenty being quietly passed among law enforcement officials now that we're finally getting smart and doing more networking, sharing info or at least uploading routinely to state and federal databases like ViCAP, CODIS, and AFIS. Anyway, far as I can tell, investigating the weird and inexplicable is apparently the specialty of this unit. And they have the reputation of getting to the bottom of any situation in record time."

Emma glanced over at the hand and partial forearm jutting up from bloody blades, then looked hastily back at the sheriff. "Then I say let's call them. Before another machine or piece of equipment gets weird with one of us, up close and personal. And before anyone else gets an enigmatic text message."

TWO

Quantico
FRIDAY

Special Agent Hollis Templeton studied the last page of the fourth report, then closed the folder and rested one slender hand on the stack, long fingers drumming restlessly. Her nails were very short, the thumbnails slightly ragged due to a bad habit she couldn't seem to break, so the drumming was quiet. "I don't get it. Why call us in for accidents?"

She was a woman of medium height and almost slight build, with no-fuss short brown hair and eyes an unusual and striking shade of blue. Her face was memorable without being in any way remarkable, her emotions generally clearly visible and lending animation to her regular features.

"If that's what they are," her partner, Special Agent Reese DeMarco, said slowly, his gaze still on the open file before him. He was a very big man with wide shoul ders and an athletic build, his face coldly handsome perfection, almost as if carved in marble by a master's hand, and not a bit softened by shaggy blond hair and watchful pale blue eyes.

"What are you seeing that I'm not?" Hollis demanded, her tone more questioning than challenging. "A car accident, a guy using too much lighter fluid in his grill, an old elevator with worn brakes and controls that shorted out, and now a very dangerous piece of farm machinery run amok. All those sound like accidents. The local sheriff even wrote them up that way. He might have hedged a bit with the combine harvester thingie, which does stand out as weird, but he still can't point to anything showing deliberate intent, by the operator or someone else, to cause any of this to happen. No signs of tinkering or tampering, that's in his reports—and I assume he'd know what to look for or has someone in a farming community there or nearby who would."

"He called us," DeMarco said. "Maybe he believes something really unusual is going on, something too unusual to put into his reports. Maybe something paranormal."

"We used to be the Bureau's guilty secret," Hollis said wryly. "Now it seems everyone knows our name. And our specialty. Oh, for the good old days."

"Cops talk," her partner reminded her. "Maybe he knows what's special about this unit, or maybe he only knows that we're called in to help investigate unusual crimes, and that we're very good at what we do."

Hollis turned her frowning gaze to their unit chief,

who sat with them at the big round table in the Special Crimes Unit's conference room, a place that was seldom used by any of them for anything except occasional briefings, unless a case was local and they could actually work out of Quantico. "Bishop?"

Special Agent Noah Bishop was another tall, wide-shouldered and athletic man with an almost-too-handsome face that was made very human by a faint, wicked scar twisting down his left cheek. An odd and seemingly inexplicable streak of white hair at his left temple almost glowed surrounded by the raven black, and he possessed a distinct yet somehow unsettling widow's peak setting off his high forehead. The overall effect was both dangerous and unexpectedly exotic.

He tended to speak quietly and few who knew him could even summon a memory of him losing his temper, but since there were rarely very many secrets or even unknown characteristics in a team of psychics, most of his agents knew only too well that the calm, even reserved outer Bishop was the surface mask over very deep emotions and a great capacity for sheer danger.

An excellent unit chief and gifted profiler even without the psychic edge, he was an unusually loyal friend—and a very bad, completely ruthless, and pitiless enemy.

Bishop seldom gave this sort of direct briefing to his teams, which was clearly setting off alarm bells in Hollis, but all he said in response to her was, "In a small town with less than ten thousand people, four fatalities resulting from seeming accidents in roughly four weeks is . . . an unusual spike, to say the least. Worth investigating."

"Sure, but by us? Why?" Hollis had never been shy in questioning their unit chief.

One of the two remaining agents at the table, Kirby Bell, said tentatively, "Training assignment? For Cullen and me?" She was younger than the other agents, still in her twenties, and with her short, very red curls and big golden eyes, she could easily have passed for a high school student. In fact, she *always* got carded at a bar or whenever she ordered alcohol, something she found frustrating and most around her found amusing.

And nobody *ever* believed she was an FBI agent, no matter how many credentials she could offer as proof.

Cullen Sheridan, the final agent at the table, was nearly as tall as the other two men but less physically imposing, wiry rather than powerful, his regular features usually wearing a friendly expression and his reddish-brown hair seemingly always in need of a trim. He had an unusually deep voice, evident when he said, "It's not the first case for either one of us. Just the first we've both been assigned." He eyed Bishop from very sharp brown eyes, one brow rising. "Testing out partners?"

"I do that on a continual basis, until it's obvious a particular partnership gels," Bishop said. "Sometimes that happens quickly, even almost instantly. Other times not so much."

"You don't have to tell me I'm a prickly bastard," Cullen said, knowing only too well that it was true. Kirby was the fourth partner he'd been paired with in the last eight months.

"A characteristic true of most members of the unit, to one degree or another," Bishop said. "Male and female alike; our lives are usually difficult and if our abilities weren't the cause of that, they certainly didn't—and don't—help."

"Ever?" Kirby asked rather forlornly. She was not only the youngest at the table, but also the newest psychic. A car accident two years previous had left her in a coma for a week, after which she had emerged with absolutely no memory of what had happened to her and one more sense than she'd had before. And even though she had found real understanding and total acceptance in the SCU and was happy she was part of the unit, Bishop had had to talk her into joining the FBI.

She was a full agent only because Bishop had over the years earned the authority to recruit people directly into his very specialized unit. Even then, before they could go into the field they were required to complete the basic law enforcement courses and the physical fitness test, or PFT.

Kirby was still astonished she had passed that one.

Hollis said to her, with characteristic bluntness, "At first most abilities can be a pain in the ass, especially if you came to them recently and/or abruptly." Something she most certainly knew about, since she had developed several of them, each very abruptly, in only the last few years.

"But just at first, right? I mean, it gets better?"

"Some of it does. And some abilities are easier than others to handle. The thing is, most everybody who does get better at it does so in the field, not in the lab. Meditation exercises and biofeedback sessions notwithstanding."

Kirby said uncertainly, "So it is a training mission?"

Bishop replied, "There really aren't any SCU training missions per se, not in the field."

"He doesn't send us out on those," Hollis told both of the two newest agents. "Subscribes to the theory that new agents are best broken in by being dropped into the deep end of the pool. Even if there are sharks in the water." She returned her almost limpid gaze to the unit chief.

Bishop's very handsome face seldom showed any emotion, but when it did it was the faint scar twisting down his left cheek that was as good as a barometer, becoming more prominent and growing pale when he was in any way disturbed.

The scar remained virtually invisible, his sentry-gray eyes were intent but calm, and a slight smile curved his mouth. "But never unarmed," he said to Hollis. And then, to Kirby, he said, "Sometimes an investigation that appears simple on the surface turns out to be anything but."

"Sometimes?" Hollis sighed. "I gather you have reason to believe this is one of those with sharks in the water." It wasn't really a question.

Bishop nodded. "I spoke to Sheriff Gordon a couple of hours ago. He confirmed that he'd just received the cell phone records from the fourth and most recent victim, Brady Nash. Before he put it in his reports, he wanted to make sure one very odd similarity between the seeming accidents covered all four. It could well be the signature tying all these supposed accidents together."

DeMarco frowned slightly. "No cell phones were found at or around the scenes."

"No. And yet all four victims had cell phones they habitually carried."

"So what was on the cell records?" Hollis asked.

"The same message was texted to each victim at the exact same time on the afternoon before the night they died. From an unknown number, most certainly a burner. Location still undetermined. And all it said was: *Wait for dark*."

Half under her breath, Kirby murmured, "Now *that's* creepy."

Not really scoffing, Hollis said, "Oh, that isn't even the doorway to creepy. I'm betting we'll find stuff a lot more worthy of the word."

Wide-eyed, Kirby said, "Am I supposed to look forward to that?"

"Stop scaring her," DeMarco said mildly.

"I'm not really scared," Kirby told him seriously. "Just . . . a little unsettled. Apprehensive, I guess? I've been working on my shield and it's pretty good, usually, but if the whole town is feeling creeped out by what's happened, I'm bound to pick up on it, and that is *not* a very comfortable sensation." She was an eighth-degree empath, which meant she was on the more powerful end of the scale the SCU had developed to measure psychic abilities. And that meant she was likely to feel a great deal of other people's emotional turmoil, shields or no shields.

She had been known to abruptly burst into tears if enough of the people around her wanted to cry but were holding back.

"Word does tend to get around faster in small towns," Bishop admitted, "but I gather from the sheriff that while people are talking about the odd run of accidents, nobody has suggested it's anything else. So far."

"So how's he going to explain us?" Hollis asked. "I'd hazard a guess most people know FBI teams don't generally investigate accidents unless they involve something like a plane crash."

With a faint smile, Bishop said, "If anybody asks, Gordon plans to explain that the FBI does sometimes assist in investigating an unusual number of accidents in a small, fairly remote area. To expose our agents to . . . every type of incident."

"And he thinks that's gonna fly?"

DeMarco closed one of the files in front of him and said, "Well, he's called in an ME from the state network, so I'm betting people are already getting curious, if not uneasy."

"Great," Kirby murmured.

"This could all stop at the four victims we have now," Bishop pointed out. "Even if they aren't accidents, if someone is behind them, he or she might not continue."

"Because one of the four victims might have been the only real target," Hollis said slowly.

"The idea has been used in enough mystery novels and TV shows over the years, *and* in reality. More than one serial or mass murderer has tried to hide a single murder by killing a group of unrelated or seemingly random people. That could be the case here. It's certainly a possibility that has to be investigated."

DeMarco said, "One the sheriff would have trouble exploring fully after he's classed all the deaths as accidental."

Bishop nodded. "Exactly. We can ask questions he can't about accidents, especially using the excuse he's giving us. And if this isn't finished yet, if there's another odd accident, I doubt it'll go unnoticed in Clarity with or without our presence. People will begin connecting the dots, that's inevitable. Still, the text messages haven't become the subject of gossip or speculation publicly. At least at this point, Sheriff Gordon doesn't plan to share any of that information with anyone except his lead deputy and us."

"Which is great," Cullen said. "Unless, of course, the victims shared those with someone else before they were killed, and it just hasn't gone public. Yet. If I got a weird text message like that, it's something I might do."

"As far as the sheriff can determine, they didn't, but it's not a question he can ask outright. Not a question we can either, as long as that text remains the only commonality to link these . . . accidents. Especially if they don't stop at four."

DeMarco said, "You have reason to believe this is going to continue? Weird accidents that are anything but?" It was just barely a question.

"If, as the texts suggest, there's a killer making his crimes look like peculiar accidents, and toying with his

victims to the extent of warning them something's about
to happen, I doubt he'll stop until he achieves his goals.
Whatever those might be." Briskly, he added, "Hollis,
you have the most experience as a profiler, so you're lead.
If there is someone behind this, Gordon doesn't believe
it's a stranger; he believes a local is most likely responsible,
and I agree. Demographics for Clarity are fairly uniform,
however."

"So nobody sticks out," Hollis said. "Small towns really do suck when it comes to victimology. Too damned
many overlaps. Churches, doctors, places to shop, schools,
even jobs. Really hard to find something specific all the
victims have in common when they have *most* things in
common."

Bishop nodded. "And worse when the victims are
composed of both genders and a wide age range. An accurate profile of this unsub may be the only way to find
him and stop him, and building that profile is going to
take more than standard victimology, more than standard police work."

Hollis duly noted that he had abandoned even the
pretense of believing they were going to investigate accidents. "Which means our psychic tools are likely to play
a major role in finding this unsub," she said.

"I believe so."

Kirby murmured, "But no pressure."

"You're part of a team; we share the pressure." Hollis
sent the younger agent a quick, slightly rueful smile, then
said to Bishop, "Do we confide in the good sheriff?"

"Play it by ear. I couldn't really get a sense of whether

he knows about our abilities or simply assumes we're a specialized unit called in on crimes that don't fit the usual patterns."

"So," Cullen said, "we keep the psychic stuff low-key."

"At least until you get the lay of the land," Bishop agreed. "Quite often, these small mountain towns lean more heavily toward superstition than science, and rumors, once started, tend to run that way. Things can get ugly in a hurry. So even if the sheriff is told, he may want to keep the info to himself."

"That happens more often than not no matter how the townsfolk feel about it," Hollis said dryly. "Very few cops want to admit they turned to psychics for help."

"It does vary, though, so take your lead from him. And even after that choice is made, it goes without saying, if and when the media becomes interested in the story, they'll know only that you're FBI agents, called in to assist local law enforcement, and you stay in the background as much as possible, away from the cameras. If cornered by media, you have no comment."

"Copy that," Cullen said.

"Sheriff Gordon is expecting you. The jet will be ready to go in half an hour. The usual SUV, stocked with supplies, will be waiting for you at the airstrip near Clarity, the nav system already programmed to get you to town."

"Is it that far off the beaten path?" Kirby wondered, clearly still uneasy.

"It's that far off a major highway, and mountain roads

can be tricky, especially at night. It'll be dark by the time you reach town since night comes early in mountain valleys, but not too late, so you can meet Sheriff Gordon, get settled in, and start fresh in the morning."

Hollis nodded and got to her feet. "You're the boss. Come on, guys, let's go cancel whatever plans we may have made for the weekend and get our go bags ready."

She didn't appear to notice that her partner did not rise with the two newer agents but stayed in his seat, and if either of them thought it odd, they didn't show it.

When they were alone, Reese DeMarco, still gazing at the folders on the table before him, said quietly, "She isn't ready."

Clarity

Sheriff Mal Gordon frowned at the man who couldn't sit still in his visitor's chair. "You want to run that by me again, Joe?" he requested politely.

Joseph Cross tried and failed to not look as desperate as he felt, but he felt things strongly and this was no exception. Given that he generally wore a hunted, even paranoid expression common to men who dealt in bootleg whiskey *and* was known to have a still of his own hidden away somewhere, it was generally next to impossible for him to hide any emotions at all. "I just know something's happened to Perla. I know it, Mal."

Perla Ferguson Cross held the dubious honor of being

married to Joe Cross, and had let it be known that if a white knight would only swoop down and rescue her or, failing that, she could get her hands on enough money to haul her own ass out of Clarity, she'd lose no time in doing so.

They had been married slightly less than a year.

The betting pool on when Perla would leave Joe had been going on at the sheriff's department for on to nine months now.

Mal wondered fleetingly who had won the considerable pot but tried to keep his mind on business.

"Joe, I know you don't want to hear it, but Perla's had one foot out the door since your honeymoon, and everybody in town knows it because she talks to people. A lot. She's left you more than once, and only returned because she barely had enough money to get to the Holiday Inn out on the highway and spend a night or two."

Even though she had a well-paying job, Perla loved to shop, especially for shoes, and had an impressive collection of heels that looked good on her but were decidedly out of place in Clarity.

Joe flushed, but then the hectic color faded and he just looked anxious. "I know that, Mal, but this time it's different. Really different."

"How?"

"She didn't take anything. No bags, none of her perfumes or makeup, not the grocery money. All her clothes *and* shoes are still where they ought to be, even that stupid little dog of hers is in the house yapping its head off. I wanted to strangle the damned thing." At a look from the sheriff, he added hastily, "I didn't touch him, I swear. Left him in the house still yapping his head off."

Mal had to admit, if only silently, that Perla was unlikely to have run away without taking any of her things, most especially the little Yorkie, whose name was Felix and who went everywhere with Perla, his head sticking up from the overlarge designer purse she carried mostly to accommodate her companion. Whether or not the pooch in the bag had begun as another fashion statement very much out of step with Clarity, it had quickly become clear that Perla loved that little dog. He frowned. "Her purse?"

"Right where she always leaves it, on her dressing table," Joe said miserably.

"How long since you've seen her?"

"This morning, before I left for work. She had the day off and said she was going to start cleaning out the attic. The attic door was closed when I got home, but I went up the steps far enough to call out to her, even though I doubt she would have been up there all day. Nothing, not a sound. And the lights weren't on. There's no way she'd be sitting up there in the dark. Too creepy."

Perla and Joe lived on the outskirts of town in his family home, which sprawled with the odd architecture of an original cottage added to as necessary to house a once-growing family of varying tastes and which could boast generations of unwanted or damaged possessions in the basement and attic.

"Nobody at the bank has heard from her?" She worked there as a teller.

"No, like I said, it was her day off. But I called the bank before closing just to make sure she wasn't called in to cover somebody else's shift. Manager said nobody had seen her since yesterday."

Mal glanced out the window of his office, which over-looked Main Street, reminding himself what he already knew. It was dark. Even in August, darkness came early to Clarity, nestled as it was in a valley surrounded by mountains.

Wait for dark.

Had Perla Cross received that text at three o'clock today?

It had been dark for at least three hours.

"You waited, hoping she'd come home," he said, not really a question and not the one he really didn't want to ask.

"She always has before," Joe said miserably. "Or at least called from the Holiday Inn by suppertime to yell at me. And since she didn't take anything, I just figured maybe she'd gone to stay with one of her friends for a while. And left the dog at home because . . . well, I don't know why she would have done that. But I called every-body I knew, everybody she knew, and they all said they hadn't seen her."

The slightly sick feeling had been with Mal for a while now, and it felt worse when he forced himself to ask the question he really didn't want to ask. "Joe, did you find her cell phone?"

A blank stare greeted that question for several beats, and then Joe Cross said slowly, "It was on the kitchen island. That's another thing that made me worry. She always has it with her. Usually in a pocket or even in her hand. Always. Her and her friends, and her sisters, they text each other all day long."

"Did you check it for messages? Missed calls? Texts?"

This time Joe's flush was an ugly red, and he avoided the sheriff's steady gaze. "She—once before, I—I looked at her cell. To see who she'd been talking and texting to. And she got real mad. So she traded it in for one she could have password protected. I . . . don't know the password."

Mal glanced at his watch, calculating. The FBI team he was expecting was still probably at least two hours away, if not more. He didn't have a large complement of deputies, but there were others he could call on at need. Retired cops or just men and women with some training, military or law enforcement, people he knew and could count on to be discreet and to not lose their heads if there was real trouble.

If a search was required once it got light, there would be plenty of volunteers.

But if Perla Cross's cell phone contained that single chilling text, then Mal Gordon didn't expect to have to send out search teams. Because so far, except for the car *accident*, all the bodies, all the remains, had been found in or very near the homes of the victims.

Oh, Christ, I don't want to find another victim.

He'd had more than his fill of dead and mangled bodies in the military; once he'd taken off the uniform, becoming the sheriff of a small Southern mountain town had seemed the best way to put his training and experience to good use without all the carnage.

Especially since he'd grown up in Clarity and knew the place and the people as well as anyone, if not better.

He rose to his feet, hesitated briefly as he considered certain facts known locally, so far, only to him and Emma, then said, "One of my deputies is good with tech; maybe she can break the code on Perla's cell. I'll bring a couple more deputies and we can search the house and that big yard of yours."

"Mal—"

Since he didn't want to answer any questions now with so many rattling around in his own head, the sheriff merely said, "Let's be real sure she's missing before any of us lose our heads, okay, Joe? Come on."

Visibly baffled and even more worried, Joe Cross obeyed.

THREE

"Hollis isn't ready," DeMarco repeated to their unit chief.

"She wants to work."

"She isn't okay. Not yet."

"It's been more than six months," Bishop said, "since the investigation in Georgia."

"I know. And we both know time has nothing to do with it."

"We also both know Hollis isn't nearly as fragile as she looks," Bishop reminded him. "Not physically and certainly not emotionally or psychologically."

"Yeah. She may well be the strongest person I've ever known. But what she faced down there . . . I've seen a lot of people face a lot of demons, Bishop. I've done it myself, and still do from time to time. But what Hollis faced . . . was pure evil. Maybe what she was able to do after we found that last victim helped, being able to fight that evil on her own terms, but it was brutal. I know she follows her instincts, and so far they've guided her true, but absorbing so much dark energy the way she did, transforming it, that went way beyond anything any of us has ever done before. We don't know the short-term effects of that. And we sure as hell don't know what the long-term effects might be."

"All true."

"Being here, being kept busy with a few refresher courses, working with some of the new agents, digging into the cold case files, it's been a break she needed. A respite. No lives in danger. No stakes too high. No real pressure. Regular meals and plenty of time for sleep, whether she took advantage of that or not. And I know the visits from Maggie Garrett helped. Maybe a lot." Maggie Garrett was a cofounder of the SCU's domestic sister organization, Haven, but more importantly she was an amazingly powerful empath with the ability to heal others, to heal the wounds of the soul and the mind as well as those of the body. "Maybe all of it gave Hollis a chance to really *begin* recovering from everything that's happened to her in the last few years, including that original attack."

"I don't know if you could ever truly recover from something like that to the extent of putting it behind you, forgotten," Bishop said. "I don't know if Hollis will be able to, even with all her strength."

DeMarco didn't like to think of Hollis hurting even a little; it haunted him awake and dreaming, the nightmare of the horrific attack that had so changed her life and her self several years before. The sadistic serial rapist and murderer who, after brutalizing his victims, took their eyes, literally, and left them for dead.

Hollis had not died. She had fought incredible odds to survive, with her sanity intact. And then she had fought to see, after a medical procedure believed to be impossible. She had fought—and now she saw.

Through the transplanted eyes of an anonymous donor.

Steadily, DeMarco repeated, "I know she's had help healing. In the beginning and over all the time since. I know being in the SCU is without question the best decision she could have made, because it's the best place for her to be, where all of us to varying degrees understand what she's been through and accept her for who she is now. And I know she's strong."

"Yes. And now she needs to work."

"She's been working."

"She needs to be in the field, Reese. I can't keep her here in the nest any longer, not without risking her self-confidence. She's been showing signs of restlessness for quite a while. She's run the trainee course three times this week. And outscored all the cadets and trainees, plus three active agents."

"Do you know she's started remembering her night-mares? Nightmares about the attack that took her eyes and triggered her abilities?" DeMarco's voice was level.

"Does she know you remember them?" Bishop countered.

DeMarco didn't react to that, although he had told no one about his ability to "remember" Hollis's dreams. In a unit of psychics, few things were secret, even those some would have preferred to bury somewhere dark.

Or thought they had.

He said finally, "We haven't talked about it. Haven't talked about . . . anything personal."

"It appeared you two had made progress on that front."

"Yeah, well. She has the habit of . . . suddenly retreating, quickly, like a cat wary of being touched." He made his voice light, almost mocking. "Just out of reach. I turn around, and she isn't there anymore. Even if she is. I don't think it's a conscious thing. And I don't know if that's better or worse."

"She'll find a way through it," Bishop said.

"Will she?"

"If Hollis is anything, she's a fighter. She won't give in to the urge to hide herself from you. It may still be a battle, but she's never truly lost a battle yet. I don't believe she'll lose this one."

"Don't you? Bishop, I . . . *see* her. And she knows it. Maybe that's the one step too far. Even if most of her worst memories have been distant for years, they're still with her. Sometimes trapped in her subconscious, in nightmares she didn't consciously remember for so long. Sometimes, now, since Georgia, not distant at all. And nightmares that are no longer forgotten when she opens her eyes. Her shield is still iffy, uncertain during the day, when she's awake, but almost always down at night, when she sleeps. If she sleeps, which is usually when she's too exhausted not to. Probably why she's been running the trainee course, with no active case to exhaust her. I'm telling you, Bishop, she isn't okay."

DeMarco wasn't what anyone would have called a talkative man, not at all given to sharing feelings with anyone, but he wasn't much surprised to find himself talking so frankly with Bishop. People tended to do that, he'd noticed. Even the most unlikely people.

Bishop was looking at him steadily. "And you believe keeping her here will help her get okay?"

"I thought it would. Maybe it still will." *Because I haven't pushed even though I've wanted to, even though I'm back at arm's length in every way that counts. Because I've given her space. Because I want that to be all she needs. Time. Just more time. Not more pain, not for her. There's been enough pain, more than enough pain she's had to endure. So time. Just more time to come to terms with . . . everything.*

After a moment, Bishop said musingly, "The first time I sent Hollis out into the field I partnered her with Isabel. You know Isabel, blunt to a fault, and at the time she had no shield of her own. She was also the only agent whose psychic awakening was anywhere close to what Hollis had endured. A violent physical assault that should have killed her. And didn't.

"She didn't think Hollis was ready, barely seven months after the attack that first triggered the abilities she was more than half afraid of. Even after Maggie helped the way she does, to heal Hollis as much as possible then, to make most of the pain and trauma seem distant, even buried, so she was protected from the worst of it. So she could go on with her life. We all knew she was still adjusting, still learning to cope with more than a new career radically different from anything she'd planned for herself. But Hollis believed she needed to work and I agreed with her, even though she wasn't yet a full agent. Even though she was still adjusting to so many things, including the differences in her sight. That was . . . just over three years ago."

DeMarco frowned. "I read that case file. Hollis was almost killed."

"One of her many near-death experiences." The words might have been flip, but Bishop's tone was anything but. "And even though many of us find our abilities changed during some cases in the field, for better or worse, with Hollis, *every* investigation so far has strengthened or changed an active ability, or activated or created a new ability. Something that is unique to her."

"Is that why you keep sending her out?"

"I hope you know better than that."

DeMarco stared at his unit chief for a long moment before finally returning his gaze to the closed files on the table before him. "Yeah, I know. She didn't nearly die in Georgia, at least not literally. She absorbed and filtered the darkest energy I've ever seen, ever heard about. And even if it didn't damage her, it changed her. She's still changing."

"And you don't know what she'll be if and when she finally stops changing?"

———

"DON'T YOU SOMETIMES wish you were a telepath?"

Hollis jumped, more than a little startled, and turned her head to stare at Kirby. "What?"

The younger agent nodded gravely toward the conference room off the far end of the bullpen, its big windows clearly showing Bishop and DeMarco still talking. "I mean, it would make some things easier, right?"

Hollis wasn't much of one for backpedaling—except with DeMarco—so she didn't avoid the fact that she'd been caught staring and brooding. Even if she did needlessly fiddle with one of the straps of the compact go bag on top of her desk as she replied, "That coming from an empath is rich. Does it help *you* to know what other people are feeling?"

"Well . . . sometimes."

Figures.

But all Hollis said was, "If everybody were meant to know what each other was thinking, we'd all be telepaths."

Kirby untangled that in her mind and nodded, still solemn. "I guess so. Do you *know* what they're talking about?"

"No." But she would have bet it was about her. "Do you?" she added unwillingly.

"No, I've caught feelings from other people, so I'm pretty sure it's not my shield blocking them. They both have very solid shields, don't they? I mean, I knew Bishop did, but I've never worked with Reese before. His shield is *really* strong."

"Double shield," Hollis heard herself saying. Because that was hardly a secret and wasn't really anything personal. Was it?

"Really? I've never heard of that."

"Neither had the rest of us," Hollis said dryly. "Far as anybody knows, it's unique." Before the younger agent could ask more questions, as she showed every sign of doing, Hollis added, "Is your go bag ready?"

"Yeah." Kirby smiled a little. "Just tell me it's none of my business if I ask too many questions. I'm just curious by nature, but I don't mind being told to quit it."

Lightly, Hollis said, "Quit it."

The younger agent nodded, clearly unoffended. "Okay. I'll go see what's keeping Cullen."

Hollis nodded, and watched the petite redhead wend her way among all the desks in the bullpen to get to Cullen's desk, where he appeared to be searching through his bag for something.

Hollis kept her gaze on the other two agents, all the while concentrating on shoring up her shield.

She didn't look toward the conference room again.

WITH A FROWN, DeMarco said, "She'll be Hollis, I know that. All I care about is that whatever changes, it won't bring her more pain."

Bishop nodded, but said, "You can't stop that. Protect her from that. Trust me, I know."

"I can try."

"Yeah, you can do that. And will. It's human nature."

"But?" DeMarco heard himself ask, totally against his will.

"But she's an exceptional woman, we've both learned to appreciate that. She wasn't supposed to live, wasn't supposed to survive that first attack. All the doctors said so. I still don't know how she did, except . . . She wants to live. With a will stronger than any I've come across yet. So when her survival or that of a team member or a loved one is at stake and she has to change, has to adapt, even to create a brand-new ability because it's what she needs, then she does."

"Without even thinking about it."

"Spontaneously." Bishop nodded. "None of us know what her true limits are, not even Hollis. Maybe especially her. But all my experience tells me that she'll never be truly healed from that first attack until she becomes . . . the person she has to be. And for Hollis, that means accepting what happened to her, all the horrific memories, accepting that it didn't leave her damaged or broken. And then leaving it behind her, where it belongs."

"That isn't what she's been doing. Being brutalized the way she was . . . She kept that buried deep, Bishop, like I said, all of it. She *kept* it inside her, part of her. Kept it in those nightmares she never remembered then. Maybe it should have stayed there. Maybe that's the only way *anyone* could live with the pain of memories that horrific."

"If that were true, she wouldn't have faced them, finally and really for the first time, in Georgia."

"She didn't have a choice."

"Of course she had a choice. The Universe puts us where we need to be, but we still have free will. We can choose to leave. To run or keep running. You said yourself that she knew beforehand what she'd find behind that closed door. She knew it was a horrific, bloody message meant for her. Meant to hurt her, weaken her, even destroy her. She could have run. Nobody would have blamed her for that. She could have just turned away. But she opened the door. Because it was time for her to face what happened to her years ago, face it wide awake and unblinking."

DeMarco shook his head. "I'd love to call that New Age bullshit, but I know you're right. It's just . . . agony like that doesn't heal just because you face it. That's only the beginning. It's still a hell of a painful journey for her. And a long way to go yet."

"You might be surprised. And, after all, she doesn't have to take that journey alone."

With forced lightness, DeMarco said, "Yeah, that's what I keep telling her." *Not that it's done a damn bit of good.*

"She's stubborn. Don't stop telling her. Reminding her. That her life has purpose. That she's helping people. That we're her family. And that she isn't damaged, isn't broken somewhere deep inside, no matter what she believes."

"But she *was* damaged. Hurt so badly there aren't even words for it. I've seen career military men fall apart in battle with less severe injuries, less severe psychological trauma, doomed to spend the rest of their lives trying to cope with PTSD."

"And some never recover."

DeMarco nodded. "Some never recover. Not with therapy. Not with meds. Not surrounded by caring, supportive people who have some idea what that kind of trauma feels like. Even with all the help, too many of them take all that pain with them to the grave. And too many of them go to that grave too young."

"Hollis wants to live," Bishop repeated.

"Even if it means struggling? Even if it means suffering?"

"Even if." Bishop's gaze was steady. "'Out of suffering have emerged the strongest souls; the most massive characters are seared with scars.'"

"Khalil Gibran." DeMarco half nodded. "A quote well known among a lot of soldiers."

"Yes. I don't know if Hollis has ever heard it. You might offer it, if the timing seems right." He barely hesitated before adding, "Because she heals herself, virtually all of her scars are on the inside now."

"Virtually all?" DeMarco heard himself ask. "Even from the first attack?"

"Most of them are gone as well. But . . . She just had a complete physical, of course, in preparation to return to the field. The doctor reported there's only one scar on her entire body now."

"Do I need to know this?" DeMarco asked steadily.

"I think so. Because the scar isn't in a place where Hollis has to see it every day. Where she has to repeatedly confront trauma from that original attack. It's on her back, low down, on her left hip. An . . . almost perfect bite mark."

DeMarco shifted in his chair in a very rare sign that he wanted to protest, wanted to stop this. Or wanted to take things apart with his bare hands.

"He's dead," Bishop reminded him, still quiet. "He's dead, and Hollis helped make that happen."

"Carrying the scars he left her with."

"She helped destroy him. That matters. That's part of what's helped build that extraordinary strength of hers. That, more than the attack itself, set her feet on the path she's been following ever since, with us.

"The absolute right path for her, because Hollis has a real gift for this work, a fascination and understanding for it that can't be taught. And she has an instinct for finding and facing the sort of evil we too often face, without allowing it to corrupt her."

"Because she's seen true evil," DeMarco said. "It can never hide from her, not for long. Never deceive her."

"Yes. She also has a partner who knows far more than the average person about the trauma of war. And the demons that never quite leave us alone afterward." He paused, then added, "She's a survivor, Reese. You're her anchor, but you can't protect her from the pain. She has to get through this herself."

"I want to help. To be more than an anchor." DeMarco hadn't realized he was going to say that, admit that, until he had.

Bishop nodded, matter-of-fact. "I know. And I think

you'll be a lot more than an anchor for her. You already have been, even if she's still skittish about it."

"And when she stops being skittish? If she does?"

"Oh, she will. She's far too bright to . . . struggle for long against inevitability. Especially when she knows she's better, even stronger, with you than without you."

DeMarco frowned just a little. "And just how will she learn that lesson? We're partners; we always work together and have since you first paired us. She hasn't had to work on her own, without me, for more than a year."

"The Universe puts us where we need to be."

Beginning to feel more than a little grim, DeMarco said, "If there's something I need to know about this case, Bishop, you'd better tell me now. If Hollis is hurt in any way because of something important you're keeping to yourself—"

"There's nothing I know." Bishop hesitated uncharacteristically, then added slowly, "Just . . . something I feel."

"Not a vision?"

"No. And nothing I can put into words. Except that Hollis needs to work . . . and both of you need to go to Clarity."

THE CROSS HOME really did sprawl. By Mal's count it had at least eight exterior doors, not counting the double garage that also boasted a doorway into the house, three levels in two sections of the house, and a rather wild assortment of windows: large, small, multipaned, single-paned, circular—and at least two shaped like Gothic arches.

It had been constructed originally of brick, but over the years the other sections added had been faced with seemingly whatever material had been available or cheapest at the time: stucco, at least three different kinds of rock, two other shades of brick, and both cedar shakes and redwood siding.

It really did look as though it had been designed by an architect who'd been either on a drunken bender or high as a kite on some mind-altering substance. But no architect had designed any part of the Cross home, just different Crosses over different years with different needs and tastes, adding a room here, expanding a room there, modernizing bathrooms and kitchens. Hanging wallpaper that was dated before the glue dried, and laying carpet over the threadbare one underneath. And nobody had ever bothered to make the various additions match or complement the others.

Both overgrown shrubbery and unpruned trees too tall and too close to the house to cause anything but trouble made the place seem weirdly claustrophobic, and Mal couldn't help thinking as he, three of his deputies, and Joe walked up the winding and slightly uneven walkway to what had been deemed the front door that it was difficult to blame Perla for wanting to leave.

If she had left.

Mal had learned to trust his instincts, and his instincts told him Perla had not left. That she was here, somewhere. Added to the heavy pit in his stomach was a weird, crawly sensation in his skin that was something new in his life. And so far, it only heralded bad things.

The porch light, billed to repel bugs but surrounded by a little flock of very-much-alive moths and other insects, glowed a dim yellow that seemed more ominous than welcoming. Joe led the way inside, merely walking through the unlocked door.

Mal sighed but didn't bother commenting. Clarity was still one of those little towns where most people didn't lock their doors, even at night, and even if their houses were miles outside town and mostly surrounded by what seemed a wilderness of forests and overgrown pastures.

Joe started turning on lights and was only on the third one when they all heard a frantic scrabbling on the mostly wooden floor, and Mal found himself holding a bundle of shaking, whimpering Yorkie. The dog had literally launched himself straight at the sheriff.

"Hey, Felix," he said a bit wryly. An animal person by nature, he cradled the little dog easily, accepting with equanimity several almost frantic licks on his chin.

Joe eyed the two with a certain amount of indignation. "I never could make friends with that little brute. Swear I have scars on my ankles where he's bitten me."

Deputy Susie Dunlap, who despite her uniform looked distinctly unlike any kind of cop, being deceptively willowy and languid, with heavy-lidded brown eyes that gave her slightly angular face an oddly fascinating drowsy expression, said mildly, "Maybe you should stop calling him a brute. He's just a little dog, Mr. Cross."

"Easy for you to say," Joe retorted darkly. "*You* don't come home every day to a yapping attack."

Mal frowned. "He wasn't barking when we came in." Shifting his hold slightly on the little dog, he added, "And he's shaking like a leaf."

"He never likes it if Perla goes somewhere without him," Joe said somewhat dismissively.

Susie said, "I didn't think she *ever* went anywhere without him."

"No," Joe said. "Hardly ever." He appeared struck by that for the first time, and even more worried. "Hardly ever. Mal—"

"We need to search the place, Joe." Mal would have put the dog on the floor, but the way Felix was trembling so violently bothered him. Felix really did seem frightened, and not only of being left alone. After a brief hesitation, Mal half zipped the light Windbreaker he wore against the faint nighttime chill of even a summer night in the valley and tucked the Yorkie inside.

"Seriously?" Joe demanded.

Without responding to that, Mal said, "Joe, show Susie where Perla left her cell phone, so she can get started trying to break the password. Then you and Ray start going through the house. Lower floors first, in every section. Then head down and check the basement areas. Brent, you're with me."

Deputy Ray Marx, who didn't need a uniform to look

imposing since he was six and a half feet tall and built like the linebacker he had been in college, and who had the deep voice to match his size, seemed utterly matter-of-fact when he asked, "What're we looking for? I thought Perla had just run off again."

They all ignored Joe's halfhearted glare.

"Maybe she has, and maybe she hasn't. Let's make sure. Brent, you and I will take the upper floor and the attic. Joe, I know there are two sections, but you can get from one to the other without coming back down here, right?"

"Yeah, there's a kind of hallway between them, across from the top of the stairs. Perla calls it a catwalk, but it's not open, 'cept for a couple windows looking out the back."

"Same thing with the attic?"

"Yeah. There's only one doorway leads to the attic, and it's roughly in the middle upstairs. Closed door, but real stairs, not the pull-down kind, and there's a light switch, like I said. Plenty of light up in the attic."

"Okay. Let's get going. We'll leave the lights on in here, and all stairwell lights, but once you've cleared a room, turn out the light and close the door."

Deputy Brent Cannon, who was average height and sturdy and looked so much more like a stolid cop than any of the others he might as well have had *COP* tattooed on his forehead, said, "I was wondering how we'd keep it straight without a grid search. This place is . . ."

"Ambitious?" Mal suggested dryly.

"I was gonna say big," Brent confessed.

"Yeah. Well, let's get going. The FBI team ought to be getting to town sometime in the next couple hours or so, and I'd like to be there to meet them." None of the deputies questioned the information, or even reacted to it, except for Susie, who briefly raised an eyebrow.

They split up, with Joe and Susie headed for the kitchen and Perla's cell phone, with Ray wandering after them, and Mal heading for the main stairs with Brent close behind.

It wasn't until they were nearly at the top of the stairs leading to the second level that Brent asked a low question. "Sheriff, are you expecting to find another . . . accident . . . here?"

Mal wasn't surprised that Brent Cannon was the first deputy other than Emma to ask that question. The deputy had more law enforcement experience *and* education than most of the others, having not only graduated from Duke with a degree in criminal justice but also having nearly five years with the State Bureau of Investigation under his belt. He'd been born and raised in Clarity, but it was only the desire of his high school sweetheart and wife to move back here when she became pregnant with their first that had persuaded Brent to put on a uniform again.

Mal was glad he'd made that choice.

"I'm not sure what I expect," he confessed to Brent. "I just know I've got a very bad feeling we're not going to find Perla holed up at some motel this time."

FOUR

"I guess we checked the Holiday Inn?"

"Yeah. She's not there. Hasn't been there, according to the manager, in at least a couple of months. And I checked every hotel, motel, and B and B within a hundred miles of Clarity just to be sure. Nada. No woman with her name or description has checked in."

Brent said thoughtfully, "She doesn't strike me as the type to hide right here in the house to give her husband a scare."

"No, I would have said she wasn't. And if she's here, why is Felix not with her—and why's he scared to death? He's still shaking." Without waiting for a response to that, since they had reached the top of the stairs and were just across from the arched opening that was the entrance to the "catwalk" hallway between the two halves of the second floor, he found the light switch and turned it on.

Just outside the hallway on the stairway landing was a single closed door, and Mal guessed that was the entrance to the attic.

The hallway had some colorful scattered rag rugs along the wooden floor and two round windows with a small table and a vase of silk flowers between them, and looked as odd as the rest of the house did.

Mal gestured with the hand not still cradling the dog snuggled inside his jacket. "You head right and I'll take the left. Pretty sure that's the door to the attic out here; whoever gets done with his section first, head up to check that out. If I remember right, it's a big, open space with big windows at either end."

"*Is* there an end?" Brent asked somewhat whimsically. "I sort of get why Perla keeps running off. This place is a little creepy, and I swear it looks bigger every time I see it. I wouldn't be surprised if it grew all on its own after dark."

"Yeah, I'm sure the house plus Joe is a bit much to take," Mal replied absently, a more plainspoken response than he might have offered a different deputy.

They split up, and Mal discovered that his "section" was composed of half a dozen decent-sized bedrooms, all with a dizzying array of furnishings from different time periods. It would have taken a sizable housekeeping staff to keep a house this size as clean as it probably should have been, and neither Perla nor Joe had ever claimed to be a housekeeper; there was a layer of undisturbed dust over most everything, and the rooms held a musty odor of disuse.

Ignoring that, Mal cleared each bedroom methodically, checked out the two bathrooms—one of which had been done almost entirely in black-and-white checks, the tile walls as well as the floor, and made him feel a bit dizzy and nauseated—and found himself the first back at the attic door.

Even before Mal felt little Felix begin to tremble even more, his skin had that crawly sensation he had come to associate with finding bad things he didn't want to find. But he opened the door and flipped the light switch, more relieved than he wanted to admit when bright light spilled down the neat but plain painted wooden stairs going up.

It looked perfectly normal.

Like the others he had a small but very bright pocket flashlight, which he hadn't had to use as yet. And it remained in his pocket when he reached the top of the stairs to find the entire huge attic very well lighted by actual light fixtures, not bare bulbs. They were a peculiar mixture of styles, from a hanging wagon-wheel fixture with two burned-out bulbs to an extremely elaborate crystal chandelier sparkling as though all the crystals had been recently polished.

At some point in its history, maybe at several points, someone had taken a stab at organizing chaos, so in the right-hand section of the cavernous space, there were numerous areas where like items had been grouped together. There was a section of old trunks; at least three areas he could see that had groupings of old chairs and tables that were damaged or just unwanted or out of fashion; a wild assortment of mirrors reflecting light and odd bits of things in all directions since, they were leaning up against two different walls; and a long metal clothes rack on wheels from which at least thirty or forty empty picture frames hung by their corners.

But Mal barely noticed all that, because as soon as he reached the top of the stairs, two things drew his attention. One was the fact that he could feel a fairly strong breeze that told him both of the big windows up here were undoubtedly open; given their placement at either end of this main section, they could and did provide a strong crosscurrent of air.

The other thing that drew his attention was a single red high-heeled shoe only a few steps straight out from the top step of the stairwell. It was one of Perla's. Mal recognized it because she had worn it the previous Sunday. To church.

It was a very bright red shoe, and shiny, almost metallic, and it was sitting there as if someone had merely stepped out of it and walked away. The toe was pointing to the left.

Felix let out a low, eerie sound that was as close to a howl as a little dog could ever make, and Mal automatically used his free hand to try to soothe him. The odd, mournful cry ended in a little whimper, and it was a sound Felix continued to make.

Mal could feel the hair standing up on the nape of his neck, even though every sense told him he and the dog were alone up here.

He turned slowly to the left, looking down a sort of

walkway between stacks of boxes and bins lining this side
of the attic. He could see the big casement window; one
side was opened all the way inward, the other side almost
all the way, filmy sheers placed there at some point flut-
tering as the breeze blew into the attic.

In front of the window and about three feet in was the
second red high-heeled shoe, its toe pointing toward the
window.

Bracing himself against whatever he was going to find,
Mal walked slowly between the tall stacks of boxes and
bins, absently still using his free hand to soothe the little
dog, who continued to whimper miserably.

The cop in him noted that the floor was surprisingly
free of dust, far more so than the bedrooms on the floor
below. He also noted that the window seemed to have
simply been opened, not forced in any way. No panes of
glass were broken, and there was no sign in front of the
window that any sort of struggle had taken place, not so
much as a scuff mark.

Just those two red, empty shoes.

The lights in the attic didn't extend to the outside,
and as he reached the window, Mal could hear leaves stir-
ring in one of the tall trees just outside.

He reached into his pocket for the flashlight and, being careful not to disturb the shoe or the placement of
the windows, he used his elbow to hold the sheers to one
side and pointed the flashlight out at the big oak tree.

At first, for a single baffled instant, he thought she was
just up in the tree for some reason, far higher than was safe

up here nearly at the roofline. He almost called out to her, because she was facing him, and her eyes were open.

But then he saw. Then he understood. That Perla Cross hadn't climbed up in the big oak tree, and she hadn't somehow climbed out of this window to reach it.

He supposed she might have slipped, but even as the thought crossed his mind, he was dismissing it. Because it wasn't a case of had she fallen or was she pushed.

Perla had been *hurled* from the window into the tree.

Because it would have taken that much force to impale her on at least six thick limbs, their ends deliberately sharpened into rough, now bloody wooden spears.

HE ARRANGED THE candles carefully, murmuring under his breath the Words he needed. He expected the FBI to arrive at any time, expected *her* to be one of them because he could feel her getting nearer, and he had to be ready, he knew that all too well. Ready for everything, but especially ready to protect himself. Ready to hide himself.

She was powerful.

She was more powerful than anyone realized.

Especially her.

So he had to be ready. He had to have power to spare, far more than he'd needed so far. And power of a different kind, really. Because she had a nose for Dark, and he couldn't afford her figuring out what was really going on in Clarity before he was ready for her.

She was the only one who might have the ability to stop him before he was finished. And he couldn't have that.

He could conjure a smokescreen or two, he knew that. He had discovered almost from the beginning that he could do that. It was, actually, easy to lay down smokescreens. To give himself more time. To keep them, to keep *her* occupied with . . . trifles. With unimportant things.

Confusing, unimportant things.

He lit the candles one by one, this time speaking the Words louder, the cadence of his voice rising and falling. Old, old words. Ancient words, in a language few if any would have understood.

Here, at least.

But even here, in this isolated little town with its modern technology and its dedicated sheriff, even here there was someone listening to the ancient words, someone who understood.

Someone who offered him power, power few of the pitifully weak minds around him could even begin to imagine, much less comprehend. Power . . . and control. Everything he needed to achieve his goals.

Of course, there was a price. There was always a price. *Everything worthwhile has a price.*

Yes. Yes.

Still chanting, but this time softly, he reached to his right and unwrapped folded silk to reveal a sheathed dagger. It was old, the symbols carved into its bronze handle worn almost smooth with much time and use, and cryptic to anyone who didn't understand. He picked up the sheathed dagger and held it aloft, almost as an offering. He laid it down directly in front of him, then reached to his left and picked up a bronze goblet carved with similar cryptic symbols.

He set the goblet carefully in the center of the design drawn in chalk, in the center of the circle of candles.

He picked up and unsheathed the dagger slowly, laying aside the sheath. The blade revealed was gleaming silver, darting out sharp, bright little shafts of candlelight as he turned it this way and that.

He closed his eyes, still chanting, gripped the handle in his right hand, and closed his left over the blade.

In a single smooth movement, he drew the blade of the dagger from his fisted hand.

Holding his still-closed fist above the goblet, he watched thick scarlet blood drip into its cup, his chanting still smooth and without interruption.

In his right hand, the silver blade was bloody for only a few moments, and then seemed to absorb the viscous stuff, leaving the blade pristine and gleaming once more.

He finished his chant, bowed his head, and closed his eyes in a few moments of reverent silence. When he lifted his head and opened his eyes again, it was to see that the goblet, too, had absorbed the blood offering.

His offering had been accepted.

He opened his fist and watched as the thin red line across his palm slowly disappeared.

There was always a price for power. Always. This time, he was happy to pay it.

Next time, it would be a price demanded of someone else.

"I SENT JOE back to the station with one of my deputies," Mal told the four agents standing in the entrance hall of the Cross home. "It was all we could do to keep him from going up there and seeing for himself, but . . . That's not a memory he needs." He couldn't help but eye the younger-looking of the two women, wondering if it was a memory she could do without as well.

"It's okay, Sheriff," the little redhead said to him, clearly in response to his glance. She had been introduced as Agent Kirby Bell. "I'm tougher than I look. And I've seen more than you might expect."

He had a feeling that was true, despite her big, seemingly innocent eyes. But he also read tension in her face and in the slightly stiff way she held herself, so he doubted she was as calm as she otherwise appeared.

"Well. I'm just sorry I had to call you all straight out to see this without even a hello. But since it's the first . . . crime scene . . . that's been undisturbed, I figured you'd want to look it over before it gets disturbed. I thought you'd have time to settle in tonight, but . . . all I know for sure is that this was no accident."

He drew a deep breath and let it out. "I've got the ME I've had in town—Dr. Jill Easton—finding out whatever she can without disturbing the body. She's qualified as a crime scene tech as well as an ME, and brought all her equipment with her, so I got lucky there. We've never needed a CS unit. Her assistant and one of my deputies set up big work lights at that end of the house, and last I checked she was up a ladder to get as close as possible to the body. It's . . . a pretty grisly scene."

"No doubt about the cause of death?" the other woman, who had introduced herself as Hollis Templeton, asked, her unusual blue eyes very intent.

"No, I don't think so. The doc wanted to check to see if she'd been knocked out or something first, but since her eyes are open, I'm betting she was wide awake and aware when she was thrown into that tree."

"Sheriff—"

"Mal, please."

She nodded. "We're all pretty informal too." They looked it, casual in jeans and light jackets. They could have been just ordinary citizens—except for the guns three of them wore on their belts and a glimpse Mal had caught of a big silver gun in a shoulder holster worn by the larger of the two men. "First names suit us fine. And if anybody forgets, 'Agent' works too."

"Good enough."

"Are you sure she was thrown from inside the house into that tree?" He had briefly explained how he'd come to find this victim and where, as much to warn them as anything else.

"You'll see for yourselves when we go upstairs but, yeah, I don't see how it could have been done any other way. At the same time, I don't see how it could have been done *at all*. It's almost like somebody had a catapult up there."

"But no signs there was anything like that?"

"No. And I had two of my deputies search the entire attic just in case something had been hidden among the junk up there. No joy. There isn't even a fucking scuff mark in front of the window. It's like somebody incredibly strong just lifted her off her feet and threw her." He frowned. "Left her shoes behind, but in two different places. I have no idea what that means."

Hollis said, "We should definitely see her before the body is moved. Oh—what about her cell phone?"

"It was here, left on the kitchen island, but password protected. I sent it back to the station, where it can be examined a little better. I have a couple of deputies good at tech going over it now. And even if they don't find anything, I've sent in a request for the cell records. We should have them by morning."

"You expect to find that text, same as before?" The question came from the very powerful blond man standing behind Agent Templeton, a man whom Mal had instantly recognized as another military veteran. The one carrying a very big silver gun in a shoulder holster barely concealed by his black leather jacket. Reese DeMarco.

"Yeah, I do," Mal admitted. "Even though there's no way in hell anybody could mistake this for an accident. She was murdered. And while solving that and finding her killer is of course vital, I also need to know how this was done *and* what it means in relation to all the supposed *accidents* we've been having up till now."

"This could be a one-off," DeMarco offered. "Somebody taking advantage of the string of apparent accidents and hoping this death would be lumped in with the rest. Have you cleared the husband?"

"Well, technically no, there hasn't been time. But aside from the fact that he wouldn't have the physical strength to do it, Joe isn't at all a violent man. In fact, the major problem Perla—his wife, our victim—seemed to have with him was his inability to even stand his ground when she felt like a fight."

He saw Hollis lift an eyebrow at him.

"Look, I know how it sounds, but she was just . . . like that. Not mean or violent herself, but she came from a local family known to express themselves pretty much at the top of their lungs. I've been called out for domestic disputes to one Ferguson home or another by disturbed neighbors just to find two or three of them having a spirited political debate. It never escalated to violence, not even the milder sort."

"No chance he finally had enough and snapped?" That question came from the fourth agent, a tall but wiry, tough-looking man who had been introduced as Cullen Sheridan.

Mal shook his head. "I don't think so. I don't think there's anything in him *to* snap. He's never shown any signs of violence, and I've pretty much known him his whole life. He works as a mechanic and he's a good one, but he also runs bootleg whiskey and is rumored to have a still of his own somewhere on this property or up in the mountains."

"Wouldn't that sort of lifestyle make him more volatile?" Hollis asked.

"There used to be a lot of violence associated with running whiskey and making moonshine, but these days the ATF has too much on their plate to worry about a small-time lawbreaker like Joe, and it's not like he has competition in the area, violent or otherwise. It's mostly a lot of trouble with very little benefit, and as far as I've been able to determine, Joe is the only one still bothering. I've never been able to catch him red-handed but, honestly, I haven't tried that hard. In the general scheme of things, it doesn't seem much of a crime to me."

DeMarco said, "Did it seem much of a crime to Joe Cross?"

"I'm guessing he considers it more of a sin than a crime, especially since his mother had him in church every time the doors opened for the first fifteen years of his life. When she died, he kept going, every Sunday at least, not that I can see any sign it's changed him much."

Mal shrugged. "Bootlegging just isn't exactly a booming business down here, and that's even more true of making moonshine. The days of bootlegging being profitable enough for violence and territorial disputes are long past, like I said. I'm not even sure anybody who buys the shine from Joe is over twenty-one; it's the sort of thing kids do on a dare or for a goof, but since you could use the stuff to strip paint, I doubt many are drinking it. At least not more than once."

"So he isn't making much money," Hollis ventured.

"I seriously doubt it. His family used to be famous—or infamous—as bootleggers, but that was generations ago. He's probably making no more than pocket change, if that. Earns more as a mechanic." Mal shook his head. "I think Joe keeps it up because his family did, and he's the last of them. More habit than anything else, just like going to church is habit. He has a paranoid streak, not surprisingly, but his response to that is flight, not fight.

"Perla wasn't happy in the marriage, she told anybody who'd stand still to listen that much, but she wasn't the least bit afraid of Joe. And far as I know, she's never been seen with any physical signs of abuse, certainly no hospital visits, and that was never a complaint she shared. Since she shared everything else . . ."

"Everything?" Hollis asked wryly.

"Oh, yeah. I know way more than I ever wanted to about what happened—or didn't happen, as the case may be—in the matrimonial bed. I don't think Perla even recognized that there were private areas of our lives most of us keep private. She sure as hell never seemed to have any boundaries of her own." He shrugged. "You're welcome to question Joe yourselves, of course, if you can get any sense out of him."

"He's in shock?" Kirby asked.

"Pretty much. In tears, and he wasn't faking. However Perla felt about him, Joe pretty much worshiped the ground she walked on. That was a big part of why I made sure he didn't see Perla and got him out of here quick as I could. Told my deputy to put him in the break room at the station and have somebody stay with him. He's the last of his family—which, as you can see, was once a very large one to need this house—but I'm betting Perla's kin will look after him, especially her sisters."

"Even though she wanted out of the marriage?" Hollis asked curiously.

"They always liked Joe. I think most of them figured once she had a baby she'd settle down and probably be happy enough. At least, that's the sense I got."

Hollis shook her head briefly, as though pushing aside something to be dealt with later. "At least one of us will probably want to talk to him. In the meantime, maybe we'd better see the crime scene so your ME can finish her work."

"This way."

The red high-heeled shoe at the top of the stairs caused the agents to pause briefly, studying its position and the small yellow crime scene marker that bore a number 1.

"Like I said, Dr. Easton brought along her CSU markers and equipment," Mal offered. "And her assistant seems to be her photographer. It's pretty clear this is not their first rodeo; they both know what they're doing and they seem to work well together." He paused, then added, "For the record, the only prints on the shoes are Perla's."

"You printed her . . . out there?" Kirby asked. "In the tree?"

"No, her prints are on file. She works—worked—for one of our local banks, and they fingerprint employees as a matter of company policy."

Hollis, who was still leading the others, looked from the shoe near the stairs down the long hallwaylike space to the distant window. The work lights outside provided no more than a glare from this angle, but the distance was clear.

"I see what you mean about the shoes," Hollis said. "It's like she just stepped out of this one and kept walking. Would she have done that? Chosen to go barefoot up here?"

"I don't know, maybe. The floorboards are old, but smooth, almost polished; she wouldn't have worried about splinters. But I'd be more comfortable considering that as a possibility if both the shoes were together."

"Yeah, that would make more sense. But if her killer is the same one responsible for the texts to your accident victims, he might have placed the shoes deliberately. Maybe a sign to law enforcement. Or maybe he just likes games."

"If this is him being playful, I don't want to see him being mean," Mal said steadily.

Hollis half nodded, her expression a bit wry, then gestured a clear invitation for the sheriff to keep leading the way, and all the agents followed him toward the window.

The red high-heeled shoe in front of the window also had a crime scene marker beside it, numbered 2. The sheriff and agents all stopped rather than going past the shoe, studying that rather than looking at the window and what lay outside it.

"It's a good four feet from the window," DeMarco said. "And close to twenty-five feet from the other shoe."

Hollis was studying that distance, but it was Cullen who said almost casually, "I think you were right, Hollis. The shoes were placed, very deliberately."

"Pointing the way to his victim?" Hollis said without looking at him.

"That's . . . what it feels like to me," Cullen replied.

"Mocking?"

"I'd say so. Mocking law enforcement. And maybe mocking her vanity. I don't know what she was like in the privacy of her home, but however much Mrs. Cross loved shoes, I think we can all agree these weren't really the sort of shoes anyone would wear to clean out an attic."

"So he knew her." It was almost a question, and Cullen replied to it in the same casual, matter-of-fact voice.

"Pretty sure, yeah. Though maybe only well enough to know about shoes being her vanity."

"What she showed in public."

"Something so obvious, sure."

Mal had been more or less fixated on this whole scene since he'd first come up here to find Perla, not really seeing or thinking about the details so much as the overall extremely violent and grisly situation, but in that moment he had the sudden feeling that there was a conversation going on that he was no part of, that the words he was hearing meant things beyond what they seemed to mean.

It was a very weird feeling.

But the funny thing was that he couldn't remember even mentioning to any of the agents anything about Perla Cross's obsession with shoes.

FIVE

"He's certainly stopped all pretense of these being accidents," Hollis said thoughtfully.

"Assuming it's the same unsub," DeMarco said.

Hollis looked at the sheriff, her brows lifting. "From what we read on the jet, my impression was that Clarity had little if any violent crime in its history." It was only partly a question.

"It's a peaceful little town, usually," Mal answered. "Until these . . . accidents . . . began, we hadn't had a death not disease or age-related in about fifteen years. And crimes are definitely on the milder side. Some vandalism usually traced to high school kids trying to be badasses when they aren't. An occasional burglary attempt that never ends well for the perp."

"Dogs?" Hollis said.

Mal nodded. "Just about every house has at least one,

especially the outlying farms and ranches that use work-ing dogs. We've had on-again, off-again drug problems with some of the older kids, and that's usually what sparks the half-assed burglary attempts."

"Dealers?"

"Not in town. As far as I can tell, the few kids that I know are using meet up with dealers in the next county over. Even so, we don't have hard-core junkies. The schools and the parents in Clarity are extremely proactive when it comes to drug or alcohol abuse, so any kid lean-ing that way tends to get help before the problems get too bad. The guidance counselors at the high school and middle school both got extra training on how to spot problem kids, what kinds of problems they likely have, and what to do in order to head off worse trouble. So far, it's worked pretty well."

It was Hollis's turn to nod. "No real criminals to speak of. So, chances are pretty damned good that who-ever did this to Mrs. Cross is also behind the supposed accidents, assuming they're also murders."

"I can't see Clarity having two killers operating at the same time. In fact, I can't see there being one. Except . . ." He gestured toward the window still several feet away from them.

Hollis glanced back at her fellow agents, then moved forward just a few steps, skirting the red shoe, far enough to see outside.

Mal, watching her closely, didn't see her expression change except that her features tightened a bit. Other-wise, her gaze was simply intent.

"I see what you mean," she murmured. "Hard to imagine how that could have been done by just one person, even an exceptionally strong person."

DeMarco stepped forward as well, his gaze even more dispassionate as he studied the body of Perla Cross impaled high up in an old oak tree. "The limbs were hacked to points beforehand," he noted. "So premeditation."

"Yeah. And it took time, because it was carefully done; we didn't find any wood shavings on the ground below, not a single chip." Mal wasn't looking at Perla's body. The sight had, he suspected, been permanently imprinted on his brain when he had first found her. "Also no signs of a ladder or anything else to show how a person got up that tree with a saw or hatchet or whatever the hell it was he used. We may see more in daylight, but I'm not counting on it."

"So he wants you to know this was deliberate and not an accident, but doesn't want to leave anything behind to point to him." She looked at DeMarco, frowning. "Four accidents and now this? A simple escalation, or something more? It seems like an awfully sudden change in his MO."

"Maybe he wanted more attention."

"Maybe, but . . . With most of the accidents, he could have been nearby, watching it happen, watching the response. Getting off on the tragedy he caused, either when it happened or afterward. Except maybe the elevator, that one kind of sticks out as being more isolated."

"Actually," Mal said, "there were quite a few people present when that elevator failed. The tallest building in town is eight stories, an office building holding, among other things, our main bank. The bank takes up more than half the ground floor, with most of the rest taken up by the building's lobby, housing the elevators and a short hallway with public restrooms.

"There's a big open space on the top floor, a sort of ballroom where local businesses and charities host board meetings, seminars, corporate meetings, fund-raisers— and where quite a few wedding receptions have taken place. Great views through floor-to-ceiling windows, and a restaurant specializing in catering one floor down."

Hollis waited, watching him.

"Double elevators in the very public lobby, with one of the cars larger to serve as a freight elevator when necessary; it creaks and groans like crazy, so most everybody takes the other elevator, designed for passengers. Ironically, it's the one that failed."

"With only one person inside?" Hollis said.

"The lobby was full of people because they'd been upstairs decorating for a planned wedding reception. Large group of friends and family helping out, partly because cost was an issue, I think. As to what happened, the way I got it was that Karen Underwood realized she'd forgotten her purse and went back up alone in the elevator while a number of others in the party waited in the lobby. The elevator car got almost to the top floor, paused . . . and then it dropped."

"No emergency brakes?" DeMarco said.

"According to the elevator company I had out there the next day, all the brakes failed, never even partially engaged. One of the guys was convinced there had been a small explosives charge set off, but even he admitted there was no evidence of any kind of explosion, and our fire chief agreed with him. Not that there was a whole lot left of the car by the time it fell eight stories and onto a concrete base."

Mal paused, then added evenly, "When the car crashed on the ground level, the doors were partially blown outward. Nobody in the lobby was hurt, but . . . they saw. The car had dropped so suddenly and with such force that Karen Underwood got tossed around like a rag doll. By the time the thing stopped, it did look like a bomb had gone off in there. Karen . . . Part of her skull was crushed, and her neck was broken. There was a lot of blood." He paused again, then finished, "She was the bride-to-be. Her fiancé was in the lobby."

HE WAS BOTHERED more than he wanted to admit that Joe had managed to bring the sheriff out to the house so quickly and in the darkness. In the night. Joe had moved too quickly, reacted too quickly.

Too uncharacteristically.

And that had not been part of the plan.

Joe was his. Joe was . . . controlled.

Or so he'd believed.

Joe was . . . Joe needed a lesson, he thought. Joe needed to *remember*. Not speak of it. Never speak of it.

But remember.

As long as he remembered, as long as he had to live

with the memory of what had been done and why, he would be unable to do anything else to disrupt the plan. His was a weak mind, and there was always the possibility of breaking something weak.

If one knew just where and how to apply pressure.

Besides, there were others.

He had spent a great deal of time selecting. Preparing all his tools. And in deciding to use the night. He wanted the darkness to be a thing, of course, that was part of the plan. Night was perfect. Because people were more afraid in the dark.

And because it was more difficult to see a threat coming.

Even so, he had worked hard on this particular scene, going back and forth several times from the Cross home to the curve in the road where an overlook less than a hundred yards away presented a spectacular view of the valley. And where in daylight it would have been impossible to miss Perla Cross dangling like a fly in a spider's web, especially once he had carefully trimmed back some of the tree limbs, and since she was a vivid redhead and would in addition likely be wearing her signature bright red, either the blouse or the cropped pants she flaunted all over town.

He thought the sight would have drawn quite a crowd.

A shocked and horrified crowd.

Would have. But instead of making the rounds of local motels looking for Perla until it was too late to do anything else, Joe had gone straight to the sheriff.

Considering the matter, he supposed he should have

thought less about Joe's paranoid and easily panicked nature and more about how well he knew his wife. Or, at least, how familiar he was with all the signs of Perla running off.

Either way, the timing hadn't worked out as he'd planned. He was surprised to find that angered him. But since he had long ago learned to use constructive outlets for his less positive emotions, he chose to channel the power of his anger into something that would both repair the rent in the pattern caused by Joe—and teach him a clearly necessary lesson.

Joe had been taken away by the police, but Joe lived here, had lived in this place his whole life, so the energy of his spirit—such as it was—was stronger here.

He had his supplies ready. Because one never knew, after all, when they would be needed.

And he'd had to be very cautious getting into position. There were entirely too many people milling about, but the house really did sprawl, and once they'd checked the perimeter as best they could in the dark, most of the people were either inside or else grouped fairly closely together near the tree.

The slope of the roof was a bit of a bother, but all the lights around the other side meant this was his only option. And he was nimble, his balance good. The backpack contained everything he would need, and he set about his task immediately.

He drew out the fat piece of chalk, blessed it, and carefully drew out the Symbol on the asphalt shingles. His eyes had adjusted to the darkness; his lines were straight and true. When that was done, he again blessed the chalk and put it away, then began setting out the candles, one by one, blessing each as it was placed precisely as it should be.

That done, he sat for several moments, head bowed. His own blood had sufficed before, but he knew this ritual required more. Because Joe had to be either punished or else better controlled.

And because *she* was here.

He had felt her the moment their dark vehicle left town, and had spent precious minutes shoring up his protection so that she would not, could not, become aware of him.

It all had to unfold as he had planned, one step at a time.

The goblet was in its special pocket in his backpack, wrapped as always in respectful red silk. He folded away the gleaming cloth to reveal the cup. He drew it out, held it aloft, chanted softly for a few moments, then placed it reverently in the center of the Symbol.

He reached for his backpack again, pulling out the dove, beak and legs taped and wings bound to its body so that it could neither struggle nor make a sound.

Well, it made a sound, a terrified little sound.

But he pushed that out of his mind. Sacrifices had to be made, he had known that from the beginning.

And he was strong enough to make those sacrifices.

He placed the dove very carefully so that it was draped across the wide mouth of the goblet that was in the center of the circle provided by the candles.

In the center of the Symbol.

He drew out the silk-wrapped dagger, held it aloft while he chanted softly. Then he unsheathed the gleaming blade.

It was a pity.

He liked doves.

He spoke the words, and then cleanly sliced through the neck of the dove, watching as its warm blood dripped into the goblet.

No one was ever going to forget what he had done.

No one would ever forget him.

Ever.

HOLLIS WINCED AS much at the image her imagination had conjured as at Mal's description of what had happened when the malfunctioning elevator had killed Karen Underwood. "That almost sounds . . . staged. I'm sure you checked into the backgrounds of the victim and her fiancé?"

"Yeah. No violent exes on either side. In fact, they'd been sweethearts since grade school. A local romance story everybody knew. They were completely devoted to each other but waited to finish college and get their careers started before they married. Went to the same college, shared a condo here just half a block from that building. Neither one had life insurance. Why would they? They were young and healthy." He heard a tinge of anger in his own voice and made an effort to control himself.

He hated senseless deaths.

"So nobody benefited financially from Karen's death. And I couldn't find a whiff of any other sort of motive."

"Hey, Sheriff—can I get her down now? It's a little awkward trying to examine her in this damned tree." Dr. Jill Easton's voice was brisk and matter-of-fact. And fairly close to the window, since the top of her ladder put her up high enough to see inside the attic.

Hollis took another step closer to the window and said, "You got plenty of pictures, Doctor?"

"It's Jill. Or Doc, if you want to be more formal. And, yeah, we got shots from every angle." She seemed perfectly comfortable on the ladder, even with the close proximity of the horrifically impaled body of a young woman.

"I'm Hollis Templeton, FBI. Just Hollis is fine." She turned her head to look at the sheriff. "I don't think we need to keep the body in place, Mal. Unless there's some reason you want to?"

"Hell, no." He leaned far enough to be able to address the medical examiner. "Do you need any of my guys to help, Jill?"

"At least one, with muscle and not too squeamish. Two would be better. We'll need to hold the body in place while we saw off the limbs behind her."

Mal didn't know which thought he found more upsetting: pulling Perla's body off the limbs impaling her, or leaving them in her body as she was removed from the tree.

Hollis glanced at him, then turned to face her team.

"We might as well go through the house while we're out here. I'm sure Mal and his deputies found whatever there was in the way of evidence, but there may be signs of behavior we need to take note of. Especially if this killer knew Mrs. Cross."

"It's mostly empty bedrooms on the second floor," Mal said. "Longtime empty, if I'm any judge. They lived pretty much on the first floor, and that's where the master is. Can't miss it. It's the one with the huge closet with a shoe store inside."

"So shoes *were* her vanity," Hollis said.

"Yeah," Mal answered, then added, "but you didn't need to know her personally to get that. These red heels are fairly tame compared to some she wore just shopping on Main Street."

"So no help in narrowing a suspect list."

"I wouldn't think so. Look, I'm going to go get a couple of my guys and help Jill get the body out of that tree. You guys need anything from me to help you go through the house?"

"No, we have flashlights and gloves," Hollis replied. "It won't take us long, especially if they spent most of their time on the ground floor."

"Okay. I'll come back in after we've helped the doc. I don't plan to let Joe come back here anytime soon, so we'll probably just lock up the house when we're done. Unless you think I should post a deputy to stand guard."

"Doubt you'll need to. But if we find something, we'll let you know."

"Good enough." He headed for the stairs, wearing

the determinedly calm face of a man about to do something he would have very much preferred not to do.

Hollis looked after him for a moment, then lifted her brows at her partner.

Answering the silent question, DeMarco said, "He picked up on something but wasn't sure what when Cullen was talking. Then he spent a few seconds trying to remember when he'd told us about Perla Cross's obsession with shoes. It distracted him a bit, but I couldn't tell if his reaction was negative or positive."

With a slight grimace, Cullen said, "Damn, the shoes. I felt it so strongly I didn't think twice about saying it. It really is a verbal minefield, trying to relay information you picked up psychically."

Despite being alone in the attic, they were all keeping their voices low.

"Well, let's keep it up for the time being," Hollis said. "Whether he's open to psychic abilities or not, Mal is definitely shaken by what's been happening in his town. He's bound to be more concerned about that than any momentary distractions from us. So as far as he and his deputies are concerned, any information we can offer without a solid basis we'll base on behavior. We're all profilers."

Kirby said, "I haven't even taken any of the courses yet."

"Sheriff Gordon doesn't have to know that." Hollis smiled briefly.

"He knew downstairs you were tense," DeMarco told Kirby, not unkindly. "Didn't try to figure out why, just assumed even his brief description of this crime scene hit you harder than you wanted to let on."

Kirby drew a breath and let it out slowly. "Well, except for the ME out there, and probably her assistant, the others are pretty damned freaked out. I'm just guessing, but I don't think many of his deputies were all that suspicious of the so-called accidents before tonight."

"Probably not," Hollis said. "And this is not the sort of crime scene you can keep quiet, not in a town this small. It probably would have been worse if her body had been discovered in daylight, but I'm still betting a pretty accurate description of how Mrs. Cross was found will be all over town before breakfast."

"Great," Kirby said with a sigh.

"You're doing fine," Hollis told her. "And looking so young is just another tool; use it. People who look at you don't expect a trained fed, far less a highly trained and psychic fed. It's an ace up your sleeve. Just concentrate when you can, but try not to close up completely. You never know when what somebody's feeling might be the key you need to point us in the right direction."

Kirby didn't look too happy to hear that but merely nodded, and it was Cullen who asked Hollis the obvious question.

"So that's the three of us; have you seen any spirits?"

"It's an old house, and a lot of people lived here."

"That wasn't an answer," he observed dryly.

With a slight shrug, Hollis said, "I've caught a few glimpses. Not the victim out there, but others. They're hanging back, though, sticking to the shadows. I get the sense nobody has anything they feel the need to share with the living."

"Even if they saw Mrs. Cross murdered?"

"Even if. Though I'm not entirely convinced they always see what's going on outside their own realm, especially those who died a long time ago. I think they see most living people the way most living people see them— the flicker of a shadow caught out of the corner of their eye."

"They never help point the way to our killers, do they?" Cullen mused.

"No, not in my experience. I have encountered a few helpful spirits over the years, but in other ways, leading me to a clue or some other information I needed." She glanced back over her shoulder as the sounds from outside the window intensified, then added, "Let's go through the house and see if we pick up anything. Cullen, you and Kirby take the second floor. Stay together. Reese and I will take the main floor. We'll meet back up in the foyer."

"Copy that."

As the other team made their way down the stairs, Hollis stopped at the top, near the single red high-heeled shoe, and stared down at it with a little frown.

But DeMarco didn't believe it was the shoe that held her so motionless. He waited a moment, then said neutrally, "We're assuming the attic was thoroughly searched. Big place. You want to start up here?"

"We wouldn't find anything." Her voice was matter-of-fact. "The whole floor's been mopped; I can still smell it. Probably one reason why both big windows are open, and have been for hours. To help disperse the smell. He used bleach."

DeMarco was only a little surprised he hadn't smelled anything until she spoke. He could smell it now, very, very faintly.

"He spent a lot of time here," Hollis said. "A lot of time. And not just tonight, killing her."

"Is that what's bugging you?"

"I suppose." Her frown deepened, and without looking at him she said steadily, "Something else, though. I just got this funny, flashing image of a goblin or gargoyle crouching on the roof. Just a flash. It's gone now, and I can't seem to bring it back."

"This roof?"

"I don't know. It flashed by too quickly for me to tell. Just a . . . creature in the dark, on a roof, crouched and waiting."

"It is a horrific crime scene," he said after a moment.

"We've seen worse."

"True. You think what you saw was real?"

"How could it be real?"

Dryly, he said, "We've both seen stranger things that were real."

She looked at him, finally, her smile twisting. "True enough. I don't know if it was real. If it was real, I don't know if it was something in the past, something right now, or something to come—except I'm not a seer. Not supposed to be clairvoyant. As a matter of fact, I'm not supposed to be anything that would show me the image of a goblin or gargoyle. I don't know if it was symbolic. In fact, I don't know a whole hell of a lot about that. Or about any of this."

"We just got here," he said.

"Yeah." Hollis stepped around the red shoe and started down the stairs, her gaze no longer meeting his. "We just got here."

Frowning a little himself, DeMarco followed her.

SIX

They made their way to the main floor, and it wasn't until they reached the bottom of the stairs across from the front door that DeMarco said, "Your shield's holding up pretty well. You saw the spirits in the house anyway?"

Since her shield was relatively recent and had, like so many of her abilities, developed in a single instant when she'd badly needed it, and because she'd spent most of her time at Quantico since that case, they hadn't yet really field tested her new shield.

That had been one of the reasons for her restless need to get back out into the field. Because she needed to learn all she could about this new ability, how strong it was—or how weak.

Whether she could trust it to protect her.

"I'm not broadcasting?" she countered, pausing briefly to look up at him.

"Not so much. Though I admit I haven't been trying to read anybody; the sheriff has absolutely no shield, so I could hardly help picking up a lot of what he was thinking."

"I doubt he'd be comfortable with that, assuming we decide to confide in him." She had taken exam gloves from the pocket of her jacket and was pulling them on.

Taking note of that, DeMarco said, "The sheriff and his deputies missed some evidence?"

"Probably not, but he said himself they were just doing a general search of the house until they found the victim. I doubt they did much searching after that. We don't know if the killer was lying in wait for Mrs. Cross or just walked in while she was up in the attic, but he definitely spent some time here, outside and inside." She frowned.

"What?" her partner asked.

"I just don't understand the escalation. Until this murder, every death could have been an accident. I gather the harvester was least likely to be, since there were safeguards to protect the farmer, but still a possible accident. Even a likely one. How do you go from seeming accidents to a . . . brutally clear murder? More importantly, *why* do you? If it *is* attention he's after, you could argue that the first two accidents gave him what he wanted. Not just the accidents themselves, the violence, but the horrified onlookers. He could easily have been among them, getting his jollies. The car crash happened downtown, and the grill explosion was during a neighborhood barbecue. Plenty of horrified witnesses to both. The elevator too, it seems."

"But the farm accident and this scene had no civilian witnesses," DeMarco agreed. "Both were farther out from town in fairly isolated locations, and few other than law enforcement and the ME saw the aftermath. Nobody really witnessed what happened the way they did at the other accident sites, at least not here. And the sheriff said the farmer's wife didn't see what happened to her husband, thankfully."

"So what changed?" Hollis mused. "Did he plan the escalation for some reason we don't yet know, deliberately? Did he . . . throw the farmer into his harvester because he couldn't make the killing work any other way, and got a taste for hands-on?"

"Some killers do develop that way, more or less."

"Yeah, but on the jet we theorized he might be a symphorophiliac, getting off on the horror of staged accidents or disasters, and that almost always includes extra jollies from watching the aftermath, the reactions of onlookers, and you have to be fairly close for that. These last two deaths were pretty damned private. Granted, there isn't a lot of research on symphorophilia because it's so rare—for which I'm thankful—but it's a very specific condition. A very narrowly focused need. If that were driving him, the first three deaths fit, but these last two don't. And that means the profile is wrong."

"It was only a preliminary working profile," DeMarco reminded her. "Based on what we had, it made sense."

Hollis sighed. "But now we start over."

"We haven't checked into our hotel or unpacked," he said, stating the reminder dryly. "To say it's early days would be an understatement."

"I know. But if he even had a cooling-off period, that's over. He's moving awfully fast. The farmer was killed sometime during the night Wednesday; Mrs. Cross was killed sometime today, Friday, presumably after dark. I don't know about you, but I'm expecting a not-very-peaceful weekend."

"Good point."

"So let's go through this house and then regroup, see if there's anything helpful here. If not, we go back to town, toss our bags into our hotel rooms, and then get set up in whatever space the sheriff has found for us. I don't think settling in and catching our breath is much of an option, much less a good night's sleep."

"You're probably right."

Hollis nodded. "There are no obvious signs of a struggle down here, but if this is where they spent most of their time, we need to check out every room. And Cullen needs to, since he's the clairvoyant. He may pick up something both of us would miss."

DeMarco nodded and followed her toward a hallway that, in a logically laid-out house, would have led to bedrooms; in this house, there was really no guessing what they might find.

But that wasn't what was occupying Reese DeMarco's mind. He had seen his partner, he believed, in just about every imaginable situation and quite a few no one sane could have predicted. He had seen her amused, mocking, exhausted, gleeful, angry, humorous, sarcastic, briskly professional, vulnerable, guarded, shocked, angry, and almost unspeakably hurt. He had seen her face evil without flinching, and he had seen her channel the darkest of energies using her own body and soul, transforming them from negative to positive without allowing them to harm her.

He had not seen this Hollis Templeton.

She wasn't so much guarded as she was . . . distant. Not in the personal sense he'd felt these last months, although he was still very conscious of that distance between them. No, this was . . . something else. She was cool, methodical, professional, matter-of-fact, watchful and supportive of the newer agents. Seeing everything and asking all the right questions. In fact, she was displaying every necessary trait for an outstanding SCU team leader.

And that was fine. That was, in fact, very good.

Except that DeMarco had the uneasy feeling that Hollis was hiding something, especially from him, and he had no idea what that could be.

All he knew was that his instincts were screaming a warning that whatever it was, it was bad. Very bad.

SHERIFF GORDON HAD provided the agents a surprisingly comfortable space, what was clearly a little-used conference room just beyond the station's bullpen and across from his own office. There was an oval table with eight chairs, a conference-type landline telephone in the center of the table with clear speaker capability plus a built-in power strip for any other devices being used, a computer station with very new equipment set up on neat desks facing each other on either side of the door, and two clear evidence boards set along the wall that separated this room from the bullpen.

That wall held windows looking out on the bullpen, currently hidden by discreet blinds, and a couple of exterior windows actually offered daylight and, according to the sheriff, a nice view of part of the valley and mountains looming not too distantly.

And between the two big windows, a large flat-screen could serve as both a TV and, if needed, a monitor.

There was even a compact kitchenette tucked into a little alcove off to one side—and the coffeemaker was already bubbling.

"Well, I've certainly worked in worse places," Hollis said, clearly pleased as she looked around.

"I've lived in worse places," Cullen said dryly. "Smaller, too."

"I can't take the credit," Mal told the agents. "The sheriff before me held the job for more than fifteen years, and this building was pretty much rebuilt on his watch. Both he and the town council saw the future as being prosperous and the population of Clarity growing, and designed accordingly. I have half a dozen offices we don't use, and a garage downstairs that's more than sufficient for our vehicle maintenance sharing the space with eight holding cells and three interview rooms." He paused, adding dryly, "The town drunk has his own cell and leaves his pillow here on the cot."

Hollis looked at him, brows rising in faint amusement. "Just like Mayberry."

"Yeah, it pretty much was, before all this began happening." He looked tired, which wasn't really surprising.

Hollis hadn't had much of a chance to study him until now, but she liked what she saw. He was about forty, she guessed, his thick hair once black but now peppered with gray which, along with his rugged features, gave him a distinguished air and one of authority. He had level gray eyes and a deep, calm voice, and she thought he was likely a popular sheriff, good at his job.

She also thought the job had cost him at least one marriage and pretty recently, since there was still a very faint pale line on his left hand where a wedding ring would be worn. He didn't strike her as the type to discard his ring if he'd been widowed, but divorces could be mean. Or just . . . weary.

"I don't know if you all plan to settle in here tonight or wait until tomorrow," he was saying, apparently oblivious to her focused attention, "but I'd advise you go ahead and check into Solomon House and get a decent meal tonight either way. Their room service is breakfast to midnight, and from the restaurant next door to the hotel, which is actually pretty good."

He looked at his watch and frowned. "Damn, it seems later than ten. Anyway, the restaurant serves up till midnight, and after that if you want food your choices are limited to convenience-store snacks or fast-food burgers and tacos."

"At least we have options." Hollis looked at the stack of files Kirby had just placed on the conference table to join two other tall stacks already waiting for them, plus the laptop case and tablets Cullen had brought in from their SUV. She was debating silently, torn between the common sense that told her they should rest when they could and the growing uneasiness she hadn't been able to shake since they had first arrived in Clarity.

"I vote for food, and sooner rather than later," Kirby said, following that by saying a bit wryly, "I'm betting the doc will have crime scene photos and even an autopsy report by sometime in the morning, and I don't think I'll have much of an appetite after that." She had very definitely *not* looked at the body of the latest murder victim, preferring to put off that horror as long as she could.

The sheriff nodded. "Yeah, what information we have now is probably all we'll have until morning. Whatever's in Jill's reports on the first four crime scenes, which even she admits don't tell us much more than we already knew from the little left behind. And we have those cell phone records I requested."

Hollis gestured slightly toward the two tall stacks of files on the table. "Your reports?"

"Yeah. The original reports you've already seen, plus witness statements, whatever background info I could reasonably get from the friends and family of the victims, and the in-person interviews we conducted after each of the deaths. I'm hoping something in all that will help you at least figure out what it is we have here."

He paused, then added, "I'm no profiler, but any cop would know that these last two deaths being so close together is not a good thing."

"No," Hollis said. "Not good at all."

"THERE WAS NOTHING else you could have said," Miranda Bishop reminded her husband and partner quietly. "No real way to warn them when we don't even have a vision to point us in the right direction." She was a tall, strikingly beautiful woman with raven-black hair she tended to wear casually pulled back and electric blue eyes, and her habitual loose sweater and jeans did little to conceal a centerfold figure that turned heads wherever she went.

It was also extremely informal wear for Quantico, but nobody ever gave her grief about it.

Bishop shook his head slightly, though not in disagreement. "We have five teams out on cases, every one of which appears, at least on the surface, to be far more dangerous than the killer in Clarity. So why do I feel such a sense of dread about *that* case, that investigation?"

Matter-of-fact, Miranda replied, "Maybe because Hollis is there. The investigations she's involved in virtually always turn out to be more deadly than we expected. It's her first time back in the field since the case in Georgia. And . . . even a cat with nine lives eventually runs out of them."

"Maybe." But he was still wearing a rare frown.

"And maybe because of what happened to Dante," Miranda added quietly. "You can't keep blaming yourself for that."

"Why not? Robbie still blames me." One of their newer agents, Robbie Hodge had been born a psychic, so her control over her telepathy and the strength of her shield were two very important attributes that made her an excellent SCU agent. And neither of those precluded her very human ability to make her feelings plain to anyone who cared to look.

"Dante was her partner," Miranda said. "Robbie cares about people in general; her loyalty to a partner is bound to be strong. It's only been a few weeks, and the first time she's ever had to kill. Or help kill. She needs more time, that's all. As much to accept the power of her own abilities as to forgive us."

"She acted in self-defense. What was my excuse?"

"A monster," Miranda answered simply. "You hunt monsters. We hunt monsters. Evil thrives when good people do nothing to stop it. So we do our best to stop it. And all too often our teams pay a price for that. We pay a price for that."

He turned his back, finally, on the window that offered only darkness as its view and looked at his wife. "I don't often doubt what we do," he said.

"I know."

"So why do I feel this way about the situation in Clarity? Why do I want to recall them all here to Quantico, ASAP?" His wife was, quite literally, the only person he could or would talk to like this, exposing the cracks in what most everyone else in the SCU saw, by necessity, as the bedrock certainty at the core of their unit chief.

Miranda, sitting on his desk as she often did, said slowly, "I'm still betting it's Hollis. We all know you have more of a connection with some members of the team than with others. Hollis is one of those. She's also one of the very first of our agents who joined the FBI and SCU after being herself a victim of a killer we were hunting."

"Are you sensing anything?" he asked her.

"No, not really. A general sense of unease, but that's from you. And not that uncommon with teams out. Especially this many teams. But . . . more restless than usual."

The two of them shared an exceptionally deep connection that was intimately emotional and psychic, and they quite often did, in a very real sense, share feelings. But they had also learned to allow the connection to exist without necessarily reaching out to each other, and even to sometimes close the "doors" at either end of that connection. It was a necessity when they were separated and working different cases, as they often were, because their unique bond was an equally unique vulnerability and could be used against them.

"Maybe Reese was right," Bishop said. "Maybe she isn't okay enough to be in the field."

Miranda smiled faintly. "I can't believe I'm saying this about Reese, but that's his heart talking, not his head. It's his nature to do his best to protect someone he loves. If you'll remember, we had something of the same problem."

"Had?" He sighed. "At least we learned to trust each other and the connection we have. Hollis is still struggling with that."

"Of course she is. Ever since that first horrific assault she's been forced to . . . adjust . . . almost constantly. Surviving a monster's brutal attack when it should have killed her. Eyes she wasn't born with looking back at her from a mirror. No longer being an artist. Being a medium. Seeing auras. Being able to heal herself and others. Channeling energy. Channeling dark energy. Facing evil time and time again. Facing her own demons."

"And now Reese."

Miranda nodded. "And now Reese. It's good that he's a very patient man. She's been fighting for control of her life for years while too many things happened *to* her; it won't be easy for her to surrender that control once she feels she has it."

Bishop wondered why he hadn't been able to put that so simply and succinctly to DeMarco earlier. "Is that what she'll have to do?"

"It's what we all have to do, you know that. We don't master love, it masters us." She smiled. "I'm pretty sure you're the one who told me that, in an earlier life."

Half under his breath, Bishop said, "I'm surprised I was able to say anything that made sense at the time."

"We were both struggling. We both had cause. Lots of demons from the past between us, never mind a case with one of the worst serial killers either of us had ever hunted. But we found our way eventually. So will Hollis and Reese."

"In Clarity. I'm sure of that much. Somehow it all gets resolved in Clarity."

"Then it was right to send them. No matter what else you feel, that's a certainty, isn't it?"

"Yeah." But he was frowning again.

"Something else come into focus?" she asked.

Bishop shook his head slowly. "Just that sense of dread I can't shrug off."

"Since they arrived in Clarity or before?"

He considered briefly. "Before they left here I just knew they needed to go there. To investigate that case. Especially Hollis. That she has to discover something there, something she needs."

"And now that they're in Clarity?"

"The dread. Foreboding. Almost holding my breath, because I know something's going to happen. Something bad. I just don't know what, or when." He met his wife's intent gaze. "That isn't how your precognition works, so it isn't how mine works."

"We get hunches. Flashes of knowledge. It isn't all visions."

"Yeah, but it's never been like this. Never been so . . . elusive. I reach, and it vanishes like smoke through my fingers."

"Then maybe it is coming from Hollis," Miranda said. "Something she's not even consciously aware of herself. Something like that has happened before. When Nell went home to settle her family's estate. She had a connection there, to that case and what was happening, that you became aware of, even though she wasn't aware of it."

Nell Gallagher was unique even among a unit of unique agents, her psychic ability one they had never found in any other person. She could, quite literally, see into time. Which had not really given her any edge at all in hunting a killer who had been able to, in a very real sense, see into *her*.

He nodded slowly. "Which, if true, means that Hollis has seen or heard or sensed something that, subconsciously, she knows is a threat to her or someone else on the team. And even if they're buried, her instincts are warning her of danger. I'm betting she feels uneasy and isn't sure why."

"And probably doubting her abilities as a team leader since this is her first time, so that may be where she believes her uneasiness is coming from," Miranda pointed out. "So even if you knew what it really is, you couldn't tell her. It's something she has to figure out—and face—without our interference."

"Who made that a rule?"

"You did. At the time, it was about our visions. But the truth is that we both know better than to believe we should always step in and do something to influence events. Or a member of the team. Once committed to an investigation, once the team is there, on the scene, it has to play out the way it plays out. We both know that."

"Some things have to happen just the way they happen."

"Yes," Miranda said. "They do."

———————

MAL LOOKED AT the agents steadily. "I've been a cop long enough to know that we're all waiting for the other shoe to drop, pun intended." He didn't smile. "Our instinct is to work the case now, without taking time to rest. But unless you guys can pull a rabbit out of your hats and figure out who our killer is tonight, I'm recommending we all get some rest as well as a good meal. I have a feeling we'll be pulling plenty of all-nighters, and it's already been a very rough week."

Hollis had just about decided he was right when a female deputy appeared in the open doorway, her arrival a distraction more because of what she carried than anything else.

A little dog, his paws scrabbling rather comically in the air as he frantically tried to get somewhere.

To the sheriff, as it turned out.

"Emma—" He accepted the dog, not so much displeased as resigned.

"Sorry, Mal, but we've tried everybody and Felix just won't settle with any of us." Deputy Emma Fletcher had introduced herself to the agents when they'd first arrived in town, assigning another deputy to lead the way for them to the Cross house since she'd been holding down the fort at the station. She was a petite, brown-eyed blonde who looked about as unlikely to be any kind of cop as Kirby did.

She probably got carded when buying anything alcoholic as well, unless it was here in town where most everyone likely knew her.

Mal tried a last protest. "Joe—"

"Definitely not Joe. Neither one of them was happy with the other, and it was probably worse because Joe was still so upset. He isn't the type to love a dog just because it belonged to his dead wife. I'm betting he won't want to keep the dog, Mal. So somebody else is going to have to take him."

"Then I hope you know somebody who will, because with the hours I work it wouldn't be fair for me to keep a dog." He didn't have to add that a little Yorkie with a little red bow holding his bangs in a topknot out of his eyes was hardly the sort of dog a sheriff would *have*.

"I'll ask around. In the meantime, I think you're stuck with him—unless you want me to roust one of the vets so they can put him in a cage at their clinic."

He frowned at his lead deputy. "You're deliberately making that sound awful."

"Am I?" Her brown eyes were very bright, not quite laughing.

"Yes, dammit. I'll look out for him until you find somebody else. But *do* find somebody, Emma, because I really don't need a dog in my life at the moment. Especially one used to riding around in a big purse." The sheriff looked at the agents and briefly explained about Felix and his usual mode of transportation.

Hollis, watching the little Yorkie snuggle into the crook of the sheriff's arm, returning her gaze with bright button eyes, half laughed under her breath. "I know enough about dogs to know this one has made *his* choice."

"God, I hope not," Mal said, again sounding more

resigned than upset about it. "Unless he likes cold left-over pizza, I'll have to stop at a store on the way home and get dog food. Damn." He frowned, visibly changing gears, and said to his deputy, "Joe isn't still here." It wasn't quite a question.

"No, one of Perla's sisters and her husband came and got him, said he'd be staying with them." Emma sobered considerably, adding, "They were still in shock. I know you didn't offer too many details when you notified her parents right after finding her, but I think word of how Perla was killed has already started spreading. Not a whiff of suspicion toward Joe, far as I can tell. He's been in tears since you found Perla. I mean, literally, the whole time. I've never seen *anybody* cry so much or look so lost and pitiful. Her family is already closing ranks around him."

"Why does that not surprise me." He sighed.

Emma looked at the agents and said, "I was pretty sure you guys would want to talk to Joe at some point, but trust me when I say he wasn't making sense at all tonight. If he wasn't crying—and I mean sobbing—he was pretty much catatonic, with tears dripping off his chin." She frowned slightly.

"What?" Mal asked.

"Nothing, nothing. I just hope they rehydrate him."

Everybody kept a straight face except Kirby, who giggled and then looked guilty about it, covering her mouth with her fingers like a little girl.

Emma looked around and cleared her throat. "Well, anyway. I figured you wouldn't talk to him tonight."

"We can wait until tomorrow," Hollis said, hoping she was right about that. Then it was her turn to frown as she looked at the sheriff, distracted once more from the idea of calling it a night. "Still no luck in finding the password for Mrs. Cross's cell phone?"

"Far as I know. Why?"

"If they haven't already, tell them to try *Felix*," Hollis suggested.

Before the sheriff could respond, Emma said, "You know, I bet that's it. I'll tell them."

As the lead deputy vanished from the doorway, Hollis continued to frown at the sheriff. "You said Mr. Cross waited at home for his wife, convinced she'd come home or call him."

"Yeah. Until he came here to report her missing."

"Did he get home before dark?"

Slowly, Mal said, "It was dark by the time he got here, but . . . I'm really not positive whether he got home at his usual time. Didn't think to ask him, to be honest. With everything that's happened, the priority in my mind was to search that house."

Hollis nodded gravely. "Something told you she was there, didn't it?"

"Yeah. A sick feeling in my gut. I started feeling it not long after Clara Adams drove her car into a streetlight pole a few weeks ago in the middle of July."

SEVEN

There was a long silence, and then Hollis said, still grave, "I believe all good cops develop instincts about crimes. And most of us tend to have some kind of physical reaction to them."

"Yeah," the sheriff said, nevertheless looking a bit self-conscious.

Hollis looked at him, then held up one hand almost as though offering the near-universal sign for *Okay!* But the thumbnail she displayed was clearly ragged. "I chew. Not on all my nails, just the thumbnails. When something's bugging me. When the instincts kick in, or the training, or whatever it is. Usually not aware of what I'm doing unless and until somebody points it out." She didn't look at her partner.

"I pace," Cullen offered.

Kirby frowned at him, then at Hollis. "I don't think I

have those instincts yet." She sounded so earnest it was almost funny.

Almost.

Mal looked at the remaining fed. "What about you?"

With a faint smile, DeMarco shook his head just once.

"He's right," Hollis said wryly. "Plenty of instincts, but no tell. At all. Don't ever play poker with him."

"Noted," the sheriff murmured with a smile, clearly no longer feeling self-conscious.

More conversational than anything else, DeMarco said, "Getting back to the matter at hand, our latest murder, I think those limbs could have been sharpened earlier, even days ago. Probably were. From what I could see, you'd have had to look out the attic window or else stand directly under that tree and look up to see anything suspicious. Especially since he didn't leave any branch tips or wood chips as evidence of what he'd done."

"Agreed." Hollis was looking at her partner now, shifting gears as smoothly and easily as he did. "But it still leaves an awfully tight time frame, even assuming Mr. Cross *did* get home after dark. It couldn't have been long after dark, not given when she was found."

Mal said, "If the killer had that tree all . . . pruned and ready beforehand, he wouldn't have needed much time to kill her." His frown deepened. "Depending on how he actually did it. And I still can't see how he did."

"A very unanswered question," Hollis said, frowning herself. "But if the pattern holds, he would have sent that text at three o'clock this afternoon, presumably while she was still up in the attic." Parenthetically, she added, "Although I didn't notice any evidence she'd been working up there, possibly excepting the unusually clean floor."

Mal frowned. "No, neither did I. And now that I think about it, cleaning out an attic wouldn't likely make Perla's list of fun things to do on her day off. Especially cleaning the floor."

"A chore that had to be done?" DeMarco suggested.

"I'd say she was a lot more likely to call in a cleaning crew if that's what she wanted. Or an insurance appraiser to see if there was anything valuable up there."

Hollis glanced at Kirby and said, "Make a note, will you, please? We need to check out all possibilities, especially if Mrs. Cross had company—of any kind—in that attic at any point during the day. Or prior to today. Maybe other days off."

"You're thinking maybe a lover?" Mal asked.

"If she was so unhappy in her marriage, maybe. And either her killer knew . . ."

"Or he was the lover?"

"It's possible, Mal."

"Jesus, that's a cold-blooded thought. Though it would explain how he could have been up there with her without even the need to use any kind of force to keep her silent while Joe was searching the rest of the house for her."

Hollis nodded. "The doc really does need to go back to the house and search the attic tomorrow. I'd also suggest she at least spot-check the whole place with luminol. Somebody used bleach up there, and you don't need bleach to clean away dust. If Mrs. Cross was killed the way it looked, impaled on those branches, there probably won't be blood inside the attic. But we don't know that for sure."

DeMarco added, "Until we know it for sure."

His partner nodded again. "And if she was meeting a lover, today or any other day, there could have been something with his DNA there. And maybe he didn't get it all, even with the bleach. Mal, with your permission, I'd like Cullen to go with Jill." She paused, then added, "There may be evidence of a behavior up there we missed before, especially since none of us really looked over the attic."

"Okay. I'll check with Jill and see what time she can go. I don't think she was planning to do the actual autopsy on Perla until early tomorrow. She's been putting in some long hours, her and Sam. He's her assistant. So I'd guess tomorrow afternoon would probably be best for her. For both of them."

Hollis was highly conscious of the ticking clock in her head but nodded. "Sooner the better, Mal."

"Copy that."

Remembering what had been said about Perla Cross's habits, Hollis said, "Didn't you say you found her cell phone downstairs?"

"Joe found it on the kitchen island." Mal paused, then added, "And he was surprised by that, since she virtually always had the phone with her."

Cullen spoke up to offer, "The killer could have left it there."

"After he killed her?" Hollis was still frowning. "He hasn't done anything like that so far. Just the opposite, in fact, since all the other victims' phones were destroyed when they were killed. Then again, this is also the first time it's very clearly, very obviously murder. And given that, given how far off-script he went in other ways, we have to wonder if he even bothered to warn her. Or if he even bothered to wait for dark to kill her."

It was Cullen who spoke up again to say, "I'd say the text matters more than the time of death. The text is the only thing we've found connecting all the victims."

Hollis was looking at the sheriff. "Mal, did the doc estimate time of death?"

He nodded slowly. "She said she'd know for sure after the post, but her estimate was that Perla died sometime between six and eight o'clock tonight."

"And Mr. Cross came here to report his wife missing when?"

"He was here a little after seven. Probably left the house right at seven to get here when he did—unless he stopped along the way to look for Perla and just didn't tell me about that. He said he made a lot of calls, to her work, her friends. Didn't say anything about talking to anyone in person."

"What time did he usually get home from work?"

"Usually around five thirty, I think. The garage where he works closes at five, so that sounds about right. After sundown but before it got really dark. We get more twilight hours than most places, since the mountains to the east and west are the highest in this part of the Appalachians. Joe said he checked the house right away because it wasn't like her not to answer when he called out."

"But he didn't search the attic?"

"No, just opened the door, saw the lights were out, and knew she wouldn't be up there in the dark."

"Not alone, at any rate."

"Yeah. Said he called out her name anyway and didn't hear a sound in response."

"So . . . if the doc is right, Perla Cross was killed either while her husband was in the house waiting for her, or else very soon after he left to come here."

"It couldn't have been while Joe was in the house," Mal objected. "Scuff marks or no scuff marks, she must have struggled, even if she knew the guy. Once she realized what he meant to do. Or cried out, at least. Joe would have heard something."

Hollis nodded. "Yeah, even in that big house I think he would have. Assuming she wasn't drugged or otherwise rendered unconscious for hours, which we have to assume she wasn't unless the tox screen tells us otherwise. So . . . the killer already had Perla with him, probably in the attic since it's the one place that, according to him, her husband didn't search. In the dark, and managed to keep her quiet while Mr. Cross was looking for her, waiting for her. Maybe her killer . . . made it a game. Something new and exciting in her life."

"My guess is that's something Perla would go for, unless and until she felt threatened. One of the words she often used to describe her marriage was 'boring.'"

"And he would have known that."

"Hell, everyone in town knew it."

DeMarco said, "So that's one possibility. That this

death, this murder, was personal for him. He didn't have to know her well to feel . . . somehow injured by her. She really doesn't sound the type to have hidden the existence of a lover—from anyone. Apparently, she talked about everything in her life, so why not a lover?"

Kirby, who had been pretty much silent since her comment about not having instincts yet, spoke up then, as serious as the others were. "If she was as visible as she sounds, as . . . dramatic and almost out of place as she sounds, she could have attracted the wrong kind of attention. What if she didn't know anything until today? Didn't even know she had a particular admirer. Someone might have been obsessed about her, watching her, for a long time. Stalking her."

Hollis nodded again. "We know stalkers invent complete relationships with the object of their obsession, and the fantasy, to them, is all too real. She could have done something in total innocence he viewed as a rejection. And that could have been enough to turn his obsession even darker, to drive him to kill her."

Hesitantly, Kirby said, "A stalker has a . . . very specific focus, right? His world was her. Would he have used the other killings to throw us off track? I mean—what if Mrs. Cross was his intended target all along, and we were just meant to lump her in with the rest?"

KEITH WEBB HAD been married to the second-oldest of the four Ferguson sisters, Carla, long enough to know that it would be a while before they had their house all to themselves again. And it wasn't that he hadn't expected they would be the ones to provide Joe Cross a temporary home after Perla had been so horribly killed; they had the largest house in what was in reality—and had been dubbed by most of Clarity—the Ferguson Compound.

When you married into that clan, you ended up in a specific small neighborhood on the outskirts of Clarity. Whether you meant to or not. And if there wasn't a house for you by the time you returned from the honeymoon, it didn't take much longer to finish building one on the considerable acreage of Ferguson family land.

Keith and Carla had anticipated having a large family, and so the house built for them boasted four bedrooms, plus a guest suite *and* a mother-in-law suite in the basement.

They'd been married for ten years, and no kids so far, but Carla was only thirty and they were both still enthusiastically working toward having those kids any time now.

In the meantime, at least for now, quite a few Fergusons were occupying those extra bedrooms, as well as other areas of the house, even if their own homes were only two doors down. And Joe Cross was going to stay in the guest suite.

If, Keith thought, the shocked and grieving widower ever made it as far as the stairs. So far, he was still in the den just off the foyer. Keith's den, where he sometimes slipped away to watch a movie or sports on his big flatscreen when the house was invaded by too many Fergusons.

All the Fergusons were shocked and horrified and grieving the murder of the youngest sister, and all of them were handling that grief the way Fergusons handled any troubles in their lives.

They stayed busy.

Joe Cross, Keith knew, gave them something to be busy *with*, so he really didn't begrudge Joe the guest suite in his home or even the far end of his very comfortable sectional in the den.

Even if he was half convinced Joe's tears had literally soaked into the one section he was sitting on.

Carla bustled into the room with yet another box of tissues, sitting down beside Joe and using a handful of tissues to mop his wet face one more time.

"I know, Joe," she said. "I know."

He let out a wail and buried his face in his hands—and in the tissues Carla had expertly slipped into place. His sobbing was a bit muffled. Just a bit.

Carla met her husband's gaze and said, "It's awful." Her eyes were bright and hard, the way they would stay until she was alone with her husband in their bedroom, tonight or maybe not until tomorrow, and she could finally cry herself.

"Yeah," Keith said, meaning it because he had liked Perla very much; she was fun in a town that was otherwise pretty conventional. "It is awful."

"The boys want to get their guns and go hunting for the bastard that killed her," Carla said.

The "boys" were her four brothers, the youngest twenty-eight and the oldest nearly forty.

"Best stop them," Keith said. "Mal won't put up with it. Besides, we don't know who did it."

"Think those FBI agents know?"

"Only been here a few hours. I doubt even FBI agents can figure things out that fast, especially in the dark."

Carla seemed struck by that. "True. Maybe tomorrow?"

"We'll see."

She nodded. Then said, "Mama's making her stew."

Joe wailed into his tissues, and she patted his hunched back several times. Rather briskly. "Perla loved Mama's stew."

Keith, who had decided he wasn't likely to see his bed before dawn, sniffed the air for the faint scent beginning to waft through the house from the kitchen. "Her chicken stew?"

"Yeah."

"I love it too," Keith said. "Is she making it for tonight?"

"She's making it for all weekend. And maybe next week. She has two big pots going, with all the chicken I had in the freezer."

"Good. That's good. Keep her busy."

Carla nodded. "June's chopping vegetables for her," she said of the Ferguson sister who was now the youngest at twenty-six. "And Ally slipped out to go hide the boys' guns." Allison was the oldest, at thirty-two.

"Boys drinking?"

"Starting to."

Keith nodded. "Good, then. They'll think better of it tomorrow. Sober."

"Or not," Carla said.

"Or not," he agreed. He looked at Joe, and for an odd moment he fancied there was a sort of shimmer in the air just above Joe's far shoulder. But then Joe wailed again, and shuddered, and began sobbing louder, and Keith forgot about shimmers in the air.

"Think we'd better call the doc," he said.

"He's on his way," Carla said.

"Good," Keith said. The sobbing of his wife's brother-in-law was beginning to set his teeth on edge. "That's good."

HOLLIS WAS LOOKING intently at their youngest agent. "His world was her. You're right, Kirby. Assuming one exists, a stalker would have been obsessed with Perla. He might have gone after someone he felt or knew was a rival, but if that were so I'd have expected him to go after Joe Cross. These other victims . . . How could they have threatened his fantasy relationship with Perla?"

"Maybe it's simpler," Mal said. "Maybe he knew he had a motive to kill her. And no motive to kill the others."

Something Bishop had suggested as possible, Hollis thought. But she had an objection. "It wouldn't be a stalker, then. Kirby's right, a stalker's world would have been her, his focus on her. All these . . . staged . . . accidents don't make sense for a stalker."

DeMarco said, "But maybe they do make sense for a serial killer with very specific tastes."

"Oh, yeah, that's always possible. Even likely. But I keep coming back to the way Perla Cross was murdered," Hollis said. "The abrupt escalation from staged accidents to an obvious murder just bugs the hell out of me. Because there's no possibility anyone, even outside law enforcement, could look at how she was killed and not know they were looking at a murder. It's not like she could have fallen out of the window and hit that tree the way she did; she had to have been pushed or thrown, and hard, with a lot of power. From all the evidence so far, he went out of his way at considerable trouble to stage accidents; this time he went out of his way to make sure we'd know this was murder. Why make murder obvious now?"

"I'd say maybe he didn't have a choice, that she somehow forced his hand and he decided to get rid of her," DeMarco said—and then immediately shook his head. "It may have been done in rage, but there was a lot of premeditation in her murder. A lot of preparation. It took time and hard work to sharpen those limbs. Whatever else happened in that attic, he meant to kill her. And maybe she realized that at some point, either by instinct or because of something he did or said that told her she was in danger. Maybe he had to produce a gun or other weapon. Maybe by the time her husband came home, the killer had her tied up and gagged."

Cullen spoke up to say, "I didn't see any ligature marks on her wrists or ankles. Though, to be honest, I wasn't really looking for signs she'd been bound."

"I didn't look at all," his partner confessed, stating what the rest of them knew anyway.

Almost automatically, Mal said, "The doc will be able to tell us if she was tied up. Or maybe she was right to look for a head wound, if the killer knocked her out."

In the same sort of tone, Hollis said, "If Perla was slammed against that tree with enough force to drive those limbs through her, I expect the doc will find the back of her skull crushed, or at least fractured. That could easily hide evidence of an earlier blow to incapacitate her."

"She definitely needs to go back and check the whole attic," DeMarco said. "If the killer was up there with Mrs. Cross, I doubt he would have assumed her husband wouldn't at least come to the top of the stairs. He wouldn't have been standing out in the open."

Cullen said, "Plenty of stuff to hide behind, that's for sure. Enough to hide him and an unconscious Perla Cross, if he had to use a blitz attack or drugged her. And if he did use bleach up there, maybe it *was* blood he had to clean up."

DeMarco was watching his partner. "What is it? You're the most experienced profiler here."

Hollis wondered if he had said that to emphasize her leadership with the sheriff or simply as useful information, but the inner question was brief and easily pushed aside. She had another fleeting thought about a good meal and the no-doubt-comfortable bed waiting for her at the hotel, then pushed that aside as well as she half sat on the conference table with a sigh.

"It doesn't make sense."

Mal asked, "What part?"

"The escalation." She brooded for a moment, then said, "I keep coming back to that. It's in my head like neon. All the so-called accidents before tonight took careful planning, and over a period of time. He was very meticulous. He knew his victims, their schedules, where they'd be at the right time for his plans. Either because he knew them personally or else stalked them long enough to learn what he had to, *and* stalked them without being seen or at least noticed by anyone else. Right?"

"Looks that way," DeMarco agreed.

"Okay. We know he took the time at some point to sharpen the limbs outside that attic window at the Cross home. That could have taken more than one trip when neither of the Crosses was home, and he had to clean up after his work, leaving no signs he'd been there, and he had to be pretty sure neither of them would notice, either from inside the house or from outside. Again, careful planning; he managed to get it done without being seen."

All three of her fellow agents nodded, but it was Kirby who said suddenly, "Oh—he had to know what time Mr. Cross got home from work. He had to know Mrs. Cross had the day off. Right?"

It was Hollis's turn to nod. "Right. If we find the same warning on her cell phone, then we'll know his *intent* was to kill her tonight. Which is why, at the very least, I would have expected some planned distraction for Mr. Cross. Or some routine behavior the killer was counting on to get his victim's husband away from the house for at least a couple of hours after dark."

Mal hesitated, then said, "I think Joe *would have* gotten in his truck and driven around checking out the hotels and motels Perla tends to be in when she's left him in a huff."

"That was his normal reaction?"

"Yeah."

"Then why not do that tonight?" With only a slight pause, Hollis answered her own question. "Because there was too much evidence at the house that she *hadn't* run away, evidence that was obvious to him. She left behind her dog, her cell phone, her purse, any money she had—and she didn't pack a bag. There was a matched set of red luggage in that huge closet of hers, and not a single piece was missing. Her jewelry, makeup, even her toothbrush, all still there."

"And all of it evidence to her husband that she hadn't run away again." Mal nodded. "That makes sense."

Hollis brooded again. "But if the killer knew her and was counting on her husband to react as he usually did, why would he have not made certain that it *looked* like Perla Cross had just run away one more time? It's clear he had the time to do that, time before Joe Cross was due home from work. Why make it so very obvious she hadn't run off again that her husband couldn't possibly have reacted as he usually did?"

DeMarco said slowly, "To up the ante? To give himself more of a challenge? A smaller window of opportunity in which to work?"

Kirby shook her head half-consciously. "That would be taking an awful risk, though, wouldn't it? I mean, nothing really stopped Mr. Cross from staying put and just calling the sheriff, right? He was probably less likely to drive all the way here after realizing none of her stuff was missing."

"Unless . . ."

"Unless what?" DeMarco asked.

"Unless Mr. Cross hasn't told us everything he knows," Hollis said. "Or unless this unsub has escalated again, this time dragging a loved one into his delusions and fantasies. Unless this time the suffering was something he wanted to inflict on someone else as well as the victim."

Cullen noted, "He pretty much did that with the elevator *accident*. Friends, family, and her fiancé saw what happened to Karen Underwood."

"But that part of it, the audience, couldn't really have been planned. Unless he was part of the wedding party, somehow managed to hide Karen Underwood's purse so she'd have to go back up and get it, *and* suggest to the others that they wait. He couldn't have controlled those events any other way."

Mal swore, not under his breath. "I have a list of everybody from the wedding party who was waiting for Karen. In fact, I have a list of every soul who was within sight of those elevator doors."

"And you interviewed them?"

"One of my deputies or me talked to every person. But only about what they saw. We weren't looking at anybody as a suspect, except maybe her fiancé. And we ruled him out pretty quickly. I'd bet my pension his shock and grief were genuine."

Hollis nodded slowly. "The significant other is usually a prime suspect in murders, but not in serial cases."

There was silence for a moment, and then Mal said, "So one killer orchestrating all these deaths. And Perla's murder was so different because the killer wanted to watch Joe mourn his dead wife. Is that what we're saying?"

"Or watch her murder destroy him. It's at least possible. And if that's it, then Joe Cross is who he really wanted to hurt, at least with Perla's murder. But I doubt that was the trigger that set him off initially. More like . . . a fun little bonus for him." Hollis reached up to massage one temple, hardly aware of what she was doing. The little headache she had felt coming on all day was beginning to explode into something very close to a migraine.

At that moment, Deputy Emma Fletcher reappeared in the doorway, this time not holding a dog, but holding a cell phone. "Got it," she announced triumphantly. "Hollis was right, the password was *Felix.*"

"I assume that's been dusted for prints," the sheriff said, not really a question.

"Yeah. Only Perla's and Joe's. More of his than hers, actually."

Mal nodded. "He probably tried to figure out her password when he saw she was gone and the cell had been left behind. He admitted to me that's why Perla got a phone she could password-protect, because he'd been snooping, trying to find out who she'd been talking and texting to. What about texts, Emma?"

"It's here," the deputy answered him. "Sent at three o'clock exactly from an unknown number. And since it isn't an unread text, I assume Perla saw it."

"Wait for dark," Mal said.

"Yeah. Same as all the others. *Wait for dark.*"

EIGHT

They ate at the restaurant next door to the hotel, so it was nearly midnight when they finally checked in and went up to their rooms. The desk clerk informed them helpfully that he had put all of them on the same floor and into a block of rooms with connecting doors in case they wanted to move around and maybe work up there.

So Hollis wasn't really surprised when, no more than ten minutes later, DeMarco knocked on the connecting door between his room and hers.

She opened her side, saying immediately, "I've been trying to decide whether to unpack. I hate living out of a suitcase. Then again, I'm hoping we won't be here long enough for it to matter." She added a muttered, "And I probably just jinxed us."

DeMarco had shed his jacket and the shoulder harness

for his gun, and that plus his carelessly rolled-up sleeves made him look very casual.

The look in his very intent blue eyes, however, was anything but casual. He might not have a tell, and Hollis might not be a telepath, but that didn't mean she hadn't gotten fairly good at reading her partner.

He, of course, had an edge.

"Is it a full-blown migraine yet?" he asked her, stepping into her room as she went to frown at the suitcase open on her bed.

Damned telepaths.

"It's just a little headache," she told him. "Are you reading me, or does it just show?"

"It shows. You're more pale than normal, you're holding yourself stiffly, and the light is obviously bothering your eyes."

"I didn't ask for a detailed summation."

When only silence greeted that, Hollis turned her attention away from her luggage and sat down near it on the bed with a sigh.

"Sorry." She looked at him, noting that he had come only a few steps into her room. "I'm just a little tense, that's all."

"You haven't been sleeping well."

Hollis frowned. "I haven't had a chance to sleep here."

"I mean over the last few months. And especially the last few weeks." He stood with his hands in the front pockets of his jeans, a man clearly prepared to remain right there, immovable as a granite boulder, until he got his answers.

Maybe all his answers.

"Have you been picking up my dreams?" she demanded.

"Yes." The reply was simple and calm.

She had been hoping for a different response, so Hollis didn't quite know what to do with that. She had only recently begun to remember her dreams—nightmares—and it horrified her that he might have shared those agonizing experiences. She could feel herself stiffen even more. She fought the urge to start chewing on a thumbnail. "That's an invasion of privacy," she muttered.

"I didn't go looking for your dreams, Hollis."

She thought that was probably true, but she also thought it was worse. Apparently, her shiny new shield *did* desert her when she slept. Or maybe . . . maybe he had always been able to see her nightmares, at least since they'd been partners.

The shield was new. Broadcasting like a damned cell tower had been the rule before that. And just because she hadn't remembered her nightmares then most certainly didn't mean she hadn't been experiencing them just about every night.

Oh, God.

"Why are you telling me this?" she asked finally, admitting some truths, however unwillingly. "I mean, it's not like I can stop you. We both know my shield is iffy at best when I'm awake. I'm sure it's totally down when I'm sleeping."

"It is," he said.

The confirmation wasn't welcome. At all. Grim, she said, "I'll have to work on that."

"You don't ever need to hide yourself from me. Any part of yourself."

Hollis shied away from that subject completely. She wasn't ready for this. She had thought she was, but . . . but she just wasn't. It was too much right now.

Maybe just too much at all. Ever.

That cost her a pang she didn't want to acknowledge.

"Listen, it's late, I'm tired, and I need to swallow half a dozen aspirin before I try to sleep. And I need to sleep. We're getting an early start tomorrow, remember?"

"We both know you're not going to sleep. You'll lie awake in bed going over and over this case in your mind. Trying to figure out if you missed something."

"It's my job, Reese. To keep this monster from killing anyone else."

"That isn't your job. Your job is to investigate, build a profile, and narrow down what's now a wide-open list of suspects. To *hunt* the monster. *Our* job is to do that. And if he kills again while we're closing in on him, that's on him. Not us."

"Words. They don't mean a whole lot when somebody dies."

A slight frown made him look nearly as dangerous as he actually was. "We do the best we can, always. That's all we can do, and you know it as well as if not better than most. So what's really bothering you?"

Damned telepaths.

"You mean you don't know?" She meant it to sound mocking but was pretty sure it missed the mark.

She was prickly as hell, and DeMarco had the strong

sense that he was picking his way through a minefield. One wrong question, one wrong step, and he could lose everything.

He kept his voice steady, as dispassionate as he could make it. "I see two possibilities. You can tell me which is right. Either you've seen or sensed something you can't quite put your finger on, or you do know what's bothering you and simply choose not to share."

Hollis wondered how he managed to make that last bit an accusation without actually accusing her.

"Hollis?"

"I don't know what's bothering me," she said finally.

"But something is."

"Wouldn't take a telepath to see that, I guess."

He ignored that statement. "You weren't bothered before we got here to Clarity, right?"

"Right." Just restless and ready to work, but he'd known that.

"When did you first begin feeling uneasy?"

"When do you think?" she challenged.

DeMarco answered immediately. "When we reached the Cross home."

Damned telepaths. She thought it was becoming her personal mantra.

She managed a shrug. "Whatever is bothering me, I can't get a fix on it. I told you about that flash I got, about some impossible creature of the night crouching on a roof. Looking for something. Waiting for something. Or maybe it wasn't that at all. Maybe whatever's bugging me *was* something I actually saw but didn't really take in at the time, something somebody said . . . Hell, maybe something I heard or smelled, I don't know."

"Maybe information a spirit offered?"

Hollis frowned. "What I said up in that attic and later was the truth. I caught a few glimpses, but no spirit stepped forward to offer anything at all."

"Were the spirits hanging back because they had nothing to say, or because they were hiding from something dark or evil in that house? It's been the latter at least once."

Her frown deepened, and then Hollis shook her head. "I didn't get the sense of any negative spiritual energy, nothing preventing them from speaking or coming out of the shadows. It didn't strike me as a *haunted* house, just one where a lot of people have lived and died, and where a few decided to stick around. I don't think they have any intention of interacting with the living, including mediums. And from all we've been told about the family, I doubt any of them were aware of spirits on any level."

"Okay. Not spirits. And yet you're bothered."

She drew a deep breath and let it out slowly. "Yeah, but whatever it might be is beyond my reach, at least for now. Maybe tomorrow, when we get a timeline up, and can study the victims, the other crime scenes, when we have the autopsy on Mrs. Cross . . . maybe then I'll know. Until then, all I can really do is stop trying to force it and just wait until it . . . floats to the surface."

"Sensible," he noted. "But not really you."

"And you know me so well," she muttered.

"Yes," he said. "I think I do."

A very painful memory surfaced before Hollis could do anything to stop it.

"Yes," he said. "I do understand. I understand that you've survived more horror and agony than any human being should ever have to bear. I wish I could take away the pain, at least. But, Hollis, everything that's happened to you has made you the woman you are today, right now. The bad as well as the good. You know that."

"I know . . . I didn't want to remember. I didn't want to think about the monster who took my eyes. But when I saw her—her face. When I saw her eyes were gone, I remembered." She drew a sudden, deep breath, and her eyes began to lighten.

And fill with tears.

DeMarco didn't hesitate. He stepped closer and pulled her into his arms. She was stiff for just a moment, resisting. And then her new walls came down, and her arms went around him.

That memory was so vivid in her mind that for a moment it took her breath away. Vulnerable. God, she hated feeling vulnerable. Feeling helpless. Out of control. Even with Reese.

Maybe especially with Reese.

The monster who had destroyed her old life and put her feet on the path of a totally different one had also done that to her, had taken her to hell and left her so broken, so hurt in ways she didn't want to think about, to remember. He hurt her and left her to die, but she had survived.

Survived to be a damaged freak with abilities that would always set her apart from normal people.

"Hey." DeMarco snagged the chair from the little desk in her room and placed it in front of her, sitting in it and leaning toward her, elbows on his knees, eyes still very intent. "What is this?"

She wondered fleetingly why he hadn't joined her on the bed, but then remembered that her suitcase was open and taking up a lot of space. *Stupid. Damn, I can't even concentrate.*

"Hollis, what is this?"

"Nothing," she managed.

Blunt, he said, "Why are you feeling like a freak? I thought you'd gotten past that a long time ago. Before we ever met."

"I guess I haven't. And stop reading me."

He ignored that last, almost desperate command. "What is it that's making you doubt yourself?"

Hollis didn't want to admit it even to herself, but that *was* the problem, this sudden sense of self-doubt. She had tried to think like a profiler earlier, to do what she was trained to do, and yet it seemed to her that the others had done most of that work, that her own mind just hadn't . . . worked properly somehow.

And she had no idea why.

She cast about for something to say, and finally said,

"I don't think I should be a team leader. Not yet. I don't think I'm ready."

"You've been doing fine," DeMarco said.

"Yeah, well, nothing's happened yet to . . . challenge me." She looked down at the hands knotted in her lap, absently noting that she had been picking at the cuticle of her thumbnail without being aware of it, a sure sign of stress.

"Bishop wouldn't have made you team leader if he hadn't known you could handle it," he reminded her.

Hollis heard herself say, "Maybe he thought what I did. That it wouldn't really matter. I thought at the briefing that it would be a good case for me to try my wings as team leader. A series of bizarre accidents, that's all. No serial killer, no monster, no evil psychic trying to get into my head. Just a simple investigation."

"When was the last time the SCU was involved in a simple investigation?"

"Don't rub it in," she muttered.

DeMarco reached over and grasped her hand, pulling it gently down to her lap and continuing to hold it.

Hollis hadn't even realized she'd been chewing on her thumbnail again. Dammit. She stared down at his very large, very strong hand covering hers.

No wonder he carries such a big gun. My Glock would look ridiculous in his hand.

Slowly, DeMarco said, "When Diana was in the hospital fighting to survive, when we didn't know whether she'd make it, I told you I never wanted to be in the position Quentin was in, sitting at her bedside afraid she was dying, knowing that between them there were too many things left unsaid. Because bad things happen, and for us, in this work, they happen suddenly and usually without any warning. A simple investigation becomes something a lot more complicated. A lot more dangerous. And before we can even get our bearings, time runs out."

HE WASN'T ENTIRELY sure he had reestablished the necessary control over Joe Cross, but he wasn't all that troubled by it; the very weak man was so overcome by grief that it occupied his whole mind, at least for now, allowing nothing else in. Not even guilt. Not even *knowing*. But it was waiting for him, the *knowing*, hovering nearby and waiting for eyes not clouded by tears and a mind not racked by grief.

And in the meantime, poor, weak Joe posed no problem to either him or his plans. Grieving so violently and surrounded by Perla Ferguson Cross's very protective family. The sheriff and the feds would probably go to interview him, and he'd be useless, worse than useless. They'd get no sense out of him.

Joe was no threat for now. He might have broken completely, and if so he'd never be a threat. But if he hadn't broken, if he became a threat, well, the plan was in place for that. A very good plan, he thought.

Suicide by cop was such a common way for a cowardly killer to end what he fancied was his own suffering, and in the dramatic style of Hollywood.

A nice, clean wrapping up of loose ends.

A nice, clean ending, when he was ready for that. And it might be a challenge, now that he thought about it, to use Joe that last time even though he was broken. It might just be . . .

However, in the meantime, he had work to do. Much work. And a very large part of that work was to make certain that *she* didn't become aware of his plans.

He thought she'd almost sensed him once, and though the impression he received before hastily shoring up his shields had been a confusing one, he was reasonably sure she had seen him as some kind of monster.

A monster.

Perhaps not surprising, since she hunted monsters. Maybe she always saw her opponent in that light. It probably made it easier for her, he thought. Such a nice, clear, black-and-white concept. No shades of gray, no real doubt. Everything cut-and-dried, with so little need to question. He thought he was probably right about that, even though all he could really sense of her was her power.

But black-and-white concepts. Good versus evil. Heroes versus . . . monsters. Evil monsters, he supposed.

He shrugged all that off for now. Bowed his head for a short but reverent prayer. Then opened the large, very thick, very old book laid out on the altar.

There was so much to do . . .

HOLLIS MET HIS gaze finally. "That was more than a year ago. When Diana was in the hospital. When we talked like that, I mean." She wasn't even sure whether that was simply a statement—or a complaint.

He nodded slowly, his gaze never leaving hers. "I wanted you to know how I felt, but I also wanted you to know I wouldn't push, wouldn't insist, wouldn't pressure you for anything. Wouldn't even ask how you felt about us. About me. Because we both have baggage, and yours bothered you very much. Still does. For a lot of reasons, but mostly because you had no shield, and so felt you had no private place to retreat to if anybody got . . . too close.

"But you have that now, Hollis. That shield. It may not be as strong yet as it will be eventually, but it's there."

"Then why do I feel like one giant exposed nerve?" she asked without at all meaning to.

"Because it's still new. Still something you can't control, can't trust."

"Georgia was six months ago," she reminded him. "Every other . . . ability . . . I've developed has been pretty much full strength right away. I mean, after the first one, when I finally accepted the fact that I was a psychic, a medium."

His fingers tightened around hers, and he spoke slowly, carefully. "Maybe that's why you can't trust your shield yet. Becoming a medium and developing a shield both came from the same source, Hollis. A horrific attack made you a medium; facing the memories of that attack fully and consciously for the first time created a shield because your mind still needed to try to protect itself from the shock."

"Still."

DeMarco nodded. "Even years later, you want to bury that attack deep and never have to think about it again. The mind is a wonderful guardian, trying always to protect us from whatever hurts the worst. But for you, the attack that changed your life is something you *have* to remember, have to accept."

"Why?"

"Because that's where your shield comes from," he repeated. "And because what happened to you made you who you are today. Hollis, I know you still grieve for the woman who had no experience of violence. For the artist who only wanted to create beauty. For the person who had a . . . a simple life, without monsters."

"She's gone," Hollis said starkly. "She's gone, and she's never coming back. She'll never live a normal life. She'll never have kids, or a boring job, or a husband who snores beside her in bed at night. She'll never live the life she expected to live."

"Very few of us do that," DeMarco said. "Live the life we expect to. That's a . . . storybook dream, what we expect when we're young and arrogant and haven't seen much of the world. The remnants of childhood hopes and aspirations. Then life happens. We turn left instead of right, make this decision instead of that one, choose one thing over another, and get hurt in ways we could never have imagined when we were so young and had never been hurt. And suddenly we're on a different path, in a different life, one we never expected to be living."

"And can't go back."

"No. But would you really want to, Hollis? Now,

knowing what you know about how much bigger the world really is, having the abilities you have, being able to do extraordinary things, to make a real difference, would you really, consciously choose that ordinary life? You've helped save lives. Without you, Diana would probably be dead. And Miranda. And who knows how many others are alive today because you helped cage or destroy so many monsters."

"It's a useful life, I know, but—"

"It's a remarkable life, Hollis. And nobody, not even you, knows what's ahead for you. Or what isn't. You're on a far less-traveled path than most people even know exists."

"'Two roads diverged in a wood,'" she murmured.

"And you took the one less traveled by. *Really* less traveled by. It isn't likely to be peaceful except in rare moments. It very likely leads to more horrors, like that poor lady tonight, killed so violently. And perhaps to more pain for you. But it's *your* path now. It's who you are now. I never knew that other Hollis, but I'm betting the one I do know is stronger and more courageous, and will go on saving people. Protecting people from all the things that go bump in the night, the things most of them don't even believe are real.

"I believe the Hollis I know is . . . amazing. I believe she's on the path the Universe wants her to be on, has shaped her for. A path even she is more comfortable on than she realizes. Because her experiences have made her more suited to a life of danger and uncertainty, of hunting monsters. I see that in her, the drive, even the instincts, to hunt monsters. To keep beating back evil no matter what form it takes. And I believe in her ability to not only survive what fate throws at her, but to triumph."

Hollis was pretty sure she had never heard him say so much in such a short time, and while a part of her knew what that meant, another part was reluctant to believe it.

No matter what he said.

Forcing lightness, she said, "So I should pull myself together and do my job, huh?"

"You have to trust yourself." He didn't seem at all bothered by her seeming dismissal of his really articulate and admiring assessment of her.

"To do my job?"

"To be the woman you were meant to be."

Hollis again looked down at his hand over hers and heard herself speak slowly. "After the attack that took my eyes and did so much damage, I knew my life would change. Had changed. I sat in the dark in the hospital room, a bandage over my eyes, for days and days, thinking about it. Even when I met Maggie, and she took away so much of the pain and buried so many memories most victims of trauma never have to deal with, I knew I was different." She paused, then added almost conversationally, "Did you know that? That most victims who survive horrific trauma never remember what happened to them? Most lose days, even weeks of memories. They wake up not knowing what happened to them. Never remembering. But a few of us do. I did. I remembered everything. Every single minute. That's how I really knew I was different."

"Hollis—"

"Even when I could see again, I knew nothing would ever be the same. I would never be the same. And there was nothing I could do about that but . . . accept it. Maybe that's why Maggie helped me bury so much of it, and why it stayed buried for so long. Because I had to forget, at least consciously. Just so I could . . . adjust to a new reality and move on. Just so I could function."

"You did more than just function. A lot more. I've read the case reports from the beginning of your SCU career. And I was there, at the church where we all faced and fought a . . . an almost bottomless evil, and saw you do amazing things. After that, even more amazing things with every case. You never turn away from the darkness, from evil; you turn toward it, face it, fight it. I've seen you channel energy, positive and negative, becoming a living conduit. I've seen you heal, yourself and others. I've seen you communicate with spirits. I've seen you help people, even when it was . . . so dangerous for you."

He paused, then added deliberately, "I've never seen you doubt yourself like this."

"I can't explain it," Hollis said finally, mentally tucking away all the incredible things he had said to her to think about later. When he wasn't touching her. "Maybe because I don't know where it's coming from. All I can tell you is what you already know. I . . . don't feel like myself."

"Could a spirit be influencing you, or a psychic unsub?"

"Jesus, I hope not." She frowned. "It . . . doesn't feel

like something alien, something outside myself. It just feels like something's wrong. Wrong with me. And that's as far as I get, feeling that, knowing that. Starting to panic. I try to look deeper, I try to think about it, and that's all I get. This sense of wrongness in me."

"You've been able to see spirits here. Can you still see auras?"

"Yeah, unless my shield is working at the time. If it is, I have to concentrate harder. For the record, all the auras I've seen have been within normal parameters, if there is such a thing. Nobody fighting off any kind of energy, or showing anything unusually negative, given the situation."

"Do you feel grounded? Anchored?" DeMarco asked after a moment.

Hollis tried a laugh that didn't quite come off. "Is that something I can feel?"

"It should be. When we met, you were only beginning to discover abilities beyond being a medium. Beginning to explore, to reach out. I became your anchor, even though it wasn't your choice. I've been your anchor, keeping you grounded when your abilities could have taken you too far."

"Reese—"

"Like into Diana's gray time."

Diana Hayes was a medium and had been one all her life, but a controlling and overprotective father had seen her gift as sickness, and for most of her life a parade of doctors had kept her medicated to the point that she was a medium only at the subconscious level. But even then, years before she became consciously aware of them, her remarkable abilities had taken her to a place she called the gray time, a sort of corridor between the living world and the spirit realm, where spirit guides had asked for her help in one way or another.

The gray time was a realm Diana was very familiar with, a place where, at least for the first part of her life, she had been strong and certain and in control of her abilities. Usually. But the gray time was also never meant to be a place for the living, and an "off the books" experiment between the two mediums had left Hollis with something of a link to a place that was far more dangerous for her than it would ever be for Diana.

Reese *had* been her anchor long before she'd accepted that she needed him to be, and he had most certainly pulled her from Diana's gray time at least twice in potentially deadly situations.

"I should probably thank you for that," she murmured.

DeMarco shook his head slightly, his gaze still intent. "You needed an anchor, and I knew it was me. In Diana's gray time. And when you poured everything you had into the effort to heal her, to heal Miranda."

"Bishop said my sense of self-preservation would have pulled me back before it was too late."

NINE

"Bishop is wrong."

Hollis felt a curious little shock and realized only slowly that she had never heard anyone say that before.

Whether he was reading her or aware of her thoughts in any sense, DeMarco simply said, "We both know I was your anchor when you stood in the doorway of an energy vortex. Your anchor, and maybe something more."

"You kept me safe," she murmured. "When it was necessary. When I needed your strength, your energy as well as mine."

"So that's it," DeMarco said, his tone less of realization than of confirmation.

"What?"

"I think maybe I made a mistake in letting you delay a very important conversation. We should have talked about this months ago."

"I don't know what you mean." She tried her best to put conviction in every word.

DeMarco unknotted her hands and held them in each of his. "This," he said. "This connection between us. It's real, Hollis. Even if we're not touching. Even if there's some distance between us. It's real, and it will always be there. We'll always be connected."

"You don't have to—"

"You believe this is a chore for me, a burden? Something I'm reluctant about?"

"I read *your* file. I know about your background. You're . . . a very private man. You wouldn't have developed that double shield otherwise, we both know that. You were always a loner."

"I was. And then I met you. I couldn't be a loner anymore. Why else do you think I joined the team fully, came into the unit instead of requesting another undercover assignment?"

She tried to pull away, tried to look away from those too-intent blue eyes, but could do neither. "I think . . . you didn't have a choice," she said finally. "I think you got stuck with me."

"And you got stuck with me?"

Hollis hesitated again. "No. I didn't mean—"

"We're partners, Hollis. Not because either one of us got stuck with the other, but because we naturally complement each other. Because I have excess energy and you sometimes need that. Because we both have the baggage of people who know what trauma feels like. Because I can protect you in my shield while yours is getting stronger."

She forced a laugh. "It sounds like a very one-sided partnership, if you ask me. You give and I take."

"It's a question of balance, and the balance is always going to shift between two people. That's true of every partnership in the SCU, and you know it. It's not a question of taking turns, but one partner's abilities are almost always more necessary to resolving a specific case than the other partner's are. Bishop and Miranda are probably the only partners who balance each other perfectly most if not all the time, and they had to go through hell, separately and together, to get to that point."

"I've already been to hell," she said almost involuntarily. "I'd rather not go again."

"Me either." He smiled faintly. "My hell was war. Yours was being brutalized. I have memories I don't want to touch just like you do."

"Nobody's telling *you* that you have to remember, have to face those memories."

"Nobody has to. Every murder victim we see, every mutilated body, every autopsy photo brings it all back. I remember because I can never forget. That was never an option for me."

Hollis had never thought about that, had never considered how war had to haunt him, and she suddenly felt more than a little bit ashamed of herself. "I'm sorry."

"Don't be. Neither one of us has been all that good at sharing things we should have."

"You're doing a pretty good job of it now," she managed, trying not to look as self-conscious as she suddenly felt.

He looked down at the slender hands he was holding, then back at her face. He thought he knew her face better than he knew his own. "Because now it's time. Partnerships develop step-by-step. Relationships develop step-by-step."

"And this is the next step?" And before he could answer that, she hurriedly added, "We're in the middle of a case. To say the timing is lousy is an understatement." She *really* hoped he'd follow her lead. But that hope was dashed when he didn't.

"You don't ever want to feel vulnerable. Neither do I. But everyone *has* to be able to feel vulnerable sometimes. We have to just let go, expose ourselves, let someone else see who and what we really are. At least one other person. You and I can be that for each other. All it takes is trust."

"Trust."

DeMarco nodded.

"I already trust you," she said.

"Not that much. Not yet."

Defensive, she said, "What about you? Do you trust me that much?"

"Yes. I knew that when you faced off with the evil in Georgia—and all I could do was stand back and watch. I started accepting it even before, when you channeled pure negative energy and all I could do was be your anchor and just hold on."

"An anchor is everything," she said slowly. "Without you, I could never have done that."

"Are you sure about that?"

"Positive." Realizing something else, she looked down

at their hands and then met his steady gaze again. "That was when the connection between us grew stronger. When we became . . . something more than partners."

"Yes, it was."

"Why didn't I know that?"

"You knew, even if you weren't ready to face it. You knew when, for a very brief time, I was able to see the spirits you saw."

Hollis had almost forgotten that. "But, if that was through the connection between us, then why was it temporary?"

"My best guess, and it is a guess, is that all the energy you channeled had temporarily . . . overloaded the connection. Once that extra energy dissipated, it went back to what it was meant to be. A connection we can use when we want to or need to."

Slowly, she said, "So we won't always share abilities the way Bishop and Miranda do?"

"I don't think so. Though we may from time to time."

"Because their connection is deeper?" It was a difficult question to ask.

"Because it's different. They're both extremely powerful telepaths, so that's the way their energy works, mind to mind, sharing their innermost thoughts. Being lovers, I would think, only intensifies that."

Hollis wanted to look away from his intent gaze but discovered she couldn't. Any more than she could stop herself from asking the question. "What would that do for us? Being lovers?"

"I don't know," he replied simply

"Guess."

"Our primary abilities are different; I'm a telepath and you're a medium. We use energy differently, interpret it differently. You interpret a much wider range of energy than I do, and in different ways. How our energy would merge . . . I'm sure it would strengthen the connection between us. I'm not sure how. Build more trust. Maybe even forge a different kind of connection. Whatever it is, you can be sure it'll be unique to us."

"All positive. No negative?"

"There's always negative. Balance. The most obvious negative would probably be that our timing is never going to be perfect. The last months at Quantico were a bit unusual and we both know it. We're usually working, often without time enough even for food or sleep. But we're also human, and it may be that we have to steal moments for ourselves even in the middle of a case. That we'll need to."

Hollis nodded slowly. "And?"

"That vulnerability we were talking about. You're vulnerable to a lover in a way you are to no one else. For some people, it's a temporary thing, in the moment and no more. It won't be for us."

"It won't?"

"No."

"Because we're already partners? Already connected?"

"That's part of it."

Hollis realized that they were both speaking as if becoming lovers was simply going to happen, and she didn't quite know how she felt about that. Except nervous.

"Reese, I haven't . . . been with anybody for a long time. Since before the attack."

"I expected as much. Even with Maggie's help, scars like yours take a long time to heal."

"I'm not sure I'll ever be ready."

"I am. And you will be too. When you're ready."

"Baby steps," she murmured.

"That's the way we've been moving toward each other all along, in case you hadn't noticed. Personally, I mean." He lifted her hands for a moment. "Just don't forget this. We already have a connection, and nothing is going to break it. You are not alone; you never have to hide any part of yourself from me. And I am a very patient man."

Releasing her hands finally, he rose and replaced the chair at the small desk. He was smiling faintly.

"How's the headache?"

Surprised, Hollis said, "It's gone. Who did that, you or me?"

"Let's call it a team effort and not look too deeply for now. We both need to get some sleep. Breakfast at seven?"

"Sounds good."

"I'll knock on your door. Good night."

"Good night." She watched him return to his room, pushing his side of the connecting door without completely closing it. She sat there for a time, just looking at the door and thinking.

Thinking about a lot of things. Because she knew he wasn't reading her right now, that he had deliberately withdrawn inside both his shields—to allow her the privacy she couldn't yet count on inside a shield of her own.

He might have done that only to prove a point, but Hollis thought that wasn't his reason.

She thought about that, about vulnerability, about sharing more of herself than she had ever shared with anyone in her life. Then she got up, quickly and methodically unpacked, stowed her empty luggage in the closet, and went to have a shower.

She came out of the bathroom ready for bed, turning off lights until only the lamp on the nightstand was still burning. And it wasn't until she was reaching to pull back the covers that she saw the foil-wrapped chocolate on her pillow—and a folded piece of paper underneath.

She unfolded what she recognized as a sheet of the hotel's stationery, and even though she hadn't seen it very many times, she also recognized DeMarco's printed but curiously light and fluid handwriting. Just a few words, a brief quotation that really needed no explanation, not for Hollis.

Out of suffering have emerged the strongest souls; the most massive characters are seared with scars.

—KHALIL GIBRAN

Hollis looked at the quotation, realizing absently that he must have slipped back into her room while she was in the shower, just long enough to leave her this . . . gift.

She thought about it for a long time, reading the words over and over. Finally, she opened the drawer of the nightstand where she almost always kept her e-book reader for sleepless nights, and put the folded piece of stationery in there as well, the foil-wrapped chocolate on top.

It was after one thirty before Hollis crawled into her bed. She was conscious of the fleeting hope that there would be no nightmares tonight, but she didn't dwell on that.

She didn't dwell on anything, in fact. Within minutes of turning out the lamp on her nightstand, she was sound asleep.

SATURDAY

Despite his calling, nobody who knew him would ever call Reverend Marcus Pilate a gentle man. Or even a particularly holy man. He took care of the administrative duties of running the Second Baptist Church of Clarity, a job at which he excelled, but when it came to having a reassuring bedside manner, Pilate was somewhat lacking in compassion and sympathy, Christian or otherwise.

Which is probably why Perla Cross's relatives ushered him out of the house where Joe was staying after he barely had the time to tell the grieving widower that Perla was in a better place now, she was at peace, he needed to forgive her killer for the sake of his own immortal soul and, by the way, would he be donating any of her personal belongings to the "yard" sale the church was having to help fund its highly successful daycare center and get a start on funding for next year's new roof? Shoes were always very popular.

Joe looked bewildered, even stricken, and then buried his face in his hands, sobbing, which he'd clearly been doing a lot since the death of his wife.

Two of Perla's sisters, excruciatingly polite, escorted Reverend Pilate from the house, offering only the information that "someone" in the family would be making the funeral arrangements soon, and that while they were very grateful for his kindness, the family would of course be making those arrangements with the church where the Ferguson family had always attended services.

Which was not his.

Reverend Pilate didn't exactly feel appreciated in Clarity. He never had. A competitive man, he had never quite reconciled himself to the fact that the Cane Creek Baptist Church, which was on the opposite end of town from his church and was not, in fact, on or even near a creek, had a very popular preacher in Reverend Martin Webb, who had cornered the lion's share of Baptists.

Including the Ferguson family. Every blessed one of them.

His own congregation was on the small side, as was his church. Neither of which matched his more lofty ambitions.

So Pilate could be forgiven for a pang of jealousy at the size of the Cane Creek parsonage, discreetly set back from the road and the church to offer its occupants privacy. It was at least twice as big as his own. Of course, Reverend Martin Webb had a *family*, so Pilate supposed that accounted for it. There was a wife and—three kids? Two? Pilate wasn't really sure. They seemed interchangeable to him, all blond hair and tanned limbs and dirty faces.

But Webb's larger family certainly didn't account for the truly excellent landscaping around both the church and the parsonage, *or* the very nice and practically new Buick Webb drove, *or* the fact that his congregation had sent Webb and his wife on a cruise the previous year because they thought the couple deserved a vacation.

Some things in life were just not fair.

Reverend Pilate got in his five-year-old Ford and headed back toward town and his own church, very deliberately not looking at the Cane Creek church or parsonage as he passed.

It was Saturday afternoon, and on Saturday afternoon he always supervised the Flower Ladies. They came every Saturday, with pails filled with flowers from their gardens, and made colorful arrangements around the church so everything would look pretty and fresh for Sunday services. Even in winter, they shared a greenhouse that continued to provide for the church.

He didn't know anything at all about gardening but felt the need to assert his authority within his own church. Not that they needed his supervision; even Pilate had to admit that the three elderly but highly energetic ladies had been growing and arranging flowers since long before he was born. But he still felt he should offer a word here and there, ignoring the inevitable and absentminded "Yes, Reverend, of course," response he always received before they continued doing just as they liked.

He parked his car in the accustomed place beside his

tidy parsonage, spared a moment to wish he had an extra room to use as a study so that he wouldn't feel he was always on duty while working on his sermons at the church, then sighed and walked across the gravel parking lot between the two buildings and went inside the church.

The Flower Ladies were busy, and he was just about to go supervise whether they liked it or not when his cell phone buzzed in his pocket.

He did not like ringtones. Especially the hymns.

He pulled the cell phone from his pocket and flipped it open, wasting a slightly bitter moment regretting that it wasn't the latest model. Or even last year's model. But it was functional, his church supplied it, and he was certainly not one to complain.

A text. Unknown name, unfamiliar number.

Wait for dark.

Huh. What was supposed to be happening after dark? Nothing that he knew of, and he'd checked his calendar just before leaving to visit Joe Cross and the Ferguson family.

Who would—

Kids, of course. The bane of his existence, kids. They probably thought he'd be outside with a flashlight come dark, and they could hide in the shrubbery or wherever and jump out and yell *boo* before running off. Laughing at him.

Idiot kids.

Reverend Marcus Pilate closed the phone with a snap and returned it to his pocket. He put the cryptic text out of his mind and checked his watch almost automatically.

Three o'clock.

Briskly, he moved forward to supervise.

HOLLIS LIFTED HERSELF up to sit on the table, frowning at the evidence boards now all set up in the conference room. They had spent most of the day doing what they could. In this room they had spent necessary hours sifting through and organizing all the information Mal and his deputies had gathered and getting a reasonable timeline up to study. They had even called in a few witnesses to the earlier "accidents" to re-interview, this time with at least one of the agents sitting in to ask a few behavior specific questions.

The interviews hadn't helped much, at least in part because word of just how gruesome the murder of Perla Cross had been not only flew around town seemingly with the speed of light but was also embellished with even more gruesome details, resulting in nervous witnesses who wanted to ask questions rather than answer them.

The whole town, it seemed, was busy connecting the dots of four strange accidents followed by a definite murder.

Hollis wondered if the killer knew, and was sure only that they should assume he did.

"Hey," Cullen said suddenly. "It's three o'clock." He

was looking at the rather large clock above the conference-room door.

Sheriff Gordon looked up from the file he had been studying with a frown. "Do we believe he'd kill three straight days?"

Hollis shook her head. "I don't know what we should believe, except that he's not likely to stop with Perla Cross. Our preliminary profile was pretty much turned on its ear even before the jet touched down. We thought we might know what was driving this unsub, and it just doesn't fit anymore. So what's driving him? Especially to do such extreme—and extremely painful—murders? Until we figure that out, I don't see how we'll have anything like a reliable profile."

Still looking at her, the sheriff said, "When I talked to Jill about sending over her official autopsy report this afternoon, she said you two were there first thing this morning for the post."

Hollis merely nodded, not about to say that after her discussion with Reese the previous evening, and despite the gift she truly believed had granted her an utterly peaceful night's sleep, she had nevertheless been determined to reclaim at least some of the distance she had tried to keep between them. She thought she needed that right now, just as she needed to keep the focus of both of them on this investigation as much as she possibly could.

And never mind that she hated attending autopsies.

DeMarco, who was also studying the evidence boards, but from a chair on the other side of the conference table, said almost absently, "I wouldn't recommend that before breakfast. Or after breakfast."

Hollis turned her head to meet the sheriff's gaze. "Unless something unexpected shows up in the toxicology report, I don't think we'll learn anything more than we have from Perla Cross's body. There was really only one anomaly Jill discovered in the postmortem." She glanced over her shoulder at her partner. "And so far we haven't figured out what it means."

"What anomaly?"

"There were no ligature marks on her wrists or ankles, but there was something very like a ligature mark at her waist."

Mal blinked. "Her waist?"

"Yeah. As if a cord or cable, and not all that thin, was tightened around her waist long enough to leave a ligature mark, even through her clothes. But since she was dressed, whatever it was never touched her bare skin, and so we don't have anything distinctive about that mark. Except that it exists. And it was deep enough that Jill found fibers from Perla's red blouse embedded in the ligature."

"What the hell?"

"That was pretty much our reaction," Hollis told him.

Kirby came into the conference room just then, accompanied by Deputy Emma Fletcher. The very young-looking agent seemed both tense and queasy, an expression explained by the very sympathetic deputy.

"The elevator company still hasn't replaced the door to close the shaft where Karen Underwood was killed. And even though they removed the destroyed car and we put up that canvas curtain thing over the opening so people could walk past to the other elevator without looking in, there's still . . . Well, it still looks pretty horrific in there. People are ignoring the crime scene tape *and* the curtain to look inside, Mal. And pictures. Some of them were taking cell pictures. We'll be very lucky if they don't post them on social media. Ghouls."

"Dammit," he muttered. "I can't lock the door or forbid entrance to the building, not with the bank and other businesses there. But I can damned well get something more sturdy to use as a barrier and station a deputy at the barriers with orders to arrest anybody who tries to get past." He reached for the phone.

Kirby sat down at the conference table and sent a brief smile to the deputy. "Thanks, Emma. I'll be okay now."

"Sure? You reacted more strongly to the elevator than you did when I took you and Cullen out to the Nash farm this morning. And since there's been no rain lately, that field still looks . . . bad." It didn't smell too good, either. And it was drawing insects. And birds.

Cullen spoke up to say, "Yeah, I told Hank Taylor that he could plow it all up if he wanted to. I mean, since the doc has gathered everything she needed, including plenty of photos, we've seen whatever there is to see there, and we have the harvester down in the garage." He paused. "I felt sort of . . . disrespectful saying he could just plow everything under. I think he felt the same way."

"He'll probably do it, though," Emma offered. "If only to spare Sue the sight of that part of the field, since she can clearly see it from the house. Besides, it's not like we can reasonably crawl all over the field picking up . . . bits . . . of Brady all mixed in with the corn and dirt. His arm and everything the doc collected is going to be cremated anyway, once she's finished with her examination."

"Still," Kirby said rather faintly, "just . . . plowing the remains still out there under with dead cornstalks really does seem disrespectful."

"Dust to dust," DeMarco said, still looking at the evidence boards. "Or the cycle of life, if you prefer. Either way, our physical bodies do tend to end up back in the earth. With Brady Nash, unfortunately, it's a more direct journey."

He must have realized he was being stared at, or felt it, because he looked from his partner's raised eyebrow to Kirby's unhidden queasiness, to Cullen's careful lack of expression, and settled finally on Deputy Emma Fletcher's face and the various emotions that flitted across her pretty features.

"Don't mince words, do you?" she said finally.

"Sorry. Just thinking out loud."

Rather dry, Cullen said, "I don't think that helps."

"Did *you* attend a postmortem this morning after breakfast?" DeMarco demanded.

"Well, no."

"All right then." DeMarco returned his attention to the evidence board, not quite frowning.

The sheriff hung up the phone and looked around the room at various expressions. He frowned.

"What did I miss?"

TEN

Instead of answering him, Hollis asked, "Is the elevator all taken care of?"

She did that fairly often, Emma thought, watching the attractive fed with her easy smile and unreadable blue eyes. An unusual blue, she thought. Almost turquoise. Like so much about this woman, her eyes were just slightly unusual. No question she knew her job, that was clear, but Emma was curious about what else Hollis Templeton's invariably calm manner and pleasant expression hid.

Emma wondered what her chances were of getting her questions asked, much less answered, and had a hunch they weren't good. With an effort, she hauled her mind back to what the sheriff was saying.

". . . he'll build a plywood barrier and fasten it securely across that opening. Other than that, I can't do much except keep a deputy or a security guard stationed at that elevator twenty-four-seven until the elevator company gets off its ass and replaces the doors and car."

Thinking of the field they had just left, Emma murmured, "You might want to get one of our guys who's good with a pressure washer to hose it down in there as well, Mal. Before you close it off, I mean."

"Shit. I should have thought of that. Now that the doc and the agents here have had a look, we might as well do what we can to get these places back to normal. Emma, could you please go ask for a volunteer or two familiar with a pressure washer? I'd really rather not make it an order."

"Copy that." She left the conference room.

The sheriff looked back at Hollis. "That mark around Perla Cross's body? The doc really doesn't know what could have caused it?"

"Pretty sure a cord or cable caused it," Hollis replied. "Maybe a rope. We're just not sure how or why. It certainly wasn't a case of her cinching her belt too tight. Plus, she wasn't wearing one." She turned her head and looked at Cullen, frowning just a bit. "Jill was planning to head out to the Cross home and search the attic sometime today. Do you know if she has yet?"

"She said she'd come by here to drop off the autopsy report on Perla Cross before heading out there. She knows I'm planning to go with her."

"That mark on Mrs. Cross's body, Cullen. We need to know as much as we can about it. And if there *is* a cord or cable, we need to find it."

"I'll see if there's anything to find," he replied calmly. "Between us, the doc, her assistant, and I may come up with something useful."

Once again, Mal had the odd sense that a silent conversation had gone on, or something had been said in a code he didn't understand. And he still found it at least briefly unsettling. Then his attention was reclaimed by the actual conversation going on.

Cullen was saying, "We have five victims so far, and the one thing they all have in common is that text message. They all got that at exactly three o'clock in the afternoon, and died later that night. The text originating from an unknown number, presumably a disposable cell."

Kirby, clearly trying to get her mind off recent unsettling sights, added, "And the cell company's records for Clarity put those calls being placed from somewhere between the two closest cell towers—meaning in the general area of downtown."

"I don't think that's going to be much help," Hollis said.

"No, me either. Between businesses and condos and that big apartment complex, most of the citizens of Clarity both live and work in the downtown area or just outside it, the area covered by those towers."

DeMarco spoke up suddenly. "The victim photos up on the board. Anybody else see a pattern?"

The photos fastened to the board above the timeline were of the victims as they had been in life rather than death: smiling, happy for whatever that moment had been.

Clara Adams had been twenty-eight when her car had inexplicably crashed and burned in mid-July. A very pretty blonde with an unusually warm smile. An elementary school teacher.

Jeremy Summers had been thirty and hosting a neighborhood barbecue, manning the grill reportedly complete with a comical apron inviting people to *Kiss the Cook*. A plain charcoal grill, large but seemingly no threat at all until it had inexplicably exploded, not only killing the friendly, happily married father of a little girl, but almost literally blowing him into burning chunks of flesh. In the photo taken for his successful insurance agency, he looked like anybody's neighbor. Everybody's neighbor.

Karen Underwood, the last of July's victims, only twenty-six and killed so near her wedding and almost literally under the horrified eyes of friends, family, and the fiancé she had adored since childhood, the victim of an inexplicably malfunctioning elevator. In her photo, she was a beautiful blonde, glowing with happiness.

Brady Nash had been sixty and looked every year of it in his photo, his broad face lined and leathery after decades spent outdoors working on his farm. But he was smiling, and there was a twinkle in his eyes that said he always had stories and jokes to tell, and told them well. Found not only dead but literally shredded only two days before, the murder weapon a combine harvester, and the murder itself inexplicable in almost every way.

And, finally, Perla Ferguson Cross, who looked even younger than twenty-three in her photo, her fiery red hair and slightly narrowed blue eyes more than hinting of spirit and temper. Another truly beautiful woman who had suffered the most bizarre and inexplicable murder of all, and only last night.

Only last night.

They all stared at the board in silence for several moments, each gaze studying the faces one at a time, all looking for something, anything, that would offer even a nudge in the right direction. And it was Hollis who got it first.

"He's alternating. Female, male, female, male—female."

Mal frowned. "You think it's deliberate?"

"Statistically significant," Cullen said. "Five victims gives us a pretty good pattern."

"So . . . if somebody else got a call today, a little while ago, it's likely to be a man?"

"I'd say the odds favored it."

DeMarco, watching his partner now, said, "What is it?"

"I'm just wondering if we're being irresponsible in not warning people about that text," she replied. "From staged accidents through to obvious murders, it's been the one constant. That he contacts them, on their cell phones, at three o'clock, always from a disposable cell, and always leaves the same text message. A message that isn't a clear warning or threat, and isn't likely to be taken as either unless people know about it."

DeMarco turned his head to look at the sheriff. "What do you think, Mal? How would the people of Clarity react?"

"Panic, probably." He was frowning. "But I've been wrestling with it myself. We put out an emergency alert or warning to everyone with a cell, chances are about a hundred percent that the unsub gets it as well. So then what? I have a town full of panicked people—and a killer who would very likely change the way he warns or tries to scare his victims, stop warning them at all—or send out a lot of texts to a lot of people just to muddy the waters and slow us down."

"You have been wrestling with it," Hollis noted. "Those are very good possibilities."

"Yeah. And I still don't have an answer." He looked around the table hopefully. "Anybody else?"

It was Kirby who said, "The fact of the text messages doesn't really help us, right? I mean, help us identify the unsub. We can't trace the calls. We don't know about the texts, don't know who gets one, until we find a body. If we tell everybody to be alert for a text, chances are we scare a lot of people, *maybe* alert somebody who got a text today at three—and put the unsub on notice. That's assuming he uses in his supposedly normal everyday life a personal cell phone able to receive emergency alerts, and he may not. Lots of people go month-to-month or use disposables. He may not get the sheriff's warning. Or he might. And if he does, he could decide not to kill tonight if he did have a victim chosen. Or he probably thinks of another way to warn them or scare them or whatever it is he's trying to do."

"Why?" Hollis asked, looking at her intently. "Why look for another way?"

Kirby was blank for an instant, then said, "He has to warn them. It's part of his game. Part of his signature. Something not necessary to the murders."

She might not have taken the profiler courses, Hollis thought, but it was clear the younger agent had more than a passing familiarity with, or simply an instinct for, the process of profiling and what to look for. Inwardly, she gave a tip of the hat to Bishop, who really did seem to have an excellent instinct or sense for which agents would or would not be assets to the Special Crimes Unit. He was definitely not a man to judge a book by its cover.

"Go on. Why?" Hollis repeated, this time with just a trace of a smile.

"Because . . . it isn't for us. It isn't even really for the victims, at least so far, because they don't know it's serious, just like you said. The victim doesn't know it's a deadly warning, so it's more likely to inspire impatience or puzzlement than fear. And we don't know about the text, about who gets one, until we find a body. So it has to be for him. It has to mean something to the unsub. Otherwise why go to all the trouble?"

Hollis nodded. "It makes sense to me. The text messages have to mean something to the unsub, and whatever it is, it's not about fear. Not about the victims being afraid, at least. His text message lacks a specific threat, so why would they feel threatened? They wouldn't. So what happens if we effectively take that away from him? We tell the public, and because the text and the murder have so far been hours apart, chances are good that anyone receiving that text today would know it *is* a threat, and would call or come here and report it immediately."

DeMarco said, "Bound to be some pranksters. Probably a lot among the kids, especially in high school."

Slowly, Hollis said, "He hasn't killed a kid. So far, the youngest victim is Perla."

"The women have all been younger than the men," Cullen offered. "Twenty-three, twenty-six, and twenty-eight. The two men were thirty and sixty. Am I crazy or is that a really wide range?"

"For the men, definitely," Hollis said. "The women all being in their twenties could mean something. They could be surrogates for a woman he really wants to kill."

"Then why kill men too?" Mal asked.

"So we don't guess who he's really after, maybe." Hollis stared at the evidence board, her gaze studying the female victims. "Watching crime shows on TV could have taught him that much. Hell, the news could have; we've had at least a few serials and mass killers over the years who killed several people to hide the murder that really mattered to them. So maybe he's hiding his intended victim in a crowd. Men—and women. Two blondes and a redhead."

Mal said, "Perla was a bottle redhead."

"She matched top and bottom," Hollis said matter-of-factly. "That was clear at the autopsy."

"Yeah, she would."

Hollis looked at him, brows rising.

"Everybody knew," he said hastily. "She has three sisters, one blond and two brunette, and if any of them color their hair they haven't flaunted it the way Perla did. She was somewhere between blond and brunette in high school. Didn't go red until she married Joe. The talk of the wedding was her hair and her shoes."

"Like glass slippers," Hollis said.

"Yeah, as a matter of fact. Dunno if they were glass, but you could see through them. And she'd had every toenail painted a different color."

Kirby murmured, "Not exactly a shrinking violet."

"Oh, hell, no," Mal said. "The third subject of gossip that day was her dress. Sort of . . . defied gravity, if you know what I mean."

Hollis and Kirby exchanged glances, and it was Kirby who said dryly, "Yeah, we know. The wedding-dress designs of the last few seasons have really made the rounds of social media. It seems clear designers have forgotten how to make sleeves. Or support for breasts, especially generous ones. And also share an apparently common desire to show off every inch of breast that isn't nipple."

Mal looked more sheepish than embarrassed. "Yeah, there was a betting pool among most of the male guests as to when that top part was going to give way."

"Did you win?" DeMarco asked with a faint smile.

"I did not bet," Mal said with great dignity. And promptly ruined that by adding, "I did pay very close attention, however."

Hollis half laughed. Gallows humor of a sort. Every cop she'd ever worked with used some variation of it from time to time during an investigation to distract the mind from horrors seen. "Did anybody win?"

"No, that dress defied gravity even when she danced. And she danced the way all the Fergusons do: energetically. But I think some of the men felt guilty betting; I heard later that the pot went into the next Sunday's collection basket at our largest Baptist church." His smile died. "I hadn't remembered all that until just now. Perla gave Joe hell, and she could be a pain in the ass, but she was also a lot of fun to have around most of the time."

"Sounds like it," Hollis murmured. "There are worse epitaphs to have."

"I guess. But she was too young. They're always too young when somebody just . . . takes away their lives. Their futures."

"Yes," Hollis said. "They are."

HE LURKED, SOMETHING he was very good at. They didn't see or hear him, he made sure of that. He also made sure he was close enough to hear the conversation going on in the rather small morgue in the basement of Clarity's one hospital.

Sam Norris, Dr. Easton's assistant, photographer, and possible lover, was sitting at a computer, scrolling through some very graphic autopsy photos. "You sure you want all these printed out?" he asked without taking his attention from the screen. He was a man of average size and average looks—except for a pair of very sharp gray eyes and a pair of very distinct dimples that appeared when he smiled. And he smiled a lot whenever the doctor was in.

Jill Easton emerged from a little alcove off to one side, wiping her freshly washed hands on a couple of paper towels. "Yeah, all of them. I don't know about the sheriff, but feds always want every single detail I can give them." She was an attractive blonde, slender enough that people were always surprised at how easily and efficiently she handled the literal dead weight of bodies.

"I printed out the other shots you wanted and put them in the folders," he told her. "From what few other remains we've had to examine."

"Good. More details for them. Make sure your camera is charged up. I sort of doubt we'll find anything worth finding in the attic of the Cross house, but the consensus seems to be that her killer could have been hiding up there at some point, with or without Perla, so the entire attic is now considered a part of the crime scene."

"Jeez, we'll be up there half the night."

"It's not even four o'clock."

"I'm just saying."

"Well, just print out the autopsy photos, will you? We'll drop them off at the sheriff's department and pick up the fed who's going to be . . . assisting us."

"They think we need our hands held?" Sam demanded, clearly about to work up some righteous indignation.

"No, while we look for any physical evidence, this fed is apparently going to be looking for signs of behavior."

He looked at her, brows raised. "A profiler?"

"So I gather. We've found shit for evidence so far, and given that, I don't blame the sheriff a bit for calling in investigators who look at killings from a different perspective."

"Have we ever worked with a profiler before?"

"Not that I know of. Though they don't always tell us anything other than the fact that they're FBI agents. I was actually pretty surprised that Hollis and Reese turned up this morning for the post on Perla Cross."

"Me too. They didn't seem too grossed out," he offered.

"No, I'm guessing this is far from their first murder investigation or their first autopsy."

Sam slid his chair over to the printer and pulled out a stack of photos. "Well, they can all pore over these for a while if they want. Which fed is coming with us to the Cross house?"

"Cullen."

"Wonder why he got the short straw?" Sam mused, but not as if he expected an answer. He got up and went to gather his part of the CSI equipment they used while Jill gathered up photos and files and grabbed her own bag.

"Ready?"

"Yeah, let's go. I'd as soon not spend any more time than we have to in that house. Place is creepy."

"Some places just are."

"Yeah, but to be really creepy—"

The door closed behind them, cutting off whatever Sam thought was necessary for true creepiness.

The lurker waited for a few moments just to be safe, then emerged into the room and went straight to the wall of very specialized freezers. It was a small town, so there were only eight perfectly square doors.

He got it right with his first guess, and smiled as he reached into the freezer to get what he'd come here after.

DEMARCO GAVE THE subject deserving of respect at least half a minute, then said, "Well, whether her killer knew Perla Cross was naturally a blondish brunette or thought she was a redhead, it doesn't appear that hair color matters to him. The first two women killed were both blondes."

"Still possibly surrogates," his partner said. "Especially if he did know Perla's real hair color and considered it more blond than brunette."

"True. And they have more in common than the two male victims, in age and general appearance. Attractive women in their twenties. If they *are* surrogates, it means that either he isn't ready yet to go after the woman he really wants to kill, or she's somehow beyond his reach. Maybe both. A woman he believes hurt him or abandoned him or somehow destroyed his life. And he wants payback." DeMarco paused, then added, "You know, given the way Perla was killed, with absolutely no attempt made to make it look like an accident, it's possible she was the one he was after all along."

Mal said hopefully, "Then no more victims?"

"I wouldn't go that far, not if he's as smart and careful

as he's seemed up to now. By making Perla Cross's death very obviously a murder, he's gone off-script. If he stopped with her, it would be almost as good as a confession, a neon sign pointing at her, and we'd be turning her life upside-down looking for someone who wanted to kill *her*."

"She's the one I really hated," Hollis murmured. "The one I really wanted to kill."

"Then he has to kill again?" Mal shook his head. "I've gotta say, I'm leaning toward a public announcement about the texts. And I'd just as soon get it out well before dark."

Cullen asked, "How are you set up for that kind of emergency announcement?"

"Ironically, the first step is a text on every cell phone reachable by the two cell towers and enabled to receive text alerts. Cheap disposables or those on some prepaid plans aren't always enabled—but unless you're alone, you're going to hear a *lot* of other people's phones going off around you, and not with normal ringtones but with clear alert signals. There are emergency weather alerts, Amber Alerts, that sort of thing. This one would read something like: *Sheriff's Department Alert: If you or anyone you know receives a text message that reads "Wait for dark," report it immediately to the sheriff's department or nearest deputy. Your life could be in danger.*"

Hollis winced. "Well, that's blunt enough." She held up a hand when Mal would have spoken, adding, "I know, I know. They have to know the text is a serious threat, or most would shrug it off."

Cullen was clearly thinking along other lines. "How do you reach the places farther out, beyond range of those towers?"

"Landlines came first, and for the outlying homes and farms, they're still used. We have a list of every number and notify them the old-fashioned way, one at a time, with everybody I've got manning the phones."

Cullen opened his mouth, then frowned.

Mal answered the unasked question. "Pretty much every person in Clarity over the age of eight has a cell phone, even those who live outside the range of the towers. The kids go to school, the parents and workers come into town, and that's when they use the cells."

"I'm guessing if you don't get an answer on a landline—"

"I send a deputy out," Mal said with a nod. "Or ask a neighbor we can contact to pass the word along. It sounds unwieldy, but it's worked pretty well for us."

"Sounds like," Cullen agreed.

Hollis looked at the big clock above the door and said, "Maybe you'd better get started on that emergency alert."

"Right." The sheriff pushed back his chair and left the conference room, headed toward what the agents had already noticed was a fairly elaborate communications center.

"You're frowning," DeMarco noted to his partner.

She frowned at him for a moment, then shifted her gaze to Cullen. "Are you sensing anything?" She kept her voice low.

Just as quietly, Cullen said, "Nothing unexpected. Nothing new. Why?"

Instead of answering that, Hollis looked at Kirby and lifted a brow.

Kirby sighed. "The people gawking at that elevator shaft were feeling all kinds of things, but what I've been getting mostly today has been the horror of Perla Cross's murder."

"So the details are out."

"Listen, when I woke up not long after dawn this morning, I knew the details had gotten out. The first shock is wearing off, and now people are jumpy as hell. Which means I am. I swear, if somebody had yelled *boo* at me anytime today, you'd have had to peel me off the ceiling."

"You've hidden that pretty well. But I guess I don't have to suggest you keep working on those shields," Hollis said dryly.

"Oh, no. I'm working on the shields almost continuously. Mostly when I'm sitting down, though. Because the problem is, when I'm really concentrating on trying to strengthen my shields, I'm lucky if I can walk in a straight line at the same time."

"Which is why Emma had to almost lead you back here by the arm?"

"Pretty much, yeah. She thought the elevator *accident* scene upset me, and it seemed easier to just let her believe that. I thought I had a pretty good shield, but . . . Is it the same way for you guys, not being able to concentrate on blocking the really strong stuff and still function normally otherwise? Because none of you look like you've had to make an effort."

"We've been at it longer," DeMarco said. "And for some of us, our shields had to be in place very early on, out of necessity. Whether we were born with our abilities or had them triggered, not having a shield would have been too dangerous."

"I can testify to that," Hollis said wryly, and added to Kirby, "I had no shield. At all. For years. And I broadcast, especially when I was upset. Well, I still do that sometimes, which you already know. And I'm still working on strengthening my shield. So I can sympathize."

"Wow. Years? How did you get through that?"

"I had teammates," Hollis answered firmly. "People around me who understood. People to help me learn, and sometimes use their own abilities to help me. Which is what you have and will continue to have. Believe that."

ELEVEN

DeMarco added, "Our minds tend to do what they need to in order to protect us. Sometimes the mind of a psychic, their nature, is stronger than they realize. They can endure more than they believe they can. And for whatever reason, the Universe insists that they endure." He wasn't looking at his partner, though the other two agents glanced at Hollis. "And for those psychics, the mind apparently doesn't give building a shield a priority."

"Why is my mind giving me trouble?" Kirby asked with a tinge of desperation in her voice. "I'm not strong, really. I mean inside. Not tough. Too many things still scare me. And feeling what others feel . . . I think it's a good bet the emotions in this town are going to be getting more intense, especially after the sheriff's warning. Panic, worry, fear. Is my mind going to protect me from *that*?"

Hollis said, "You haven't been in this kind of situation before, right? With a whole town, even a small town, feeling way too much to be calm about it?"

"No, I haven't. My abilities were triggered by a car accident around two years ago. And it wasn't long after I started freaking out the nursing staff at the hospital that Bishop paid me a visit. I don't have any family except distant cousins I never kept track of, and since I'd left Chicago to move to New York and had the accident on the way, there were no friends nearby. When I was discharged, Bishop was there to take me directly to a big house up in the mountains here in the South. Really high up, like a sort of . . . aerie. I don't know if you guys have been there, but it was like someone's private home, only it had half a dozen guest suites and a pretty amazing communications center, and incredible views out of every window. And a helicopter pad, which is good because I'm not sure there were roads."

Hollis glanced at her partner, their eyes meeting briefly as both of them remembered that particular aerie. It was where they had met for the first time. At that amazing place that was part home and part business, where Bishop and Miranda occasionally met up with teams during their cases and where they tended to spend what off time they could carve out together. But neither Hollis nor Reese interrupted the younger agent as she went on.

"From what I saw and what I was told, I gather that's where Bishop takes some of the more . . . fragile . . . psychics before he decides whether they belong in the FBI or at Haven. Or neither. There were other people there, other psychics including Miranda, almost all of them with shields, so it felt very peaceful to me. And there were tests, I suppose to see what I was capable of. I honestly don't know why Bishop thought I belonged at Quantico, but he convinced me. About six months after the accident I joined up, took the tests the FBI required, somehow passed them, and he and Miranda have been working with me ever since. Other agents as well. Some tests in the lab, but mostly learning or trying to learn to develop that shield. They didn't seem to feel I needed to work as much on the empathy."

"That's because you're a very strong empath," Hollis said calmly. "You tested at the upper end of the scale. So the priority was to teach you how to protect yourself from being hurt."

"I don't think I'm there yet."

"Probably not. But if I know Bishop—and I believe I do—he reached the conclusion that you and I share a trait, and it's probably why he put our teams together on this case."

"What kind of trait?"

"Our minds and abilities adapt, usually quickly, especially when there's danger, and they do what's necessary to protect us or help us survive. It's not something that happens in the quiet moments of concentration, or in the lab. We've figured out that much. If it happens at all, it's virtually always in the field, and because of the intense pressure of an investigation."

Uneasy, Kirby said, "Isn't that assuming a lot? That this case will help me rather than hurt me?"

"Bishop rarely assumes," DeMarco said dryly. "And he's virtually always right about how our abilities develop. That said, our shields develop to protect us, usually, from a threat, and often enough the threat does at least some damage initially, enough to . . . wake up the defenses of your mind. So chances are good you'll find yourself being overwhelmed by the emotions of those around you, and may well also face some kind of threat, maybe more than one, before your shields are truly strong enough to protect you."

"Great," Kirby said faintly.

"You have us," Hollis told her. "We're a team, remember? In most cases, we can help protect each other. You're not alone, Kirby. Never forget that."

"Okay." Her voice was still rather small, and her almost childlike face was anxious.

Hollis hadn't really expected to fully allay the younger agent's fears and uncertainties, but it was a start, and sometimes that was all they got. She nodded, then looked back at her partner. "Have you picked up anything?"

"Same thing from Mal a couple of times today, that he had the sense there was a conversation going on around him somehow, and he wasn't invited."

"Does it bug him?"

"Momentarily. More puzzlement than anything else, and so far brief. I don't think we need to confide in him about our abilities. Not yet, at any rate. Hollis, have *you* picked up anything?"

She hesitated, glanced at the other two agents, then nodded. "There's something, I just can't get a fix on it."

WAIT FOR DARK   183

Kirby said, "But isn't it easy for you to see—spirits?" She lowered her voice hastily on the last word and actually ducked her head a little, obviously realizing she needed to speak quietly because the conference-room door was open.

"Yeah, it is. Has been for years now. This isn't about that." Hollis kept her own voice quiet. And she didn't tell them that several times during the day the spirit of a deputy had walked through this very room without, seemingly, taking any notice of the living.

"Then what's it about?" Cullen asked.

"Energy," DeMarco said. "It almost has to be energy. Even if our auras appear normal to you, that doesn't mean there isn't some kind of unusual energy in this place the rest of us can't sense and aren't threatened by. You're probably more sensitive to energies of all kinds than anyone else in the unit."

"That's what I keep telling myself, that it's energy, and since it's not negative I don't need to worry," Hollis responded. "But if it is energy, it's unlike any I've ever sensed before."

"In what way?"

"That's the hell of it. I don't know. It just feels . . . wrong. Not negative, not dark, just . . . wrong." She felt the way she'd felt the previous evening, that whatever was wrong, it was somehow wrong with *her*. And that was not something she wanted to confide in the newer agents unless and until it was necessary.

But DeMarco wasn't going to drop it so easily. "Wrong enough to be worrying you. The same as yesterday?"

"Sort of the same." She rubbed both temples, frowning. "Hell, I dunno. Sometimes it seems almost like everything is . . . slightly out of focus. So maybe it's just me. My eyes. Maybe my eyes—"

"Your eyes are fine." DeMarco didn't touch her, but he did lean toward her until her gaze met his. "Whatever this is, it isn't because of your eyes."

After a long moment, Hollis nodded. "Okay. It's not my eyes. So what is it?"

"Beats the hell out of me."

Hollis half laughed. "Right."

Kirby said, "Should we be worried?"

DeMarco answered her. "Any anomaly is a reason for concern. That said, as you both probably know, Hollis has a history of developing entirely new abilities during a case, spontaneously, and there's nothing to say that's not what's happening."

Hollis frowned at him. "Seriously?"

"It's as likely as anything else, isn't it? And it certainly fits the pattern with you. So far, nobody's extra senses have helped us figure this thing out. You know we're on a tight timeline, that he could kill someone tonight, and that could easily be enough of a threat. In an investigation, you instinctively reach out with everything you have. Maybe this time, like other times, you need something you didn't have when we got here."

Kirby said suddenly, "My head hurts."

"It's confusing," Cullen sympathized.

"No. I mean my head *hurts*. Like something hit it."

She was very pale, her gaze fixed on nothing. Then she flinched, and her nose began to bleed.

"KIRBY—" CULLEN PRODUCED his handkerchief and quickly rose and moved to her chair. "Here, tip your head slightly forward."

She accepted the handkerchief, saying rather thickly, "I thought you were supposed . . . to tip your head back."

"Forward is better. Keep the cloth pressed to your nostrils; keep them gently but firmly closed. Breathe through your mouth. I'll get some ice."

Luckily, the conference room's small alcove kitchenette had an under-counter fridge with an ice maker, so he returned to the table only a few moments later with two small bundles of ice wrapped in several layers of paper towel. Using the best angle, he stood behind her chair and carefully pressed the makeshift ice packs to both sides of her face, touching her cheeks and her nose.

Kirby's eyes were a bit glazed, but she fixed them on Hollis, an obvious question in them.

"Nosebleeds are fairly common with psychics," Hollis said, calm and matter-of-fact. "Sometimes we push too hard, or just get slammed by thoughts, emotions, or information when we're not ready for it. Most of us have learned what to do." She sent a glance toward her own partner. "Though we usually don't need ice."

"Or don't have it so handy," DeMarco said. "Aren't headaches more common with empaths?"

"Yeah, usually, at least as far as we know, if only because they can feel what people around them feel. This . . . this looks like something she's picking up from someone else."

When Kirby would have spoken, Cullen said immediately, "Keep still for now. It can take ten minutes or more to make sure the bleeding has stopped. That's the important thing for the moment." He sent a glance toward the two senior agents, then looked at the wall clock, obviously monitoring the time.

"Too early for the unsub," DeMarco murmured.

Keeping her voice just as low, Hollis said, "Maybe not too early for him to already have his victim. We think it's at least possible he was with Perla Cross for anything up to a few hours before he killed her. Could be the same thing again. And he could have used a blitz attack, for whatever reason, to disable this victim quickly. It could be the blow Kirby felt."

"Hell of a blow," DeMarco noted.

"Yeah. I'm not happy that she had an actual physical reaction. Empaths often do, but . . . she needs those shields."

"Then we'll help her build them."

"I hope we can," Hollis said.

DeMarco nodded, then said in a normal, not-so-quiet voice, but almost musing, "The texts really are for the unsub, not the victims."

This was what profilers did, Hollis thought. Gather information, signs of behaviors, and possible answers—

and then just consider what they had, including hunches, musing, examining from every angle.

Shuffling the puzzle pieces, examining them, turning them this way and that until they started, finally, to drop into place and show what the whole picture really was.

Hollis nodded. "And I can't think of a way for us to find out or figure out *why* that phrase or why dark is important to him. Or why just sending the text is important. It doesn't make any sense to me no matter which way I turn it."

DeMarco frowned. "How much juice do you figure Bishop has?"

"As much as he needs. Why?"

"I'm just wondering what sort of assets we could call on."

"Pretty much anything within the realm of the possible," Hollis said. "We're really on borrowed time with the media as well as the unsub, and once they show up they'll only cause chaos in a town this small, never mind slowing us down. We need to get as much accomplished as we possibly can before that happens. Bishop will be on alert already, especially since the body count went up even before we could get here. I don't know if he'd send in the military, but probably anything short of that. What did you have in mind?"

"Media or not, I also think we're definitely on a very tight timetable, especially if the unsub *does* kill again tonight. Given that, given the ongoing threat, I think we'd be justified in asking that the top analysts available at

Quantico do complete background checks on every soul above the age of sixteen in Clarity."

"Especially our victims," Hollis said slowly. "Clara Adams, Brady Nash, and Perla Cross have lived in Clarity all their lives, with the exception of college in Clara's case and a military school in Mr. Nash's. Except for her honeymoon to Aruba, Perla Cross never left this town, at least as far as we know." She was gazing at the board, her gaze studying the photos of the victims one more time.

DeMarco nodded. "We also need someone who really knows what they're doing to comb through all available public records and documents for the town, going back at least ten years. It's the fastest way we'll get enough information, especially since we're looking for any sort of event that could have created this monster. My guess is, it won't be an insignificant event even from our point of view, though it's likely intensely personal, even if for most people it went unnoticed. A divorce or broken engagement, maybe a death or some other kind of abandonment. Involving an attractive woman in her twenties."

Hollis blinked, then said slowly, "It's a pretty small town, so I'm sure it's doable even though it'll probably take a couple of days for the background checks at least. The public records and other documents on the town can likely be searched more quickly. Though without a warrant I don't think even the FBI is going to want to get caught searching through any records or documents that contain private information."

"No way a judge would sanction a search that broad and at the same time that intensive."

Hollis reached a hand to rub her temple briefly and almost absently. "Probably depends. Bishop seems to know a lot of judges. And either they're all on our side or else they owe Bishop big-time, because he's been able to get us legally into some pretty protected places. We both remember Samuel's church. Judges really are reluctant to act against a church even if it's really a cult—and we didn't have legal proof it was. You were already inside, but the rest of us wouldn't have gotten past the gates without that warrant."

"True. But we did have cause there, if not actual physical evidence. Just my testimony could have put Samuel *and* his inner circle away for a long time." He watched her rub her temple again, and again she didn't seem to be aware of doing it. "Say even Bishop can't get a warrant for this one. Do you think he'd balk at something on the shady side of legal?"

Dryly, Hollis said, "He gave each of us a set of lock-pick tools and taught us how to use them. What do you think?"

"I think we should report in and make the request. He's the boss. If he knows the right friendly judge or is willing to take the risk, then he will. If he says no, it's no."

"I somehow doubt he'll say no. He seems to view this sort of thing as a challenge. I think."

"In his position, I imagine he has to. Building and running a unit like the SCU is very much outside the norm for the FBI."

"True," Hollis said.

"Hey," the sheriff said from the doorway. "What the hell happened?" He came in, staring at Kirby and Cullen.

"Nosebleed," Hollis answered. "Nothing to be concerned about."

"You sure? She looks awfully pale."

"I'll be fine," Kirby said in that weird voice everyone has with their nostrils pinched closed.

"Okay, if you say so." He eyed her a moment longer, then looked at Hollis. "The warning about the text has started going out. The majority of Clarity's citizens will be notified in the first hour, but making sure everyone got the message is probably going to take tonight and most of tomorrow. We've even asked all the downtown stores to make the announcement via their own PA systems, every half hour from now until they close tonight."

Hollis said, "Virtually all the victims have been killed and left either at their homes or somewhere near. Even the car crash was—what?—about two blocks from Clara Adams's condo?"

"About that, yeah. What're you thinking?"

"The emergency warning system for cell phones, is there a response when the message is delivered?"

"Yeah, it pings back, and our communications system records the response. The cell company that installed the system is trying it out in several places around the country, both small towns and big cities. Trial runs, they said. They want to take it national. Big warning sirens and the emergency-alert signal on TV just don't reach everyone, not anymore. But I gather the tech people are expecting more cell towers, and more smart watches and cell phones and tablets and other handhelds, until that'll be the way virtually everybody can be alerted in case of an emergency."

"Sounds like a good idea." But she was frowning slightly. "What response do you get if somebody's cell is off or dead? Because I forgot to charge mine last night, and just noticed a little while ago that it's dead." She lied easily, which bothered her somewhat, but there was no good reason to go into even a nonpsychic reason why her cell phone could never carry a charge more than a few hours. Especially since she knew the other members of her team had the same issue. DeMarco had been known to carry a watch, though she had noticed that he stopped doing that not too long after he'd left his undercover assignment and come fully into the SCU.

Clearly incurious, the sheriff was nodding. "Well, in the case of you four, if those are Bureau-issued cells, when you powered up or checked your phones, you'd get the text warning but no alarm, and they won't ping back. Same thing with any law-enforcement-registered cell. Basically, the system is designed to alert—but otherwise ignore them. Something about frequencies, and the fact that any of us could be in situations where it wouldn't be wise to have alarms going off, or our locations pinpointed."

"Impressive," Hollis said. "And if a civilian's cell is dead or off?"

"The system attempts to deliver the warning a second time within five minutes, and then it logs an alert that notifies one of our operators. Same thing with the landlines, except that the emergency message is spoken, a recording, and the system logs a successful contact even if the phone has voice mail."

"So you wouldn't necessarily know if people living at that home got the warning."

"Not with the existing system, no. That's one of the bugs they're trying to work out."

"And you?"

He didn't have to ask her to explain the question. "I have operators listening in on the landline calls; that's one reason I expect those contacts to take longer. If a machine or voice mail picks up, the operator cuts into the automated system and calls the number at least twice more, leaving the message for them to call the sheriff's department immediately."

"Do you wait?"

"No, not if the emergency is dangerous in any way. An Amber Alert is one thing; a severe thunderstorm warning or flash flood warning is something else entirely. It's passed on to dispatch, which immediately alerts the nearest patrol car in that area. They have orders to knock on doors and even shine their flashlights through the windows, *especially* if the family vehicles are there. Anything suspicious, they're authorized to break a window to get in."

Curiously, DeMarco said, "It sounds like a pretty elaborate system for a small town that I'm guessing doesn't experience too many emergencies."

"Yeah, except for regional or national Amber Alerts, our emergencies tend to be weather related. We get some rough storms up here, and there's always the danger of flash flooding from all the streams and creeks, so warnings are taken very seriously. There are several outlying homes and farms that can be cut off by flood-level streams, sometimes for several days, and so they need immediate warning. It doesn't happen every year, but we've had rough springs the last two years I've been sheriff."

"So you've had chances to work out the kinks," Hollis said.

"A few, yeah."

"Hey, what's happened here?" Jill Easton came into the conference room, followed by her assistant, Sam. She had an armful of file folders, which she absently handed to the sheriff, her gaze on Kirby. But it was Cullen who answered.

"A nosebleed, no big deal," he said, then glanced at the clock and added, "Unless the bleeding hasn't stopped when we take away the pressure and ice in two minutes. If it hasn't, Jill, then you're up."

She nodded. "Sure. Do you know what caused it? Not really high enough here for elevation to be an issue."

"I just get them sometimes," Kirby said, and rolled her eyes at the funny sound of her own voice.

Jill merely nodded gravely, but her assistant seemed to have an abrupt urge to turn away and hunt through his equipment bag for something.

Mal couldn't quite hide his own smile, though it died as he began looking through the autopsy photos. He sat down at the conference table with a sigh to really go through the files, his face more grim by the moment as he studied them.

But he was the only one not either openly or covertly watching Kirby, and Hollis knew Kirby hated being the center of this kind of attention, so she drew the doctor's attention to herself. "Have you had any more thoughts about that seeming ligature mark around Perla Cross's waist?"

"Not about the source or the reason, but I'm pretty sure there was some kind of cord, cable, or rope tied pretty tightly around her waist while she was still alive. Left quite a mark, as you saw this morning. And it's deeper and more pronounced on the front of her body than on the back."

Slowly, DeMarco said, "As if she was pulled backward?"

"More like jerked backward. With considerable force."

Hollis said, "With enough force to impale her on those sharpened limbs?"

"I'd say so."

"Could a single man have done that?" Hollis was thinking of the attic, the tree, the angles involved. She was no geometry whiz, but it just didn't seem possible that Perla had been killed the way she had been killed.

"Not without a little mechanical help, if you want my opinion. Mal's catapult idea would have worked just dandy, but if it had existed, it wouldn't be a small thing, it would have left marks on the floor—and I don't see how anybody could have taken it apart and gotten it out of the attic in the time available."

"I kept picturing one of those giant medieval cata-pults," Hollis confessed. "The things they used to throw giant boulders or balls of burning pitch."

"While storming a castle or trying to set an enemy's ships on fire?" Jill nodded. "It's what I pictured first, but I had a pal whose longtime hobby is machines of war send me some info, and according to him, a person-sized catapult is not only possible, there are directions on the Internet on how to build one. And it's not all that hard. But it would have a lot of moving parts and you'd have to have some pretty advanced knowledge of construction. In addition, the same problems for us exist if your unsub used something like that: it still would have been too large to hide intact in that attic, taking it apart and hid-ing it would have taken time, *and* the parts would stick out as something unusual even in an attic. And there just wasn't time for something like that to be removed from the attic, not given Perla's time of death. And I am sure of that window for time of death, by the way."

DeMarco said, "So the unsub used something more basic, more common?"

Jill nodded again. "Some kind of block-and-tackle setup, maybe. A pulley. Ropes or fairly thick but flexi-ble cable. Something to give him leverage. And I'm not sure where he would have been positioned to get the necessary leverage to apply that much force. I'm guessing there was something rigged higher up in the tree as well as in the attic, or outside the attic at the peak of the roof. And we just missed it the first time."

Her assistant joined the conversation with a resigned

expression and muttered, "Christ, I'm gonna have to climb that tree. I knew it. I just knew it."

Jill glanced over her shoulder at him, more amused than annoyed. "Afraid so, Sam."

"Dammit. Then can we go now, please? Aside from not being able to see shit, I'd rather not be up in that tree after dark for all kinds of other reasons."

"We can leave as soon as Cullen's ready."

The words were barely out of her mouth when Cullen replied. "We can leave anytime. The bleeding's stopped."

Kirby, the makeshift ice packs removed, dabbed at her nose with the stained handkerchief a bit gingerly, but they could all see that her nose was no longer bleeding.

"Breathing okay?" Jill asked her professionally.

Kirby breathed carefully in and out through her nose. "Yeah, fine. Thanks, Cullen."

"That's what partners are for." He took the now-soaked ice packs back to the kitchen area for disposal, then returned to the conference room, rubbing his hands together. He got the light Windbreaker from the back of the chair where he'd been sitting and shrugged into it. "Ready when you are," he said to Jill and her assistant.

"Watch your back," Hollis warned, her voice light but her expression showing a fleeting anxiety.

"Always," he replied in the same tone.

TWELVE

He watched the small team leave the sheriff's department and smiled, unworried. If they found what he'd left for them to find, it would just present them with more questions. And if they didn't find it, well, they'd still have questions.

And another body to offer more questions, after tonight. He was ready, everything in place for his plan. *Reverend* Pilate was in place, and had provided the added benefit of his cell phone and the emergency-alert text from the sheriff.

The sheriff.

He wondered when Malachi Gordon would catch on to what was happening. Or if he would. He was generally a good cop but in this case was quite likely blind to the truth.

Most people were, when it was hiding in plain sight right under their noses.

MAL CLOSED THE Perla Cross autopsy file with a muttered curse, then proved he had in fact been paying attention to the others in the room, asking Hollis, "Why'd you warn Cullen to watch his back?"

Hollis gave it a beat, then said, "Because I think we could be targets."

"You said this guy wasn't picking random targets."

"We wouldn't be random. We're a threat. Or, at least, he could see us as a threat."

DeMarco nodded toward the evidence board. "And if we're right about that male-female pattern holding, the next victim will be a male."

Mal rubbed his face with both hands in a slightly weary gesture, then said, "I really hope you guys are wrong about there being another victim. But I don't think you are."

"Did you see anything you didn't already know in that autopsy report?" Hollis asked.

"No. But I heard you and Jill talking about there likely being some kind of equipment or device that helped the killer slam Perla into that tree. Which makes sense, given how hard she was thrown. Do you think they'll find signs of whatever was used?"

"They will if he wants us to find something."

Frowning, Mal said, "No offense, but I really hope this guy isn't as bright as you think he is."

Hollis shook her head slightly. "None taken. But I don't think it's as much his intelligence as it is his meticulous planning. I think he's been planning all this for a long time. Until Mrs. Cross, he made sure his victims' bodies were pretty much destroyed, or at least left so damaged there'd be no evidence to point to the killer. Of the first four victims, only Karen Underwood's body wasn't completely destroyed, and with a falling elevator car as the murder weapon, what could we possibly find to help us? Nothing."

"But he left Perla impaled on those limbs. Didn't do anything to destroy the body."

"No, he didn't. So the question is, did he lose it with her? Or was the manner of her death always part of his script? And if it *was* part of his script, then why did he decide to so abruptly stop arranging accidents? Why make it so obviously murder? The question I keep coming back to, no matter how far away from it I get." She sounded just a little frustrated, and there was a tiny furrow between her brows, her expression almost but not quite a frown.

"You think it was part of his script, don't you?"

Hollis nodded immediately. "We do. Especially now that we believe there's a good chance he used some kind of device."

"That sticks out?" Mal was definitely frowning.

"Mechanical," Hollis said. "Except, possibly, for the grill, all of the first four deaths were caused by something mechanical, some kind of machine that failed, or worked in a way it wasn't designed to work, or was sabotaged."

Mal looked over at the evidence boards briefly. "Another commonality?"

"It will be," DeMarco said, "if there's evidence that some kind of constructed device was used to kill Perla Cross."

Returning his gaze to the agents, Mal nodded. "And it hasn't been part of the profile—as least what you've told me so far—because as soon as you got here, there was Perla."

"Right," Hollis said. "We had a few initial ideas in mind after studying the reports you sent on the first four victims, but the grill was always iffy, and then we had no real evidence that some kind of equipment threw Mrs. Cross into that tree. All we had was our conclusion that no single person could have thrown her from the attic with such force. And we knew we weren't looking for a team."

"God, I hope not," Mal said, looking startled.

"This type of killer, apparently playing games or trying to be creative in how he kills, almost always works alone," Hollis told him. "He's trying to be clever, to challenge himself or us, or maybe just to hide what he believes is an obvious motive by varying his methods and victims so much."

"Still . . . we could be looking for somebody who's mechanically adept," Mal said slowly.

"We could," Hollis agreed. "He pretty much has to be, as a matter of fact."

"Joe Cross is a mechanic."

DeMarco asked, "Is he good with machines other than cars, electronics in general?"

"Well . . . I don't know."

Hollis waited, smiling slightly.

Mal snapped his fingers. "Perla's cell. He couldn't get past a simple password. And there's not even a computer in the house, at least not that I saw."

"We didn't see one either. Pretty good signs his knowledge of electronics is probably limited to cars. So *maybe* he could have sabotaged Clara Adams's car, but an elevator? A giant piece of farm machinery? Not very likely. Plus, from what you and Emma told us, Joe Cross is not only not the type to kill at all, far less five people including his wife, but he appears to be grieving her death, and deeply." She paused, then added, "But we still need to talk to him, Mal."

"Of course. According to talk, a doctor had to knock him out last night. He's staying with one of Perla's older sisters, Carla, and her husband, Keith Webb. Apparently the house is pretty much filled with Fergusons, all of them characteristically trying to keep busy. Lot of cooking, I hear. And there's solid sympathy for Joe, but apparently he just couldn't stop crying. So a doc knocked him out."

Hollis nodded, not really surprised.

Mal looked back at the evidence board, frowning again. "But if some kind of device *is* found at the Cross home, then the killer has to be somebody good with electronics—as well as fairly ordinary tools like a hacksaw or hatchet or some kind of knife. Sharpening those limbs sounds easy, but I'm betting it wasn't."

Hollis said, "And he took as much time as he needed to plan. Planning means he was definitely on-script."

DeMarco said to the sheriff, "Something you may not

have noticed in Jill's reports. She's certain that the tree limbs were sharpened as much as a week before Perla's death."

Mal blinked. "A week before? But that means—"

Hollis was nodding. "That means he was already prepared to murder Mrs. Cross—or at least murder someone in that tree—when he murdered Brady Nash."

"Did he get them out of order, or—"

"It feels more like he planned to kill them just the way he did, when he did. He knew their routines, Mal. Even Clara Adams was coming home after the night class she regularly taught at the community college about ten miles outside town."

"Yeah," Mal said slowly. "She was. And the barbecue hosted by Jeremy Summers had been the same weekend in July for the last three years. The whole neighborhood looked forward to it. Not only is his yard the biggest, with a pool that has elaborate slides for the kids, he always provided dozens of steaks, and asked neighbors only to bring hot dogs or hamburgers, plus sides. And he always had three big grills going, different places in the yard, charcoal only. He claimed you could always taste the propane in foods cooked on gas grills."

Mal paused, then added, "It was his oldest grill that blew. And a miracle he was the only one standing close enough to be even seriously hurt, let alone killed. There were some minor burns on a few of the other people there, some because they rushed toward the area seconds after the explosion, hoping they could help, and a few because they were hit by falling . . . debris."

All of them were silent for a moment, all thinking of what that debris had consisted of. Shards of hot and burning metal. And burning flesh.

Finally, Hollis said, "According to your reports, Nash routinely went out to the barn to check on his cows before bed, same time every night, regular as clockwork, even if he didn't have a cow ready to calve. And even on a day off work, Mrs. Cross would have been home between six and eight, probably getting ready to go out since it was a Friday and she always went out on Fridays."

"Not without Joe," Mal said immediately. "That was one of the things they fought about, that even if she went out with her sisters or other women friends, he lurked around the edges."

"Didn't trust her?" Hollis asked.

"Didn't trust every other man in town. And everybody knew it. So what you said before makes more sense. That the unsub had Perla under his control somehow, and made sure all the evidence downstairs said she was gone but hadn't run away again. He could have figured Joe wouldn't look closely enough to see stuff there that shouldn't have been, that he'd just find no Perla and think she'd gone out to be with friends or family, slipping out on purpose before he was due home from work. The unsub probably expected him to do his usual panicked routine of checking all the motels in the area, or even just take off for town to hunt for Perla there. But instead it all just felt too wrong to Joe, and he came here right off to report her missing."

"Sounding more and more like the unsub's still

on-script. He might have had less time to kill Perla, but it doesn't seem to have rattled him."

"What the hell. Getting that tree ready ahead of time, somehow rigging the grill, sabotaging the elevator and Clara's car, knowing where all his victims would be . . . It's like he's stacking up planes to land. Just how long do you think this maniac's script *is*?"

"Sorry, but no idea. There's been less and less time between each kill and the next, but given his preparations at the Cross home alone, it doesn't feel like he's doing that because of any external factor, any unexpected pressure. It feels like all this is in his script."

"And there's nothing in his behavior that moves us any closer to finding out who the bastard is?"

Hollis glanced at her partner, then said, "The thing about profiling is that it's a process. Every bit of information we learn is a piece of the puzzle. And sometimes the pieces don't even look like they fit. But they will. Sooner or later. That's why Reese and I spent the whole day here going through all the information you'd already collected and getting a timeline up while Cullen and Kirby visited the Nash farm and that elevator shaft.

"There's nothing left in the Summers backyard to remind Mrs. Summers and her little girl that Jeremy Summers died there; shocked and grieving neighbors very kindly cleared away all the signs as soon as you allowed them to, even cleaned the pool and laid new sod and turf over the crater left by the explosion. And even though you classified it as an accident, you have Clara Adams's burned-out car safely stored in a rented garage just outside town."

The sheriff frowned at her. "That isn't in my report."

Hollis lifted both eyebrows at him. "We're profilers."

Mal frowned, but as soon as he spoke she realized the frown was directed at himself. "I'm sorry, guys. It feels like you've been here for days. But it's not even quite twenty-four hours, is it?"

"Something else that tends to happen in serial-killer investigations," Hollis said. "Time . . . changes. Or at least our perception of it does. Sometimes it rushes past, then it drags. You lose track of what day it is. Of when you last slept or when you last ate. Hell, one of the reasons we get a timeline of the murders up on the board as quickly as we can is to ground ourselves as much as to look for some kind of pattern."

"Yeah, I think I get that."

Quietly, DeMarco said, "When was the last time you got a decent night's sleep?"

"Sometime around mid-July, I think," Mal answered frankly.

"Around the time of the car crash. What made you think it wasn't an accident?"

Mal didn't have to think about it. "Clara Adams was a good driver, a safe driver. And her car had just been inspected not a week before. If there was a short in the electrical system, it should have been found. She had a newer car, the kind they hook up to a computer and do a diagnostic on. I checked with the dealership where it was inspected. I saw the diagnostic report. There was nothing wrong with that car. Unless somebody tampered with it just before the crash. And did that skillfully enough to leave no evidence, or at least to be sure any evidence would be destroyed in the wreck. I don't even know if he somehow arranged for the car to go up in flames."

"You had that checked out," Hollis said, and it wasn't a question.

He answered anyway. "An army buddy who specializes in bombs, explosions, took a look at the burned car for me about a week after. No signs of any explosive device or accelerant. But he couldn't rule out something that could have been destroyed in the fire."

Kirby, who had been sitting so still and silent that the others had nearly forgotten she was there, said suddenly, "You didn't believe any of them were accidents, did you?"

He turned his head and looked at her. "No. No, I didn't. My gut told me that much. But I didn't have any proof. Nothing to connect them. Until I hit on the cell texts, checking records pretty much out of desperation."

"And because all their cell phones had been destroyed when they were killed," Kirby said.

Mal nodded. "Even Karen Underwood's. She'd forgotten her purse, but like so many people these days she tended to carry her phone in her hand. In the crash, it was broken into about a zillion pieces."

"I wonder if that was part of the script," Hollis mused. "To make sure the phones were destroyed—and see how long it would take you to check the records."

"What, you think this bastard is challenging me?"

"This type of killer, with such elaborate, meticulous plans, is always out to challenge law enforcement. That's part of his fun. He needs to prove he's smarter than the people hunting him."

"Do you think this is personal?"

Hollis glanced at Kirby this time before replying, "You probably know him, in a town this size. He probably knows you better, or believes he does. You're visible on a regular basis. You represent authority. He could have a personal grudge, but it's more likely, given his victims so far, that trying to outwit you—us—is just a fun bonus, not the reason why he's killing."

"But you do believe that a woman is his real target. Is or was, if it's Perla Cross."

"Alternating gender and always killing women in their twenties is, as Cullen would say, statistically significant. Mrs. Cross's bright red hair makes her appear to stand out, as does the fact that he either wanted us to know it was murder, or just didn't care. That escalation bothers me, obviously, but . . . it still doesn't point us in a clear direction moving forward. Hard as it is to accept, what he does next is likely to help us, or at least clarify a few of our puzzle pieces. Because we do believe he's after a specific woman. And if it wasn't Perla Cross, then it's very likely more women will die."

BISHOP SAID, "I'M fairly sure we have at least three analysts available to do those background checks for you. I'll get them started on it right away. All the adults?"

"Yeah, I'd say so," Hollis responded. "Everyone over the age of about sixteen, at least. We think he's older, probably in his late twenties or thirties, but . . . there's an element of childishness in some of this. Hell, maybe he just didn't get picked to play Red Rover in school, and he's still pissed about that." She was using the landline on the conference table, partly because her cell was indeed dead as a doornail, as per usual, and partly because she knew the sheriff's department communication system was pretty literally blasting out cell calls constantly, still trying to reach everyone with a cell.

She was half convinced she could feel the damned things—and couldn't help wondering if DeMarco did. She knew she was edgy, and all day she had alternated between oddly brief but pounding headaches and equally odd sudden urges to look over her shoulder to see . . . whatever was behind her.

To say she still felt there was something off, something wrong inside her would have been an understatement. And to say she had done her best to shore up her shields and minimize if not hide her uneasiness from her partner—and everyone else—would have been a greater one. She didn't want anyone picking up on her weird, unsettled feelings.

Mostly him.

Sheriff Gordon had been called out of the conference room to be updated on the emergency-alert warnings, and Hollis had used the momentary privacy to call Bishop. She was reasonably sure that Mal wouldn't like the idea of his people being investigated, even if his cop's mind told him it was the thing to do.

Not that she was hiding it. Exactly.

"Copy that," Bishop said. "And the other thing?"

Damned telepaths. Even at a distance . . .

Hollis held the receiver away from her ear for a moment and glared at it, then put it back against her ear. "What other thing, Yoda?"

"What sort of energy are you sensing?"

"Do you live in my head, or just visit occasionally?"

DeMarco was smiling slightly, and so was Kirby; one thing everyone in the unit knew was that Hollis could get away with questioning their unit chief when others really couldn't or didn't dare, and also that—for whatever reasons—he tolerated, even seemed amused by her sometimes disrespectful comments and questions.

"I just visit. Out with it, Hollis." His voice took on a more serious note. "It isn't negative energy?"

She sighed. "Not as far as I can tell. Doesn't feel negative *or* positive. All I know is that I started feeling it at the Cross home. I'm not even sure it's energy, though Reese seems to be."

"Well, you are very sensitive to energy."

"Yeah, that's why I know there's a storm on the other side of the mountains and I'm really hoping it stays there." Her free hand lifted to massage her temple. "As for whatever I'm sensing here . . . I dunno, Bishop. It just feels weird."

After a brief silence, he said, "I don't have to remind you to follow your instincts."

"No, you don't have to do that."

"Okay. Is Reese handy?"

"He's right here."

"May I speak to him?"

"Sure."

Hollis held the receiver out to her partner, making sure *not* to lower her voice when she said, "He wants to talk to you."

Reese accepted the receiver, immediately saying, "I'm being glared at."

"I'm not surprised. Want to put me on speaker?"

"What can I say? She owns me."

"Then put me on speaker." Bishop remained calm.

Kirby happened to be looking at Hollis in that moment, and her amusement became astonishment—because she had never seen the other agent look so totally shocked and almost painfully self-conscious.

Seriously, how could she not know? He doesn't even try to hide it from anyone. Jeez, even I know . . .

Without looking at his partner, Reese leaned forward to press the speaker button on the conference phone. "Okay, you're on speaker. Kirby is here as well."

"And Cullen?"

"With the acting ME and her assistant, going back over the scene at the Cross residence. She thinks there may have been something mechanical involved, maybe a block and tackle or some kind of pulley."

"Sounds more likely than not, given where and how the body was found. How does Cullen feel about the town?"

"He says nothing really sticks out. Just some tension and anxiety, which you'd expect. Probably getting stronger as the sheriff's department warning goes out. And as

Hollis told you, Kirby had a very strong physical reaction, possibly to a new victim being incapacitated by the unsub."

"On a third straight night."

"Not even night yet but, yeah. He could be getting set up to kill again. Don't know if he's in a hurry, maybe to distract us from Perla Cross's murder, or whether it was always planned this way, for some other reason."

"Kirby, how are you holding up?"

"I'm okay, Bishop. Still working on the shield, obviously, but I'm okay."

"Glad to hear it. Hollis?"

"Yes?" Her expression now could best be described as mutinous, and she did not look at her partner.

"You know I can't hang up with you mad at me." His voice was uncharacteristically solemn.

Even Hollis had to smile at that, however unwillingly. "I know you're full of shit," she said roundly. "Just . . . get us any background checks flagged with the parameters on our list, will you, please? I don't like how fast this unsub is moving, especially if we find out tomorrow that somebody else died tonight."

"Copy that. Everybody watch your backs."

"We will."

DeMarco leaned forward to end the call and had barely leaned back when Sheriff Gordon said from the doorway, "What parameters on what list?"

THIRTEEN

Cullen leaned carefully out the attic window, his flashlight shining upward, and said, "Yeah, there's a new-looking metal ring up there that could have easily supported a block and tackle of some kind." He moved the flashlight slowly downward until he was examining the outside and underside of the upper part of the window frame. "I don't see a friction burn on the window frame, but there are a couple of very small marks I don't recognize. He could have fastened something smooth and metallic here, I suppose, to make sure there weren't any friction burns from a rope or cable."

The flashlight was necessary because even though the sun had not yet fully set, it was cloudy over the western mountains, and the entire valley was in a kind of twilight. The attic, being shaded at both ends by very tall trees, most definitely required artificial light.

From outside the attic, quite a bit higher up in the tree than where they'd found Perla Cross's body, Sam Norris's voice came with the swishing, crackling sound of leaves and limbs being shifted.

"Yeah, looks like there was something fastened here too. Around the trunk and a couple of branches." He raised his voice. "Jill, I don't think there's any reason to collect evidence—unless you want me to saw off one of these branches showing the marks?" Clearly, he wanted a negative response.

Cullen glanced over his shoulder at Jill, who had just worked her way back to him after covering one side of the attic, and she grinned at him.

"Sorry, Sam, but I think we should take a much closer look at one of those marked limbs, at least," she called out.

They could both hear muttering from the tree—and then the slow sound of someone carefully using a hacksaw.

Cullen stepped farther inside the attic and away from the window. "You can check the top frame of the window and the peak of the roof if you want. Maybe you'll see something I missed. How about the rest of the attic?"

"I've only gone over this one side, following the wall to make sure I didn't miss anything. Have to say, I'm still not seeing any signs that she was held captive up here *or* that there was some kind of lover's tryst. I will say it looks like most of the exposed flooring was either thoroughly dusted, and recently, or else mopped."

"Hollis smelled bleach. I don't, but I don't have a very sensitive nose. How about you?"

"I can smell it, faintly. Haven't found any damp spots,

but it's August and breezy; if the windows were open long enough, that could have dried anything that was wet."

"Could Perla have cleaned up here?"

Jill pursed her lips thoughtfully. "If she did, she would have had to wash up afterward or wear rubber gloves to protect her very nice manicure and very long acrylic nails—and something besides those black leggings and the red blouse she was wearing when she died. I found one pair of rubber gloves in the storage closet off the ground-floor kitchen, and that appears to be worn by the cleaning lady who comes in twice a week, just to do the main floor. My guess is that Perla wasn't the sort to clean an attic."

"Even though that's what she told her husband she'd be doing yesterday?"

"Yeah. My bet is that to her, *cleaning* the attic would have meant no more than looking through all the stuff stored up here, hopeful of finding a treasure of some kind. Box of old jewelry, maybe. Or more shoes."

"But no dusting or mopping."

"Not likely. I didn't find anything under her nails, on her clothing, or on her body that would indicate she'd been cleaning. Certainly not anything containing bleach. In fact, I don't believe she spent much time even looking around up here. The floor may be free of dust, but there's plenty on the trunks, boxes, and bins she would have had to look through, and so far I've found no sign anything was touched in months at least, far less opened. If she *did* spend any time at all up here looking around, she had to have changed afterward, because there was no dust on her clothing. Bits of bark and dirt from the impact with the tree, but no dust."

Jill indicated a couple of vials on a handy sort of tool belt she was wearing. "I took some scrapings of the dust here and there, but I can already tell you it doesn't look like anything I found on her clothing or body."

Cullen shifted slightly, not even aware he had moved as something caused him to focus his attention inward. Almost absently, he said, "You haven't found any signs of blood, and there was nothing on her body to indicate how he might have . . . subdued her. Maybe even kept her immobile for hours."

"Well, what I can test for in the field is limited to drugs and other substances most commonly found in murders or accidental deaths; we won't get the tox screen back for days at least, maybe longer. So I can't be absolutely certain he didn't drug her. I didn't find an injection site, and I looked everywhere. With a magnifying glass. Stomach contents looked normal, organs looked normal—except for those punctured, of course."

Cullen blinked and looked at her, saw her. "Oh."

In a polite tone, she asked, "Where were you just now?"

"Here. Obviously."

"Part of you was," she agreed blandly.

He looked into her unusually pale brown eyes and slowly said, "Why do I get the feeling you know a lot more about me than I know about you?"

"I can't imagine."

"Jill."

She smiled faintly. "How's Bishop?"

He glanced back over his shoulder to where sounds of sawing and muttered but colorful curses were audible, then looked at Jill and nevertheless lowered his voice.

"You're not SCU?"

"Not even FBI." Still smiling, she added, "Some of us were already committed to our schooling or professions when Bishop came calling. We didn't all want to be feds. Or cops of any kind. But that doesn't mean we can't be . . . useful . . . from time to time. And you know how Bishop hates to waste a psychic."

He lifted his eyebrows in a silent question.

"Like you. Clairvoyant." Jill's voice was low, but calm and almost casual.

He crossed his arms over his chest and didn't— quite—glare at her. "Why do I get the feeling that Sam being up that tree and me being here in the attic with you was totally unnecessary?"

"Hey, I could have missed something. There's nothing wrong in double-checking your . . . assumptions."

"Dammit," he muttered.

Jill's smile widened, but her voice turned brisk when she said, "I'm not sure what your senses are telling you, but mine say that after Joe left the house, she had a visit from someone and they came up here. Not a lover's tryst. Maybe she did believe there was something valuable among all this stuff, and wanted a second opinion."

Slowly, Cullen said, "I was getting the sense of a man, but I couldn't tell if it was the sheriff I was picking up on."

"I don't think Mal stayed up here any longer than he had to," she said frankly. "Stationed a deputy at the bottom of the stairs *outside* the closed door, then called me. The only others up here since the body was discovered have been the four of you and me. Sam's been outside the whole time on both visits."

"So you think Perla invited her killer up here?"

"Yeah, I think it's possible. Or he already had her under control somehow. I think he followed her or lured her to the other end of the attic, where there's a narrow alley between stacks of boxes. And I think he put her out, however he did that." She paused, then added, "No scuff marks or fiber evidence, but that space is just deep enough and wide enough to conceal a body if anyone came to the top of the stairs and glanced around."

"You think he left and came back later?"

"That's the way it feels to me. I think when Joe came back home and searched the house, Perla was up here unconscious. And I think as soon as he left, the killer came up here to finish the job."

Slowly, Cullen said, "The block and tackle, the rope or cable . . . he had to have some of that ready and ready to hand."

Jill nodded. "I believe he did. And even though he had time to clean up after himself, I think he expected to have more time, that he expected Joe to find her . . . eventually. Maybe this morning instead of last night. I noticed on the way out here this time that there's a bend in the road with a pull-off vantage point where you can look out over the valley. If you happen to be looking toward this house rather than out at the view, you could have seen Perla, impaled on those limbs. It wouldn't have been a perfect view, but you could have seen that bright red blouse."

"Another bit of stage management from the killer?"

"I think so," Jill said. "Don't you?"

"Hey!" Sam yelled from the tree outside the window. "Can somebody get out here and help me down from this fucking tree?"

AS PREDICTED, MAL wasn't at all happy to have the lives of the people in his town minutely examined by analysts at Quantico. Also as predicted, he was too good a cop not to see the sense in it.

"Dammit," he muttered.

"Sorry, Mal," Hollis said. "One of the not-fun things we have to do sometimes. But we narrowed the parameters as much as we could, and our analysts are very discreet. Any histories they flag will be sent to us, and we'll all go over them. You'll undoubtedly help us eliminate even more, before we have to start talking to people."

Sitting in his usual chair at the conference table, Mal rubbed his face with both hands in what seemed a characteristic gesture of weariness. "Nobody's reported getting that text. At least, nobody credible." He nodded at DeMarco. "A few teenagers thought it would be fun to scare each other, you were right about that."

"Grounded?"

"Oh, yeah. One of the boys' dads was so horrified I'm not sure that kid's going to be going anywhere except school and church—three times a week—for the next six months."

Hollis had been sitting near the sheriff, carefully avoiding making eye contact with her partner as she absently doodled on the legal pad in front of her, something she'd been doing whenever her hands weren't busy with something else. But as Mal's dry statement sank in, she focused on what she'd been doodling.

A church.

"Hollis?"

She still refused to look at DeMarco. "Something I saw," she murmured. "Or something somebody said. Why can't I *remember* what it was?"

Mal leaned forward a bit to better see her face. "Hollis?"

Abruptly, she flipped the legal pad around and slid it across the table toward him. "Is that a church here in Clarity?"

Clearly surprised, he stared down at the drawing. "This is . . . really good."

"I was an artist in another life," she said a bit impatiently. "Mal, is that a church here in town?"

"Yeah. It's the Second Baptist Church."

Hollis looked at her partner, finally. "We need to be there."

"Okay," he said immediately, pushing back his chair and rising. "Then let's go."

Mal looked bewildered. "Do you think—"

"I don't know how I know," Hollis told the sheriff honestly. "But we need to get there, Mal. As soon as we can. And I think you should bring at least a couple of your best deputies."

Kirby got up and glanced at the big clock on the wall. "It's not much after five. Do we need our vests?"

Hollis hesitated. "I don't know."

Mal was climbing to his feet. "Better safe than sorry."

"Yeah, you're probably right. Ours are in the SUV."

"Should I call Cullen?" Kirby asked.

"There's no time. We need to leave right now." Hollis was already moving toward the door, snagging her light Windbreaker along the way.

Mal and the rest of her team were right behind her, with DeMarco pausing only a moment to look down at an astonishingly complete sketch of a church. Since he'd been watching her, he could say with authority that she had "doodled" the sketch in less than five minutes.

Considerably less.

He turned the legal pad facedown, then continued. He was already wearing the light jacket that almost concealed the big silver gun in its shoulder harness; it was the reason they all wore light jackets, really, because August nights weren't all that cool.

And yet, when they emerged from the sheriff's department and headed for their vehicles, he somehow wasn't surprised that the coming night promised to be decidedly chilly.

"Damned storm," Hollis muttered. She had the SUV

keys but tossed them to DeMarco and headed for the passenger side. Kirby hurried to get their vests from the back, then climbed up into the seat behind Hollis, handing two of the vests forward.

"Follow me," Mal called as he reached his Jeep with two of his deputies, both of them hastily adjusting vests with the uncertain touch of cops seldom if ever required to wear them.

DeMarco lifted a hand in acknowledgment, opened the driver's-side door, and found his vest tossed at him by Hollis.

"Vest first," she said as she began putting her own on. "Yours takes longer to be adjusted properly because of that damned cannon."

It really didn't, but even with Velcro fasteners, he had to shrug out of his jacket first. Luckily all the SCU agents were a lot more familiar with the vests than the deputies, so he got his on, adjusted his gun, and reclaimed his jacket by the time Mal was just pulling out of his parking place.

DeMarco slid behind the wheel and started the SUV, one glance showing him that Hollis was frowning and rubbing her temples.

"Is it really the storm bothering you?" he asked.

She'd tried to hide the odd pain and anxiety all day, but enough was enough. "Yeah, that's part of it. But there's something else too. I am beginning to get a splitting headache, and I don't know why."

Kirby pulled herself forward and looked at their team leader. "Do you get headaches?"

Hollis sort of laughed. Sort of.

"Oh, hell, yeah. Headaches, the occasional nosebleed, and at least a few times I've gone out like a light without warning."

"Not without warning," DeMarco said. "You just weren't paying attention to that part of it."

"I'll take your word for it."

"I should hope so," he murmured, remembering at least two occasions when he had caught her before she could hit the ground.

Hollis said something under her breath, but before anyone could question her, said in a louder tone, "I think that's the church up ahead."

"It's all lit up," Kirby said. "Should the church be all lit up on a Saturday?"

"No," Hollis said. "It shouldn't."

THEY WERE CAUTIOUS in entering the unlocked church, even though it was all lit up. Or maybe because it was.

They came in from three different doors, but it looked almost like they'd timed it to the second, because they all got just far enough inside to see what was waiting for them.

What he'd left for them.

Hollis slowly holstered her gun and looked at her partner. "Maybe you and the deputies can search the rest of the building? I doubt we'll find anything, but . . ."

"Yeah." DeMarco kept his own big silver gun in hand

as he went to join the two shocked and horrified deputies and got them busy searching the rest of the church.

She was vaguely aware that Kirby had slid into a pew, probably because her legs had gone weak, either because of the body or the emotions of all who had found it. Or the fact that she was trying desperately to shore up her shield, and that took every bit of concentration she had.

Mal came to stand beside Hollis, his gun held slackly at his side. "Dear God."

"I don't think God was here today," she said.

Automatically, Mal said, "The Flower Ladies come on Saturday to get the church ready for Sunday services. They've been here. But they didn't leave the flowers like that."

"No," Hollis said. "They didn't."

This was a more unusual Baptist church since there was a raised little balcony on the left side where the pastor would stand, above his flock, while he preached. At the front of the church was the section for the choir, and at the right was a lower balcony, a sort of alcove with a rather impressive organ.

In front of the choir section were four very plain wooden chairs, and in front of them, on the slightly raised front platform that elevated the choir and, in most Baptist churches, the preacher, was a long, fairly narrow table, covered in a white cloth. Normally, it probably held a cross, with perhaps a couple of candlesticks on either side.

Normally.

And normally the white cloth would have been spotless.

In a flat voice, Mal said, "He is—was—Reverend Marcus Pilate, pastor of this church for some years now."

Hollis took several steps closer but didn't have to reach Reverend Pilate or touch him to know he was dead.

Being disemboweled tended to end life quite efficiently.

The body was stretched out on the table, on the once-white cloth now drenched in blood. He was fully dressed, his arms at his sides draped by his own glistening intestines, still dripping. It was easy to see that his body had been opened from his breastbone to his crotch.

Hollis took a few more steps, drawing her gloves from one pocket of her jacket. "You should call Jill," she said over her shoulder to Mal. "Or do you want us to?"

He just stood there, staring at the pastor's body.

Kirby cleared her throat, but her voice was still a little thick when she said, "I'll call Cullen."

"Okay," Hollis said. "Go outside if you need to." She moved forward steadily, breathing through her mouth because she had to. Moving her gaze over the horribly mutilated body because she had to.

His legs were slightly parted, and between them, where his genitals would have been, his heart had been placed.

She didn't want to speculate about what had been done with his genitals, since they were nowhere to be seen.

Many of his organs had been removed and placed with apparent care around the body. A lung on each side of his head. His stomach between his feet. A closed Bible with his liver on top was placed as a macabre pillow underneath his head.

And there were flowers.

Big arrangements, undoubtedly done by the Flower Ladies not so many hours ago, had been removed from pedestals at either side of the choir section and placed on the floor at each end of the table where the pastor lay.

It was clear another arrangement had been brought to the table from somewhere else in the church, its flowers . . . distributed all around the table. There was no attempt at artistry.

Just mockery.

Hollis was dimly surprised at the calmness of her own voice. "Mal, I know we don't have photos yet, but there's something in his mouth, and I need to see it."

"Yeah. Sure." His voice wasn't so much calm as it was numb.

Hollis moved carefully near the table, doing her best not to step on anything but the carpet, and leaned over just far enough to reach his slightly open mouth.

She didn't look at his eyes. They were open too.

Slowly, she pulled a cell phone out of his mouth. It was an older flip phone. She flipped it open.

From the corner of her eye, she noted that her partner had returned from searching the rest of the church and was holstering his gun.

"Nobody's here," he said. "Jill needs to go through the place, and Cullen, but I don't think he was anywhere except this room."

"And not long ago," Hollis said.

DeMarco looked at the still-dripping body, fully aware that if he touched the body, he would find it still warm. He also knew that wasn't what Hollis was using to gauge time.

"What is it?" he asked her.

She moved carefully back around the table, gesturing slightly for him to join her where the sheriff was still standing.

"Mal," she said quietly.

He blinked, looked at her. "Yeah?"

"He left us a message this time." She held the phone out so all three of them could see it, flipped open. There was a text timed at no more than fifteen minutes before they'd arrived. And it was simple.

Next time, move faster.

EVEN AFTER JILL, her assistant, and Cullen had arrived, Hollis insisted on walking through the entire church itself, slowly, studying everything she saw, reaching out with every sense she could command. She did the same in the small parsonage, which was very, very tidy and clean, doors and windows locked, nothing disturbed.

"You're broadcasting," DeMarco told her quietly.

Since it was only them in the parsonage, Hollis merely shrugged. "Am I? What am I broadcasting?"

"Frustration, mostly. Disappointment in yourself."

"I should have been faster."

"He didn't even wait for dark," DeMarco said, catching her hand so she turned to face him. He didn't release her hand. "How could you have expected that? How could any of us have expected that?"

"I should have. Something was wrong. Something is *still* wrong. I've missed something. I should be able to focus on this energy just out of my reach. I should be able to understand it."

"Why should you? It's something you never sensed before. New things in our world don't come with guidebooks. Hell, they seldom come with definitions."

"Still."

"Still what? Hollis, as you so recently pointed out to Kirby, this is a team. I am your partner, and Kirby and Cullen are the rest of your *team*. This is not all on you. It's not all on any one of us. We're hunting a monster, and if we had any doubts before, finding an eviscerated pastor laid out in his own church pretty much confirms this monster is of the totally evil variety."

"That does not make me feel better," she muttered.

"It wasn't supposed to. It was supposed to simply point out that we came here to investigate four suspicious accidents, and in about twenty-four hours, we've had two horribly murdered victims on top of the accidents we're now reasonably sure were also murders. We've barely *started* investigating. And more often than not, it takes us more than a day or two to unmask the killer. Yes, even us."

She had to smile, albeit faintly. "Hubris?"

"I didn't use that word."

"No, but it's what you meant."

"Look, I know that for a brief time when you were channeling all that energy at Alexander House, you felt like a superhero. But things got normal pretty quick, right?"

"Well, except for my eyes. Still a weird shade of blue."

"An unusual shade of blue. Big difference. The point is, we are none of us superheroes. We do the best we can. You know that. We will do the best we can here. And we will catch and cage, or destroy, this monster. Because that's what we do."

She hesitated, then said, "Part of me wants everyone . . . wrapped in body armor head to toe. After what happened with Robbie and Dante . . . I don't think I've ever seen Samantha that shaken. As a matter of fact, I don't think I'd ever seen her shaken until then. At all."

"And you don't want to lose a team member. That's perfectly natural. And largely beyond your control."

"But it shouldn't be. I'm the team leader. I should at least be able to keep my team safe."

"You're doing it again. Piling all the weight on your own shoulders alone. Hollis, you know as well as I that a team leader's job is to keep everybody focused and moving toward the goal of catching our monster. Which is what you've been doing."

She drew a deep breath and let it out in a rush. "You can be very annoying, you know that?"

"So you've told me."

Hollis opened her mouth, obviously to ask a question, then closed it and turned away, pulling her hand gently from his. "Well, let's keep going, then. We have a monster to find." She sounded just a touch self-conscious.

DeMarco smiled slightly but didn't push. Instead, he continued to follow her from room to room, both of them studying the small parsonage for anything that might provide something helpful to the case.

They found absolutely nothing—until they were passing back through the tidy living room toward the front door. They had passed through the room earlier with no more than a cursory look around, but this time Hollis stopped dead in her tracks.

She was staring at a Bible, lying in a position of honor and respect on top of a lacy cloth covering a small table. There was a candlestick on each end—and both of them looked just a little too large for the table. The Bible seemed oddly out of scale as well, one of the larger varieties that tended to be family Bibles kept in some place of honor in the home. But this . . . The whole tablescape looked wrong, too large for the space.

Not really a mistake such a neat and tidy man as the Reverend would have made.

"From the church?" DeMarco ventured.

"Think so."

He stepped slightly to one side so he could study her face. "What else?"

"He handled them. Our monster."

"I'd guess he had to."

"They have auras."

"I thought only living things had auras. And electrical things, of course."

"Mmm. You know that thing Bishop tells us about how some objects retain the energy of whoever handles them?"

"Yeah."

"Well, I think there are only three possibilities for what I'm seeing."

"Which are?"

"These candlesticks have a long and dark history. Our murdered pastor had a very dark soul. Or our monster has way more energy than his body can contain, and he set all this up for us."

"Is he psychic?"

"No. But there's something wrong with him. I don't mean the evil, I mean physically. There's something not natural about him somehow. I dunno. An injury . . . an attack . . . an illness or sickness. Something."

"You don't want to touch those candlesticks, do you?"

"No way in hell," she answered immediately. "The auras are . . . black. With some red streaks. That is very bad."

"Okay." He took her hand in his. "In that case, let's go ask Cullen to take a look and see what he picks up."

"And Jill," Hollis said absently.

"Looking for evidence?"

She looked up at her partner, for a moment puzzled, and then shook her head. "No, because she's also clair-voyant."

He let out a low whistle. "One of Bishop's?"

"Sort of. He knows about her. But she likes being a doctor and a sometimes medical examiner and wasn't interested in becoming a fed." Hollis frowned. "You know, I never think about the ones who turn Bishop down for perfectly good reasons."

"Maybe you can talk to Jill about that."

"Yeah. Maybe." Hollis glanced back at the candlesticks one more time, then said, "Let's go. I'm not looking forward to being in that church again, but we need to know if Jill sees something the rest of us missed."

FOURTEEN

It was nearly midnight when the small task force gathered once again in the conference room of the sheriff's department, and every single one of them looked weary, tense—or both.

Jill and her assistant had done their crime scene investigating and then removed the body of the Reverend Marcus Pilate to the morgue of Clarity's one hospital, where Jill had promised to do the postmortem—first thing in the morning. It would be her second straight early-morning autopsy, but having started out this extremely busy day with Perla Cross's autopsy and ending it with processing an even more bizarre murder scene, she had decided that her day had been long enough. She was tired and didn't mind admitting it. She had also been uncharacteristically shaken by something found in the Reverend Pilate's horribly mutilated body and had announced she wanted to take two showers, drink at least two glasses of wine, and fall into bed, trying her best not to think.

Sam had pretty much shown the same intent.

So it was just the agents and the sheriff who gathered for a brief meeting in the conference room.

"Emma's been on duty all day, so I'm sending her home," Mal said. "And going home myself. I have a couple of senior deputies who can handle the shop overnight. The warnings are still going out in every way we can send them, but I can't believe this guy aims to kill two in one night. What he did to Reverend Pilate . . . that took a lot of muscle, according to Jill. If he's not superhuman, he has to rest sometime."

Cullen murmured, "More like hibernating."

"What?"

"Oh—just a really deep sleep. Usually comes after extreme exertion."

"Well, he had that, all right."

Hollis, sitting at the far end of the conference table, said, "Tonight answered one of my questions. Thought the unsub might have been physically weak, given all the machines he rigged in some way. But this . . . He has to be strong. And Cullen's right; strong or not, that kind of butchery takes muscle. He has to be exhausted."

Mal shook his head, then said, "When I realized it'd likely be after midnight before everybody headed back to the hotel, I called Solomon House and asked that some kind of meal be left in each of your rooms. I wasn't specific, so it may be a sandwich or crackers and cold cuts, but you all need to eat. None of us has, since lunchtime."

"Thanks, Mal," Hollis said. "How about you?"

"They sent over a boxed meal for me, some kind of sandwich and potato salad, I think. May be what you guys got as well. It's waiting at my desk. I'll grab it on the way out." He shook his head again. "I know none of us has an appetite after what we found, but I'm betting tomorrow's going to be a bitch of a day, so please try to eat, and try to sleep tonight. Since Jill's doing the post on the Reverend in the morning, there's no reason why any of us has to be back here at dawn. Sleep in. Whenever you get here will be soon enough."

"Yeah, you too," Hollis said. She didn't move as Mal turned toward the door, but said, "Hey, I've been meaning to ask. Where's Felix? Don't remember seeing him all day."

He looked back at them with a spark of amusement. "Well, after he insisted he sleep with me last night, it was pretty obvious you were right and he'd made his choice. Hate to admit it, but I actually slept better with him snoring beside me."

Hollis couldn't help but smile. "I've never heard a Yorkie snore."

"I hadn't either. Sounds remarkably like my ex-wife." Without following that interesting tangent, he added, "I brought him back here this morning, put a crate with toys in my office for him, and the junior deputies have been taking turns walking him every couple of hours. I'll grab him too on the way out. Looks like I have a dog."

Shaking his head, he left the conference room.

Her smile fading, Hollis leaned forward in her chair,

resting her forearms on the table, and looked at Cullen. "Hibernating?"

"Yeah, it's weird. Jill felt it too. Oh, she's—"

"Clairvoyant, yeah." Hollis didn't seem to realize that was a sort of knowledge she usually didn't pick up. "What did you two sense?"

"Something really off anywhere near the candlesticks, though not the body, which is also odd."

Hollis nodded. "I thought so too. Can you describe what you felt near the candlesticks?"

"Something old. And really, really tired or somehow . . . spent. The word I got was *hibernating*. Jill got it too. I mean the actual word. I think this unsub is . . . burrowed in somewhere. And I don't think we'll see or hear from him for at least a day, maybe two."

She frowned. "Do you usually pick up actual words?"

"Well, not like that. It was practically in neon. For Jill too. But enough odd things have happened over the years that it didn't really surprise me. Except the old part. I mean, this guy can't be old, right? Not and do the things he's done."

After a moment, Hollis said, "Maybe it was just the candlesticks. They're old, they must have a history. We'll check on that in the morning. Kirby, are you okay?"

The younger agent, who had sat down silently at the table as soon as they'd arrived, started slightly and looked around the room as though noticing the presence of other people for the first time. "Oh—sure. I mean, it was tough in the church, with everybody so sickened by what we found. And . . . what we found. But I'm okay. Like

Jill, I plan to shower twice, maybe three times, and then probably take a couple of those sleeping pills the Quantico doctors gave me for—nights like this."

Grave, Hollis said, "Shower, eat something, and take the pills. If you absolutely can't face the food, at least drink a glass of milk. Most of us have used meds at one time or another, especially early on. We can't function without food and rest. You—both of you—hang out your DO NOT DISTURB signs and sleep until you wake up."

Kirby looked like she thought that was a wonderful idea. "I will, thanks."

"Come on," Cullen said, offering her a hand up. "I'll walk you over."

"Thanks. Night, guys."

Both Hollis and DeMarco bid them good night, though again, neither moved to leave the room.

"Did you take meds?" DeMarco asked her.

Hollis looked at him steadily. "Not once I healed from the attack. I've been tempted a few times. But not since I met Diana. You know her story."

"About being medicated most of her life by her controlling bastard of a father?" His voice was level. "Yeah. And I know what it cost her. Lost years. Lost experiences. Even experiences in how to interact normally with other people."

Hollis nodded. "It made me realize how lucky I was. I mean, I knew surviving the attack was some kind of victory, and finding something useful to do with the rest of my life was another one. Diana talked about . . . moving through years of her life in a fog, not caring about anything, and I realized how easy that would have been for me to do after the attack. I thought about it while I was in the hospital. A lot. But it seemed . . . cowardly . . . to hide from life just because I'd gotten a raw deal. Like Diana, I realized I didn't want to follow that path. I didn't want the easy way out."

HE HADN'T EXPECTED that killing the good Reverend would leave him so drained. It hadn't been like that with the others, or at least he didn't think it had. He thought he'd had the strength to perform the Ceremony to ask for more strength.

Hadn't he?

All he really knew was that he was tired, exhausted, and he needed sleep. Because tomorrow he had to be normal. Tomorrow he had things to do. Ordinary things, but important things to do.

The Plan. And . . . timing. He had to be certain everything happened in its own time.

A final sacrifice. A final sacrifice, and then you'll be done.

"Then I can rest."

Yes. Then everything will be fine. Absolutely fine.

NO MATTER HOW tired she was, Hollis never gave herself up gracefully to sleep. Or gratefully. Because of the dreams, of course. And because . . . there was no way for her to control the dreams.

Not remembering them in those first years had been necessary, she knew that. Remembering them now was just as necessary, no matter how painful, because no trauma could be left in the past until it was faced. And accepted.

Accepting seemed to be the problem.

Bishop had told her something odd once. Well, he had told her many odd things over the years, but this one had been very specific—and yet very vague. There would come a time, he'd said, when she would rediscover whatever it was that the attack had cost her most dearly. The one thing that monster had ripped from the core of her being.

And when she rediscovered that, faced that, then the nightmares would truly fade from her nights. From her life.

Hollis had wondered once or twice if it was her ability to have children. If that was what Bishop had meant, what her attacker had ripped from her—literally.

Except . . . when she thought about that, though it cost her a pang of regret, it wasn't an agonizing thing. She hadn't thought much about having kids until that choice was taken out of her hands, and when it had been she hadn't grieved about it. She had the notion that children had never been part of the future she had seen for herself, even before the attack. That not becoming a mother would not be something she would regret.

No, she didn't think that was the loss Bishop had spoken of. She wondered if he even knew. Sometimes, and even though he had the uncanny ability to be right about way too many things, she had a hunch even he wasn't sure where some of the words came from. The warnings. The . . . alerts.

Hollis thought about that as she both showered and then soaked in the wonderful old claw-footed bathtub her room boasted. She generally didn't linger long over bathing. There was still one physical scar remaining, and though all the others had faded and the final scar was in a place she couldn't see unless she turned her back to a mirror, she was always aware of it.

It marked her.

Branded her.

Hollis had the notion that she herself could remove that final scar. Because all the other scars were gone. This one could be too. When she was ready. When she could let it go.

But not yet.

Not just yet.

Tonight she didn't want to think of scars. Or nightmares. She soaked in the hot water until it cooled, then reluctantly pulled herself from the tub. She never did much more than towel-dry her short hair and run her fingers through it, and a drugstore moisturizer served for her face.

She got into what she favored for summer sleepwear, a tank top and boxer pajama bottoms, and wandered out into the bedroom. Her bed was turned down invitingly—a foil-wrapped chocolate on the pillow.

And in her nightstand was the gift Reese had left for her the previous night, something neither of them had spoken of today even though Hollis was grateful, because he had given her a different perspective on her scars.

Out of suffering have emerged the strongest souls; the most massive characters are seared with scars.

Definitely something to think about.

But tonight Hollis was almost too tired to think.

The storm on the other side of the mountains was still rumbling around, which kept her just a bit on edge. She had this weird mental image of a storm slowly moving among the old mountains and along the valleys, gradually working its way to her.

Hunting her.

Man, I need to sleep.

She also needed to eat. Not that she had an appetite after today, but she was too sensible, and too aware of her responsibilities, to skip a needed meal.

A rolling table had been left in the little sitting area by one of the windows, and Hollis explored to find tea in a carafe, an ice bucket that already held a smallish bottle of milk—and coffee that was still reasonably hot. All the best options for a before-bed meal, she thought.

She also discovered under a silver cover what looked like a very nice club sandwich and potato salad, so Mal had been right about that.

She turned the TV on, absently choosing a favorite channel that aired crime documentaries. It wasn't that she couldn't get enough of crime in her everyday life and work, it was just that she didn't feel like the news and had no particular urge to channel surf this late on a Saturday night.

It was a documentary about Bonnie and Clyde, and for some reason Hollis found that amusing.

She decided on tea and poured out a glass, unwrapped her silverware from the napkin, and was just beginning to pick the roast beef out of the club sandwich when DeMarco spoke from the connecting door between their rooms.

"Hey, you decent?"

"Enough. Thought I'd better eat before bed. Come on in."

He did, carrying his own glass of tea and, oddly enough, wearing the same sort of sleepwear, except his sweatpants were long.

"You always pick out the roast beef," he noted, sitting down on the love seat at right angles to her chair and the table.

"I don't like roast beef. I like turkey and ham and chicken."

"Just as long as you eat something."

"Did you?"

"Yeah, after my shower. Same menu, except I got two sandwiches."

"I'm sure they thought, big man with a big appetite. They do seem to be very efficient here, in a nicely discreet way."

"True enough."

He idly watched as she destroyed the club sandwich and then began to eat, and thought, as he often had, how odd it was that they were very comfortable with each other—sometimes.

And the odd thing was, he could never predict when those times would be. They had worked together long enough to be comfortable as partners, of course, so both tended to slip easily into the familiar partnership roles. But in private, and especially since he had first made it clear to her that he wanted to be her partner in life as well as in work . . .

He just never knew. Never knew if he'd find Hollis guarded, or tense, or wary—or perfectly comfortable and casual. If they would find themselves suddenly at some kind of emotional crossroads, as they already had at least once in this case, or if the last thing either of them wanted to discuss was how they felt in the moment. If she would be distant, or so intently focused on him that sometimes he wondered what it was she searched so intently to find.

And whether she had ever found it.

Tonight, at nearly two a.m., she was relaxed, thoughtful. Not yet sleepy, but not especially tense—or at least he thought so until she flinched very slightly and sent an irritated glance toward the window.

"That storm still bothering you?"

"Well, it won't just *happen* and be done with it. It hovers, just close enough to this valley to make me feel it."

"Will it wake you if it hits before dawn while you're sleeping?" He suddenly found it odd that he didn't know that.

"Depends on how bad it is. How loud it is. I tried

traveling with a sound machine, but usually I'm so tired by the time I get to bed that I kept forgetting I even had it. Besides, hotel rooms almost always have a fan, if only for the heat or AC, and they're usually not quiet. And, half the time I forget to turn off the TV, or set the timer for it to go off after I'm asleep."

He glanced at the TV, which had the sound turned really low, and lifted a brow at her. "Bonnie and Clyde?"

"Historical criminals interest me."

"You don't get enough crime on the job?"

Hollis sipped her tea, considering the question seriously. "That's different. That's . . . happening. Historical crime has already happened."

"So you can be detached."

"I guess. Is it important?"

"Just curious."

Over the rim of her glass, her eyes narrowed at him. "You're never just curious."

"Of course I am."

"No, you're like Bishop; there's always a motive lurking."

"I think I'm offended by that."

"You can be offended all you want, it's still true. So what is it you're really asking me?"

DeMarco considered for a moment in silence. "We've talked about this before. Sort of. I think . . . you try very hard not to care. About the cases we investigate. About the people. Victims. Families."

Hollis set her glass down on the table. "That isn't a question."

He chose his words very carefully, aware, as he often was with her in these moments, that he was picking his way across a minefield.

"You know, when I first read your file, read about the attack and how your abilities were triggered, one thing stood out to me." And something Bishop had pointed out as very important for Hollis.

"Just one?" she muttered.

"You helped the police find him. Catch him."

"Well, sort of. I mean, I wasn't the only one. We'd never have been able to do it without Maggie, and—" She half laughed. "And that first spirit I saw."

DeMarco shook his head slightly. "Hollis, you were still in the hospital. Maggie had helped you, you badly needed to help her—and that was when you were able to see."

"Why did that stand out to you?"

"Like I said, I never knew the Hollis you were before the attack. By the time we met, you'd been with the SCU a while. You'd been in the field, had learned to be more comfortable with your abilities. And had started developing new abilities. Seeing auras. Being able to heal yourself—that one manifested almost literally in front of my eyes."

"And certainly came in handy."

"Yes, it did."

Hollis waited a moment, then said, "Okay, what am I missing? It feels like you're . . . tiptoeing all around something."

"Does it really." It wasn't a question.

She frowned at him. "Reese, it's after two in the morning. I know Mal said for us to sleep in, but I have a hard time doing that no matter how late I go to bed. Especially when we're on a case."

"I know."

"Then what are you trying to say to me?"

"Maybe I should wait until tomorrow," he said. "I have a feeling it'll keep you up, and—"

"Reese."

He cleared his throat. "Okay. It's something I've noticed. When you hold yourself aloof, try to be detached from a situation, you're . . . very closed up."

"My shield—"

DeMarco shook his head. "This has nothing to do with your shield, because I noticed it before you had one."

"Noticed what? How am I closed up?"

"You block yourself. It's not like a shield protecting you, it's something inside, a . . . reluctance to let yourself feel what's going on around you. A need to pull back, to think and not feel."

Hollis rubbed her forehead. "I'm either really tired or you're just not making sense. Or both."

"Hollis, two very important things happened yesterday. Saturday, while we were working. You're team leader. You felt responsible for the team, especially Cullen and Kirby, so you opened yourself up. You needed to . . . be aware of how they were doing, even if they weren't in the room with you."

"Okay. So?"

"It's been little things, mostly, at least so far. But it's like I've said before, when you need a sense or ability you didn't have when you got here, to solve a case or help someone, that's what you get. You're picking up information in a new way, Hollis. I'm honestly not sure if it's telepathic, empathic, or clairvoyant, but you're developing another ability."

She stared at him for a long moment, almost expressionless. "Another ability."

"Yes. If I had to guess, given how you try to close yourself off from feeling too much, I'd say it's empathic."

"But none of us have been in trouble or danger. I mean—my abilities develop like that, suddenly, because I need them."

"Yes. And as team leader, you needed to know how your team was feeling."

"I didn't feel like myself," she murmured.

"Yeah. And I think that was one of the reasons. It's the first time you've developed or tapped into a new ability gradually."

She drew a deep breath and let it out slowly, her expression now more bemused than anything else. "A new ability. Fun new toy. Except being an empath isn't fun. It's painful. That's clear watching Kirby. And as for Maggie . . ."

He nodded as she realized. "In a way, you've come full circle. Maggie helped you years ago. An empath helped heal what a monster had done to you, so you were able to go on. You've healed yourself since then, first just healing from an injury a bit faster than usual, and eventually healing from a different sort of attack that really should have killed you. You helped heal Diana. Probably saved Miranda. At the time, I suppose we all assumed it was that similar energy mediums often have. To be able to tune into the energies of death—and life. But with you . . . it's so often the case that you're more than anyone else guesses, much less expects. Even you. Which is why I believe that eventually you'll be an absolute empath."

"An absolute empath. You mean if I try to heal someone with a wound—"

"The wound will disappear from them and appear on you. And stay on you until you heal that too. Which will demand an incredible amount of energy and strength from you, especially if you heal a serious, possibly even mortal, wound or other injury. Even more than helping to pull yourself *or* someone else almost back from the dead. Because then it'll be both."

SUNDAY

"Is Hollis okay?" Kirby's voice was low.

DeMarco looked at her, wishing he could answer that question fully. But all he could say was, "I don't think she got much sleep."

Kirby didn't appear quite satisfied but nodded tentatively and reclaimed her seat at the conference table, a laptop open in front of her. They were hoping to hear from the analysts at Quantico, but so far nothing had come through.

Hollis came out of the kitchen alcove in the conference room with a cup of coffee, looking deceptively fragile.

DeMarco knew it was deceptive because he knew Hollis. She might need an arm now and then after expending too much energy, but even then there was nothing in the slightest bit fragile about her. He agreed with Bishop on that point, that she had the strongest will to survive of anyone he'd ever known.

He wondered then, as uneasily as he had wondered when it had first occurred to him, if her sense of self-preservation, her will to survive, would stop her from sacrificing herself to save someone she cared about. Bishop said it would stop her, and Hollis had appeared to believe that as well. DeMarco had expressed his own doubts.

He had seen her risk death more than once on the job, for the sake of the team or to face off against the evil they had hunted; as contradictory as it seemed, her instinct to help those she cared about was every bit as strong as her will to survive.

Hollis sat down, in one of the chairs rather than on the table this time, and stared across at the evidence boards that now contained more photos and additions to the timeline.

"Okay," she said, "there was no camera on the morgue, so no visual on who took it. Does anybody want to venture a guess as to why our monster unsub felt the need to leave Brady Nash's arm inside Reverend Pilate?"

"God, I can't even wrap my mind around that," Cullen said, leaning back in his own chair as he stared at the evidence board. "I can't decide if it's incredibly twisted in a dark way or—a childish way."

"I thought the same thing," Hollis said, frowning. "There really is something childish about some of these things. Like a kid trying to shock people."

Cullen glanced toward the door to make sure Mal hadn't returned, and said in a lower voice, "And yet both Jill and I felt something really old. At least around those candlesticks."

"Where are we on them?"

"Far as I know, Mal's still in his office with that antiques expert he called in. You think it's just the history of the things? Religious objects should soak up positive energy, shouldn't they?"

"That," Hollis said, "depends on who had them and how they were used. Religious objects have been bought, sold, traded, used in very disrespectful ways. Even used in dark rituals."

"Satanic?"

"I wouldn't be surprised, depending on how old they are and how many hands they've passed through."

DeMarco leaned back in his own chair and said, "We should probably be careful with that word. People panic when they believe some evil ritual took place, but whisper that it might have been satanic and they totally freak out."

Kirby said, "They're already freaking out. One of the two main churches in town is circled with crime scene tape and has deputies posted at the doors. They know Reverend Pilate was horribly murdered—and the details are getting out. Anybody murdered unsettles people even if they didn't know the victim. Murder several people, and everyone starts to panic. Include a holy man in that victim pool, and panic doesn't begin to describe it."

She was rubbing the nape of her neck and was definitely more pale than usual.

"Kirby?" Hollis was looking at her.

"Oh, I'm okay. I'm fine. I'm absolutely fine. The pills let me get a good night's sleep, and that always helps. It's just that people are really getting scared. Very scared. I don't think Reverend Pilate was all that well-liked, but he was a pastor, a holy man." She frowned suddenly. "Some doubt about that, I think, but still. People are terrified. If this monster would kill a man of God, nobody's safe."

Hollis looked at her partner. "I'm guessing just about everybody, even the usual part-time or holy-holiday-only attendees, will be in church today. They need to come together as a community. And they need reassurance, which their pastors will hopefully give them, at least for now."

"You're probably right."

"The Ferguson family took in Joe Cross, right?"

It was Cullen who answered. "Yeah, one of Perla's sisters and her husband." He looked through a stack of files on the table before him and found the one he was looking for. "Um . . . Yeah. Carla and Keith Webb. And looks like they, along with the rest of the Ferguson clan, live in that cluster of houses out between downtown and the Cross residence. Says here the whole family goes to the same church, Cane Creek Baptist."

Hollis said, "That's the big church with the elaborate landscaping? Opposite end of town from Reverend Pilate's church."

"Yeah."

DeMarco said, "I'm betting Joe Cross isn't in any shape to go to church today. Probably at the Webb house with at least one of the family watching over him."

"Might be our best chance to talk to him without a dozen protective relatives hovering around."

Kirby ventured, "Is he a suspect? From everything we've been told about him, he doesn't sound very likely."

"Yeah, well, that's the thing. So far, all we've had to go on when it comes to Joe is what other people have told us. I'd like the chance to talk to him ourselves."

DeMarco lifted a small day planner lying atop files and legal pads on the table before him. "And then there's this. According to his list of appointments, the last visit Reverend Pilate made yesterday afternoon was to Joe Cross. Presumably to offer his condolences, even if none of the family attended his church."

FIFTEEN

Admitted to the Webb residence by Perla's brother-in-law Keith, DeMarco and Hollis found him more resigned than welcoming. A stocky man of about thirty-five with a pleasant face and calm brown eyes that barely glanced at the credentials they offered, he seemed to have an extremely unshakable temperament—which probably made him an ideal husband to one of the reportedly volatile Ferguson sisters.

"I figured at least one of you feds would want to talk to Joe," he said, leading the two through the foyer and into what was obviously a den or family room. "Especially when we heard about what happened to Preacher Pilate last night."

"Were you here when he called on Mr. Cross?" Hollis asked.

"Yep. Joe seems calmer when it's just me. Have to

warn you, though. He hasn't said much of anything." He paused in front of the near end of a big sectional sofa, where a young, very thin, and very pale man sat staring straight ahead at something only he could see.

"Carla'd skin me if I left you two alone with him," Webb said, still calm. "So if it's all the same to you, I'll go back to my chair over there. Good luck getting him to talk to you."

He waved a hand in what appeared to be a general invitation for them to sit wherever they liked, then went himself to sit at the opposite end of the sectional, reaching down to pull a lever that swung a footrest up under his waiting legs. Then he used a remote to unpause the game he'd been watching, but hit mute before more than a second or so of a roaring crowd could be heard.

Hollis glanced at her partner, then slid the folder holding her credentials into a pocket; she doubted Joe Cross would know or care who was talking to him. For a moment, she studied the younger man, the blanket draped over his shoulders emphasizing his thinness and making him appear even younger than he was. Both hands lay limply in his lap, loosely holding a wad of tissues that looked damp. On the arm of this end of the sectional was a big box of tissues; beside Joe Cross's sock-clad feet was a wicker trash basket overflowing with used tissues.

"Mr. Cross?" She kept her voice quiet. "Do you feel up to answering a few questions?"

After a long moment, he murmured, "Feel? I'm fine. I'm absolutely fine."

"Told you," Keith Webb said laconically, without taking his eyes off his very large flat-screen.

DeMarco said, "Mr. Webb, did Mr. Cross leave this house after Reverend Pilate visited?"

Webb grunted. "He hasn't left here since Carla and me brought him home from the sheriff station Friday."

"Has he been alone at all since then?"

"Nah. Even when the doc knocked him out, Carla and her sisters and their mom took turns sitting with him. Yesterday after Preacher Pilate left, we had to get the doc out again." He paused, then continued, "Pilate was better preaching fire and brimstone than helping anybody through grief. Less concerned with Joe than with a possible donation of Perla's things, 'specially her shoes. Likes to hold what he calls yard sales to raise money. Daycare center, new roof. Churches always seem to need new roofs. Anyway, he wasn't here five minutes before the girls showed him the door."

"Your family didn't attend his church."

"No, we all go to Cane Creek. Preacher Webb—no relation—his sermons are a lot more cheerful. Sees the glass half-full 'stead of half-empty, if you know what I mean."

"I wonder if he will today," Hollis murmured.

It hadn't really been a question, but Keith Webb responded, "I had the same thought. Mostly why I said I'd stay here with Joe. Preacher Webb always said this was such a peaceful town. He kept up a good face when the accidents started, but by last Sunday he was pretty damned depressing. He didn't care much for Pilate, was my take, but I'm betting today's sermon is going to be even darker since the maniac that murdered poor Perla decided to butcher a man of God."

"SO JOE CROSS is off our suspect list?" Cullen asked when Hollis and DeMarco returned to the sheriff's department.

"We haven't got a suspect list," Hollis reminded him. "But if we had one, I don't see Cross on it. He's tall, but thin, and looks years younger than he is. Maybe wiry, but nowhere near strong enough to do some of the things our unsub has done. Besides, he has a solid alibi for the time Reverend Pilate was killed. And if he's not genuinely mourning his wife, I need to hang up my profiler's hat."

"You're frowning," DeMarco said.

Kirby added, "You're also chewing your thumbnail."

Hollis forced herself to at least stop gnawing on her nail and didn't bother to waste a glare on anybody. "Yeah, yeah. Something's still bugging me and I still don't know what it is."

"Well," Cullen said, "at least we were right in saying the unsub would kill a man next."

"It does confirm the pattern," DeMarco agreed.

"Yeah, but where does that get us?" Hollis shook her head, frowning now at the evidence board. "We couldn't profile the first two murder scenes because there was nothing to profile. Nothing really at the third scene, with the elevator car already removed. And even if Brady

Nash's . . . remains were at the scene of his murder, they weren't any use to us. Jill didn't find anything unusual in his arm, the only part of his body left relatively intact."

Kirby said tentatively, "For the unsub to—to steal the arm right out of a freezer in the morgue and put it *inside* Reverend Pilate's body . . . That has to mean something. Right?"

"I dunno, it feels to me like twisted humor. Or maybe he's just messing with us."

Cullen lifted an eyebrow at her. "Messing with *us*? Us, specifically?"

"Well, the way he left the body was certainly enough to shock and horrify anybody who saw it. The cell phone left in the victim's mouth, a text that had to be for us, for law enforcement. The arm . . . Jill was the first to find that. I didn't notice it at the scene."

DeMarco said, "The warning text was also on the cell."

"Yeah, and it had been read. But there was no sign of the emergency alert. It wasn't an old phone but also wasn't the latest model; the tech people here say it should have received the emergency alert."

"Another sign he's technically savvy," Cullen offered.

Hollis nodded. "If we needed one. So far, the analysts at Quantico haven't found anything worth flagging in the backgrounds of the victims—including Reverend Pilate, and thank you, Cullen, for thinking to call them last night to add him to their list of victims."

"I was almost asleep when I remembered," he confessed.

"I'm just glad you did. At least we know that the best

analysts we have can't find a commonality among the victims. They didn't find anything we missed. That's both reassuring and—frustrating."

The words had barely left her mouth when the sheriff came in, carrying one of the big candlesticks they had found in Reverend Pilate's parsonage.

"This is weird," he announced.

Hollis only just stopped herself from asking him to take the thing away, or at least put it down somewhere *not* near her or anyone on her team, because its aura was still black shot through with red streaks, and all she knew for sure was that it wasn't good. At all.

"What's weird?" she asked him, relieved when he set the candlestick down on one of the desks flanking the doorway, which was at least not too close to any of them. "And where's the other one?"

He answered her second question first. "The antiques expert is drooling over it in that little office beside mine. He's been communicating with another expert, this one over in Europe. They're both very excited."

"Is that where the weird part comes in?"

Mal frowned. "Now that you mention it, the reason he isn't still in my office is because Felix was getting more and more upset. I thought it was because he didn't like the guy, but eventually I realized it was the candlesticks."

Hollis exchanged glances with her partner, then returned her attention to the sheriff. "Animals sense things we can't," she said mildly. "So there's something weird about the candlesticks?"

"You could say. Expert says they're very, very old.

Talking hundreds of years. They're not as heavy as you'd expect because under the bronze surface, they have a copper core."

"Copper," Hollis said slowly. "One of the first metals ever used by humans. And it has very high thermal and electrical conductivity. Why copper wiring works so well."

And why they have such a distinct aura?

Hollis blinked and looked at her partner, startled to find his voice in her head. Because he didn't broadcast, surely—

"That's pretty much what the expert said," Mal told them.

Hollis returned her attention to him. "Sounds like they're weird all the way around," she said.

"Oh, I saved the best for last." He was still standing beside the desk, and picked up the candlestick again, this time holding it so that the agents could all see the bottom. With his free hand, he carefully peeled back the felt that had been attached, possibly to avoid scratching fine wooden surfaces. Or to hide the symbol carved into the metal.

A pentagram.

"Shit," Hollis said.

Mal said, "That was my reaction. Exactly."

THE PROBLEM, AS it turned out, was that their expert insisted the candlesticks exactly matched a pair that had been stolen from a museum in France. And if these candlesticks *were* what he thought they were, they were not only stolen and priceless, they were also, Mal told the agents with a grimace, cursed.

Hollis waved off the curse, more interested in another of the possibilities. "When was the robbery?"

"Uh—he thinks it was around five years ago. That's one of the things he's checking with the other expert."

"Another parameter for the analysts?" DeMarco suggested.

"That's what I was thinking," Hollis said. "Find out all they can about the robbery itself. How was it viewed by Interpol? Did they have a suspect? Do they believe it was stolen by or for a collector? And how did they end up in Clarity? Possibly someone who moved here since the robbery. Someone who traveled to Europe around the right time. Someone with the means to buy priceless things and a very good reason for doing so. Along those lines."

"On it," Cullen said, and went to the desk opposite the one with the candlestick to use the landline phone there.

Mal had put the candlestick back down and looked at Hollis in some disappointment. "Don't you want to know about the curse?"

She was tempted to reply that she knew all about curses but said instead, "Sorry, Mal. Hardheaded and practical."

DeMarco murmured, "I can testify to the first."

Hollis ignored him. "I'm more interested in all the symbols worked into that decorative design."

He blinked. "Damn. You really don't miss a thing, do

you? I thought it was all just frills and flourishes. Then the expert got out his magnifying glass and got even more excited. He and his . . . counterpart . . . over in Europe are compiling a list, with each of the symbols drawn and defined, and it may take a while. Ancient symbols, apparently. But he said some are definitely pagan, and others could match up with that pentagram."

Hollis sighed. "I was afraid you were going to say something like that." She looked at her partner, brows lifting. "Is he a killer because he believes in Satan or does he believe in Satan because he's a killer?"

"Probably depends on how long he's been practicing."

"Yeah. And how long he's been killing. We haven't really turned up anything similar to our crimes, but maybe the analysts at Quantico will."

Kirby, who had indeed looked both uneasy and curious about the curse, was clearly trying to keep her mind on more concrete details when she asked, "Is it more likely he's using the—the beliefs to justify murder if we find out he's done the same thing somewhere else?"

"Probably," Hollis answered. "And because he's perverting the beliefs."

Mal said, "How on earth do you pervert—" Clearly as conscious as they were of the power of the word alone, he also chose not to use it aloud. "—beliefs like those? I mean, aren't they perverted to begin with?"

Hollis shook her head. "Just a belief system, like any other religion. And traditionally—if I can use that word—not at all violent and not inherently evil."

"Are you telling me Reverend Pilate butchered in his

own church wasn't evil?" Mal objected, sounding more than a little disturbed by the whole conversation.

"It was absolutely evil," Hollis said promptly. "Everything this sicko has done is evil. But all religions have ceremonies, rituals, the . . . frills and flourishes. Sacrificing human beings doesn't fit. Sacrificing anything living doesn't fit. There are only a few blood rituals, and those involve a practitioner pricking a finger or cutting a palm— their own. It's more symbolic than anything else."

"But Reverend Pilate—"

"Mal, what we have here is a serial killer. Every serial killer has a reason or reasons for killing. The more . . . perverted . . . the murders are, the more likely the killer has ritualized them in some way. And rationalized them. In all likelihood this monster knows on some level how sick he is, and justifies that sickness by blaming it on an external influence. A higher power."

Slowly, Mal said, "He doesn't kill because he believes in Satan, he believes in Satan because he kills. Because he *needs* to kill."

"Exactly," Hollis said.

HOLLIS HONESTLY DIDN'T know whether DeMarco was right in believing she was any kind of an empath, but as the day wore on and they continued to gather information, sometimes one dry fact at a time, she felt more and more unlike herself.

There were flickers of emotion, jolts of fear, irritation— and more than once she had to fight a sudden urge to burst into tears. And it was that last bit that convinced her he was at least partly right. She was picking up on the emotions of people around her. And since the gruesome murder of one of their pastors had horrified everyone and the emergency alert had told them how the killer sadistically warned his victims beforehand, there had been a steady stream of worried citizens of Clarity in and out of the sheriff's department—some of them trying to turn their cell phones in as if that would save them a deadly text and gruesome death—and emotions were everywhere.

Mal came and went, often supplying another bit of information. Such as the fact that the apparently very excited antiquities expert none of them had even met yet now had a third specialist he was consulting using Skype or one of the other videoconferencing programs.

"Why another?" Hollis asked, fighting the urge to raise her voice.

"I take it this one's in Italy. Specializes in ancient religious artifacts. He's at his home, but all his reference books are there. I dunno, he thinks he might have information even the museum they were stolen from doesn't have about the candlesticks. I'm mostly just watching and listening, and don't have a clue about the parts in French and Italian. They all seem to be in their own world; I ask a question and it's like I'm a fly buzzing around them." He shrugged. "I'll be back when he—and I—know anything."

"Okay. We're still waiting to see if the analysts at Quantico find anything useful."

"Well, let me know."

"Right."

DeMarco rose from his chair and said pleasantly to Cullen, "You and Kirby stay here and do whatever you can, okay? Call my cell if we get word from Quantico. Hollis's is already dead."

"I didn't tell you that," she nearly snapped.

Cullen's brows rose, but Kirby looked as if a question had suddenly been answered.

"You didn't have to." DeMarco went around the table and took her hand, drawing her to her feet. "Come on, we need to get out of here for a while."

"And go where?" She still sounded snappy.

"Away from people," he said distinctly.

Hollis started to speak, then closed her mouth, frowning.

"We'll hold down the fort, don't worry," Cullen said to her.

She merely nodded and allowed her partner to lead her from the room. And it wasn't until they were in the SUV and headed out of town that she spoke again.

"I have a lot of sympathy for Kirby."

DeMarco nodded but kept his gaze on the road. "Every empath I've ever known has said it's completely overwhelming at first. Once you can shield consistently, it will get better."

"Promise?" She sounded even to herself like she was about to cry, and added an irritated, "Oh, shit, this is going to drive me nuts. And I thought spirits were hard."

"I wonder if you'll pick up their emotions," he mused.

"Oh, *shit*."

He glanced at her, trying not to laugh. "Sorry. I know it's hell on you, but I have to say, watching you cope with new abilities is . . . sort of fascinating."

"Dammit." Hollis leaned her head back and closed her eyes, wearing an expression that immediately struck him as odd.

"Hollis?"

She had her eyes closed. "Oh, man, get me out of town. We just passed the hospital, didn't we?"

"Yeah. Why?"

"I think somebody's appendix just burst. Damn. *Damn*."

"Wow," he murmured, and immediately increased the SUV's speed, losing no time in moving away from the hospital and the town. "Better?" he asked after several miles.

"Yeah. Yeah, I think so. I so have to get a handle on this. I thought you said it was happening gradually?"

"It was *triggered* gradually," he corrected. "I think. I guess once you knew, the brakes were off."

"That's a lousy analogy." She held up a finger in a silent demand that he not speak until they passed a couple of houses on the outskirts of town, then said, "Sorry. There was a wife back there *very* pissed at her husband."

"I'll try not to take it personally," DeMarco said.

"It's all your fault, you realize that, right? I'm willing to bet if you hadn't told me about it, it *would* be happening more gradually."

"It's possible. Sorry. The situation's a new one for me too. I wasn't sure whether to say anything."

Hollis breathed in deeply, then out, clearly working on control. "Why don't we stop at that overlook place near the Cross house. That's about as remote as you can get and still be within cell range of town. I don't want to get too far away from Kirby and Cullen."

"Okay." It was only about five minutes later when he pulled the SUV off the two-lane blacktop and into the overlook space that was just about large enough for three cars or a couple of larger vehicles to be safely off the road and pointed at the view.

Hollis was less interested in the view than in fresh air and the blessed lack of emotional turmoil all around her. She got out and walked toward the railing that protected the careless from a deadly leap down into the valley.

DeMarco joined her. "First time we've had a chance to stop up here during the day," he said. "It is a beautiful view."

Hollis blinked, then really looked. "Yeah, it really is. The valley is a lot bigger than it seems in town, too." She scanned the valley, looking slowly from left to right. Then she frowned again.

Always alert to her expressions, he said, "What?"

"Was it Jill who said that Perla Cross's body would probably have been visible from up here?"

"I think so. Something about the way the tree's trimmed, and the bright red blouse Mrs. Cross was wearing."

"She was right. I can just barely make out the ends of the branches they had to saw off to get the body down. Pale, fresh-cut wood against the trunk."

DeMarco squinted for a moment, then said, "You have damned good eyesight."

It was rather telling that neither of them even thought about the fact that the eyes she had were not those she had been born with.

"Spider sense. These last months at Quantico, Bishop was helping me learn to control it better. Especially with sight. At first it was like a raw nerve I couldn't protect. Quentin's best at it, really. His sight *and* hearing are drastically better. With me, it was mostly sight right from the beginning, so that's what we worked on."

She opened her mouth to say something else, then closed it and squinted again, concentrating.

"You aren't still looking at the tree, are you?" It wasn't really a question.

"No," she said slowly. "Not the tree."

He was silent a moment, then said, "Friday night, when we were leaving the attic. The goblin or gargoyle you saw on the roof."

"Stop reading me."

"Then talk to me."

There was a brief pause, and then Hollis said, "The rain we finally got before dawn this morning nearly washed it away. I can barely make it out. And I think . . . I'm seeing the energy rather than the actual marks he drew on the shingles. Chalk, probably. And he must have used blood. He would have needed the power of that. To keep us—to keep me distracted. Unsettled. Blocked, but convinced it was inside me, that there was something wrong with me . . ."

"Hollis?"

She finally blinked, then lifted both hands to briefly rub her eyes with her fingers. "Oh, man, I can't believe I let him do that."

"Hollis."

She looked at her partner. "It wasn't a goblin or a gargoyle, Reese. It was him. He was there, physically there, on the roof. Friday night. Casting a spell."

SIXTEEN

DeMarco lifted a brow at her. "Casting a spell? You don't mean an actual spell, do you?"

"Well, for want of a better word. He has power, Reese. The real deal. Or at least . . . he can call on it."

"Call on it? As in summoning the devil?"

"He's using power. Drawing it from somewhere else. Or someone else."

"Is he psychic?"

"I don't think so. If he were psychic, I would have known it. Because I was the one he needed to block." She frowned again. "Why was I the one?"

"You're the most powerful psychic on the team," he said matter-of-factly.

"Arguably."

"No. You are the most powerful psychic on the team."

She looked up at him for a moment, then nodded.

"Okay. We need to get down there and look around. Now, in daylight."

"Let's go."

It took less than five minutes to get down to the Cross house; it had seemed closer to Hollis, but the road was so curvy it definitely required careful driving. The driveway was rather long and curvy as well, and as they parked and got out of the car, Hollis said, "I didn't remember all the curves."

"We were just focused on getting to the house," De-Marco said. "And when you focus, it's like a laser."

She had started to go around to the side of the house where Perla Cross had died, but paused to look at him with her brows raised. "Really?"

"Yes, really."

This time, she frowned at him. "You've been telling me an awful lot about myself on this case," she said.

"Oh, you noticed that." He strolled past her and led the way around the house.

"Yes, I noticed. Are you going to tell me why?"

"After the case."

"Okay, now *that's* going to drive me crazy." Hollis knew him well enough not to push, and sighed as she stood looking up at the weirdly trimmed oak tree and the attic window it shaded.

"You've got that look," DeMarco said.

"What look?" Her voice was absent.

"I can almost hear the wheels turning. Puzzle pieces clicking into place. What is it?"

"There was a reason," she said slowly. "A reason this

happened. A reason it happened here. He drew power here. He *used* power here. Intention."

DeMarco kept his gaze on her face. "Intention to do what?"

"Blind me." Her voice was soft. "That's it. That's why I felt all along that something was wrong *inside me*. Because he needed me not to see him. And—deep down, I never trusted these eyes. Never trusted they wouldn't . . . just stop working. That my body wouldn't reject them someday. So when he worked so hard to blind me, I blamed myself."

"It's a tendency you have," he murmured.

This time, she didn't argue. "I wonder if he knew that."

"How could he have known that? The SCU might be more visible to law enforcement in recent years, but all of us still go out of our way to keep personal details within the team."

"I don't know how, but he knew I was coming. Maybe even before *I* knew I was coming."

Accepting that, DeMarco said, "Okay. Say he knew before we got here. Why's he afraid of you? Because you're the most powerful?"

Hollis shook her head half-consciously and finally looked at him. "It's still about . . . me seeing him. He was trying to blind me in a very real sense, distract me, because he knew if I saw him, I'd know who and what he was. And then we'd be able to catch him."

"Can you break through that now?"

"I'm . . . not sure."

The expression on her face was uncharacteristically

afraid. And DeMarco knew he had never yet seen Hollis afraid, not like this, not something on such a deep, almost visceral level. He had only seen that kind of fear in her when she had nightmares remembering the monster who had brutalized her.

"You can do it," he told her.

"Can I?"

"Whatever he managed to make you feel, it isn't real, Hollis. It's not a barrier of energy, or you'd feel it. So it has to be . . . an illusion."

"I'd see through an illusion," she objected, her voice actually shaking a bit. "I've seen *evil*, real evil. And if evil can't hide from me, how could I be fooled by an illusion?"

"You said it yourself. Somehow, he knew about that deep down. The fear about your eyes. And he used that fear against you. He made that the barrier you couldn't look past."

Hollis didn't want to accept that, but hard as she'd tried, she had not been able to come up with another reason. "Then I guess I'll have to find a way past it," she said.

"Hollis—"

Whatever he'd been about to say was lost forever. The instant he broke off, Hollis saw it in his eyes. That sharpened, yet inward-turned look she'd seen only once before, his eyes and his aura going silvery in a split second.

He lunged toward her, carrying her to the ground, but even as they were falling, she felt the impact of something hitting Reese, and then she heard two sharp cracks of the rifle that had fired.

For just a moment, lying under the heavy weight of a very big man who was not conscious, Hollis froze, the breath literally knocked out of her. But then everything kicked into overdrive. Her training, her instincts, every psychic sense she could lay claim to blasted past any and every barrier that existed.

Because she had to use everything she had. She *had* to.

The way they'd landed, she couldn't see Reese's face, and she couldn't get to her gun. But his big silver cannon was right there, and she was just—barely—able to move her hand and forearm enough to get the gun and pull it from his shoulder holster. It felt huge and awkward in her hand, and she'd never fired it or any gun as powerful, but she wrapped her fingers around the grip, looked automatically for a safety, and then held on hard.

She didn't move after that, but her senses reached out even as her mind feverishly tried to calculate the angles and she tried to guess whether he would come toward them from where he had fired, or be more wary, more careful.

He was arrogant. She had to remember that. He was arrogant, and he'd fooled a lot of people for a long, long time, people who weren't easy to deceive. He had fooled the people of Clarity.

He had fooled her.

She hadn't moved a muscle that would have been visible to him, she was sure. So he would come straight at them. Maybe deciding to fire again when he got closer just to make sure.

Federal agents. He had to know they'd never stop

hunting him if he killed two federal agents. Did he know? Did he even care? There was a wilderness in these mountains, where he'd grown up; he could probably hide for years—

She heard the snap of a twig underneath a work boot.

Her hand tensed even more on the gun. She'd have to move fast, she knew that. She'd have to shoot before he realized she could. And she couldn't miss.

She couldn't miss.

She couldn't miss.

Another snap, softer—but she knew he was closer. She focused her spider sense with everything she had, not her eyes this time, not yet, but her hearing. She was desperate for it to work. So it did.

The soft scuffing of a boot on rough ground. That would be about fifteen yards away, she thought.

Another soft sound. Twelve yards.

The sounds of small rocks and pebbles crunching underfoot. Ten yards.

Hollis knew she was taking a potentially deadly chance in lying underneath Reese's limp body, as if she herself had been hit. Because she couldn't know for certain whether *he* knew which one of them he had shot.

Crunching, finer gravel underfoot. Eight yards.

Somehow, using a strength that came from some place she'd never needed to tap before, Hollis was able to push Reese off herself and sit up in the same motion.

Across less than six yards, the oddly glazed, surprised eyes of Joe Cross met hers. She saw the tip of his rifle start to lift—and the cannon in her hand went off with an ungodly roar, knocking Hollis back down to the ground and knocking the breath out of her again.

But she struggled to sit up again, gasping, to see Joe Cross on his back, legs splayed—and his rifle at least a foot from his hand.

Without hesitating, without daring to pause to even look at her partner, she pushed herself up off the ground and went quickly but warily to check.

The monster's eyes were open. And just above them was a very large hole that had quite literally taken the top of his head off.

Even so, Hollis bent to get his rifle and carried it and Reese's pistol back to him, tossing both aside and out of her way without giving a thought to whether it was safe to do so.

She rolled Reese onto his side, knowing the bullets had gone into his back and also knowing they had not gone completely through his body. But when she saw where the bullet holes were, her mouth went dry.

"Oh, God. Reese? *Reese?*"

He was unconscious, and his face was far too pale, but he was breathing. He was breathing.

Hollis fumbled at his belt to find the cell phone he carried, the one in the special SCU-designed case, praying that when his primal sense had punched through his shields, that primitive sense of a gun pointed toward him, he had not rendered the cell useless.

"Please, please, please," she whispered, fumbling now to find the right button. It was on, a little dim, but there were bars, and Hollis quickly hit two buttons on the screen, the speed dial that would call Cullen's cell, and the speaker. Then she put the cell on the ground and pushed it at least a foot away from her.

Later, all she would be able to say was that she didn't think about anything she was doing, just acted. Pushed the phone away from both of them because the last of its power could be drained just by being close to them. And especially by what she was about to do.

The speaker on Reese's cell was a good one and the volume was turned all the way up, so she could clearly hear Cullen answer.

"Reese? We just got info from Quantico—"

"Cullen, it's Hollis. Cross is dead. Reese is down, he's been hit. We're at the Cross house. Send EMS and the sheriff, and get your ass out here." She did not yell, but Cullen afterward swore he had never heard a voice sound so utterly distinct in his life.

"Copy. Hang on, we're coming."

Hollis was on her knees beside Reese. She checked his carotid with astonishingly steady fingers, almost holding her breath until she was sure his heart was beating.

But faintly. Too faintly.

"Don't you die on me," she told him in a hard voice. "Don't you *dare* die on me. We have things to talk about, don't we? *Don't we?* We have things to say and things to do, and we are *not* finished yet. Do you hear me, Reese? *We have time.*"

His pulse was growing weaker.

Quickly, Hollis got her Windbreaker off and bundled it into a rough cushion under his head, holding his shoulder to roll him onto his stomach, with his head turned to one side.

"You're not going to die," she said, conversationally now. "You're just not. I'm not going to let you."

She heard, dimly, the sound of sirens, but ignored them. On the curving mountain roads, the EMS would not get to Reese in time.

There was almost no blood around the neat bullet holes in his back, but she knew it was because the real damage was inside. She bent over him and carefully placed a hand over each of the wounds. And then she closed her eyes and focused every bit of energy she had into the desperate need to heal.

She could feel her very life force flowing from her, down her arms, to her hands, into Reese. And then she felt even more, only dimly aware that she was tapping into something else.

She opened her eyes for just a moment, and it seemed very bright around her. She thought she saw other hands cover hers on Reese's back, almost transparent hands, one, then two, then three, maybe more, touching him and touching her, and she felt more energy surge through her and into Reese.

Hollis closed her eyes again and concentrated everything she had and everything she was into the healing. Because he wasn't going to die. Not Reese. She wasn't going to let him die. She *owned* him, that was what he'd said. He was hers, and she wasn't going to lose him. No matter what.

"Hollis . . ." It was barely a whisper, she thought.

She ignored that. There were sharp pains in her back, two of them, as if a heavy board had cracked against her, and then deep inside her a fiery pain that made her breathe raggedly through gritted teeth. But she was no stranger to pain.

She could take it.

She thought her nose was bleeding, or maybe it was tears dripping down onto her hands, but she didn't care, it didn't matter, she just had to make sure Reese didn't die. Nothing else mattered to her.

Nothing.

"Hollis . . . Hollis, stop it. You're— Hollis, you have to *stop. Now.*"

She didn't stop until he pried her hands off his back, until he gathered her into his arms, and even then she was busy . . . healing   still.

"Hollis . . ."

She felt him cradling her, and even with the fiery pain inside her, it was wonderful, it was enough. She let go with a little sigh, the sirens fading away, and blackness surrounding her.

HOLLIS WAS VERY tired, and for a little while, or maybe it was a long while, she wasn't sure she would be able to make it back. But they were with her, the spirits who had helped her save Reese, spirits she had helped in the past. They all had names, and she knew them, and thanked them while they helped her back through an odd sort of veil, a hazy space that was bright and warm, and was definitely not Diana's gray time.

It's not time, yet, Hollis. Not for you. You have to go back. You have to go back to Reese . . .

"Stay with me. Don't leave me. I won't let you leave me."

She opened her eyes slowly, the lids scratching as if she'd slept a long time, or maybe hardly any time at all, because her voice sounded normal, she thought, when she murmured, "I own you. That's what you said. I own you, and . . . I'm never going to lose anything else that matters to me. Reese . . . you matter to me . . ."

She realized, in the few seconds granted to her, that she was in a hospital bed, which was ridiculous since she knew her wounds were healed now, there wouldn't even be a scratch—

And then he was there, bending over her, that amazingly beautiful face and those eyes that had always seen her so clearly, even the parts of her she hadn't wanted anybody to see, and he was kissing her and muttering rough words the whole time, words that probably made no sense to anyone but them. But that was okay, that was fine, because nobody else needed to understand.

And more time passed before Hollis could think about anything remotely sensible. Reese was stretched beside her on the hospital bed, holding her close, both of them drifting pleasantly in the twilight that came just before and sometimes just after sleep, when she murmured, "There's two things . . . I need to tell you."

His breath warm in her hair, he murmured back, "What're those?"

She thought that was funny, but her laugh was only a small sound. "First, I love you. I always have, you know that."

"That's good," he said. "Because I love you too." His arms tightened around her.

"Good," she said. "You can drive."

"Drive where?" he asked, not sounding very interested.

"Prob'ly back to the sheriff's department first. Get backup. Finish the job. The case. Catch the monster. We still have to do that."

"You shot him, Hollis. He's dead."

It took an effort she really didn't want to make to move at all, because she was tired and sleeping in his arms sounded like the best thing in the world right now.

Except right now there was a very bad thing in the world. Their world. Her world. A monster needed to be stopped. Quickly.

So Hollis made the effort, shifting around, turning until they faced each other. His eyes opened and she instantly knew he wanted to kiss her.

"Not yet," she told him, with regret obvious in her voice. "What time is it? Is it still Sunday?" The hospital room was an interior one with no windows. And in hospitals, as in casinos, there was maintained an everlasting day.

Casinos. Jeez, why did I put that in my analogy?

"Yes, it's still Sunday. Not quite six o'clock." He rarely

wore a watch, but Reese always knew the time and could be counted on to be accurate to within five minutes or so.

"Really? Wow, a lot happened today. And more to come. We need to get going."

Reese touched her face with one hand. "Hollis, what are you talking about? You need sleep. Hell, I need sleep. We both nearly died today."

"Yes, but the monster didn't."

"Joe Cross is dead."

"He wasn't the monster. I saw his eyes before I shot him. They were . . . glazed. Distant. Like a sleepwalker. Which I think is what he's been. The monster just . . . used Joe. To deflect suspicion from himself, maybe. Definitely because he needed a tool he could control. And Joe, poor Joe . . . You saw him, Reese. He really *was* grieving the loss of his wife. Even if he did help the monster kill her. Something I think the monster taunted him with afterward. It would explain his extreme grief. That's all I felt from him, but I'm betting a stronger empath could have looked deeper and felt guilt as well."

"What? Hollis—"

But she was pushing herself into a sitting position, carefully testing her back by twisting slightly side to side. "That doesn't feel half bad, actually. Are you okay?"

He was propped on an elbow, the two of them barely fitting in the hospital bed, and he was fully dressed except for his shoes. "I need to sleep about a month, but other than that . . ."

"Good." Hollis swung her legs off her side of the bed, realizing both that she was in a hospital gown and that there was no IV. "No needles or tubes?" she asked, remembering other hospital stays.

"There wasn't so much as a speck of blood on you by the time the EMS crew got to you. Or on me, though the bullet holes in my jacket and shirt gave them pause. Anyway, I threw my weight around, and called Bishop so *he* could throw his weight around, and they basically just checked to make absolutely sure neither of us was bleeding and our vitals were normal. I told them you needed to sleep, so they gave us this bed." He paused, adding, "They're very confused."

"I imagine so." She slid off the bed, relieved when her legs held her with hardly a quiver. Then she remembered what she was wearing and turned around to face the bed, hastily reaching back, only to find that the hospital gown was not open in back.

"They've redesigned them," Reese said, not without a note of regret. "They tie on the side now. And close completely."

"Where are my clothes?"

"On that chair behind you. And you're lucky I stopped them from cutting them off you. Mal should have taken everything by rights, since there were no witnesses to what happened, but he accepted my word you'd had no choice. He's very confused too. Relieved, but confused."

"Well, let's go unconfuse everybody." She got her clothes and placed the folded garments on the bed.

"I don't think that's a word."

Somewhat impatiently, she made a gesture with one finger indicating he should turn around.

"Seriously?" he demanded.

"Well, for now."

Grumbling under his breath, Reese sat up and swung his legs over the side, with his back to her, though he remained on the bed. "I could tell you I was in the same room when they stripped you for the examination," he said.

"You could. Were you?"

"No, I was in the next cubicle, explaining why there was no reason for me to take off my pants."

For some reason, Hollis found that amusing. "Bet it disappointed the nurses," she said as she got into her own jeans.

"I didn't notice," he retorted. "Listen, do you know who the real monster is?"

"I do now."

"How?"

Hollis didn't even have to consider. "Well, I sort of knew before. Not who, but how. Today I found out who. Because his trick failed when I had to reach out with every sense I had and at least one or two I didn't know I had. It was . . . really, it was like punching through cardboard. Damned trick never would have worked if he hadn't used my own weakness against me. Once I knew there was nothing wrong with me, with my eyes, it was only a matter of time before I could see him even better than he saw me."

Reese didn't comment on the fact that what she had described was more like clairvoyance or even telepathy than any ability Hollis had possessed before this case.

Though he wondered, for the first time, if Hollis would end up with every psychic ability they knew about and a few she'd create out of thin air for herself, continuing to rewrite the psychic rule book—if there was such a thing. But all he said was, "Does the monster know?"

With some satisfaction, Hollis said, "I'm blocking *him* now."

"You're not broadcasting," Reese said. "But your shield—"

"I know," Hollis said, coming around the bed still adjusting the V-neck T-shirt she'd been wearing underneath the light jacket and Windbreaker. She held the Windbreaker in her free hand, absently shaking it slightly because the last time she remembered touching it, she'd balled it up and put it on the ground underneath her partner's head. "Where's my gun?"

"Mal took yours and mine back to the sheriff's department. I think the docs and nurses here were uneasy about unconscious and nearly unconscious patients having lethal weapons."

"That's understandable." She shrugged into her jacket. "We'll need our guns. And there's a stop I want to make before we get there. I want to meet Sean Brenner."

"And who is Sean Brenner?"

"Sean is an eight-year-old boy. I could feel him once the block stopped working on me. Because he played a part in all this, was connected to all this. He was used as a tool just like Joe was. Not to kill, but to help cause a death. I need to make sure the kid's all right, and protected from our monster."

"And you can do that?" Reese asked mildly.

"I can try. And he might know something he doesn't know he knows, which could be important."

"To us? To the case I thought was over?"

"Important things are important things," she told him seriously. "More puzzle pieces. I don't know where they'll fit. Or even if they'll fit. People, places, events. Things I see, but things I feel as well."

"You appear to know more about the puzzle than I do," he told her wryly.

"Weird how we pick up knowledge, isn't it?" She looked thoughtful. "I'm not sure I've ever picked up stuff like this before. It's more than emotions now."

"Yeah, I know. What I don't know is why."

She smiled at him. "We need to go. Right now."

Reese got off the bed and found his shoes, but said as he put them on, "Are you not answering me on purpose?"

"Not answering you about what?"

"Innocent is not your best face."

She waited, brows raised.

"You're going to be an extremely stubborn life partner, aren't you?"

Hollis smiled faintly but reacted as matter-of-factly as he had reacted to her—finally—declaration of love. "Well, you can't say you haven't been warned."

SEVENTEEN

"That is true." He took her hand as they left the quiet room and went out into the equally quiet hallway.

"Are we checking ourselves out?" she asked.

"We were never really checked in. At least, nobody asked a zillion questions or presented a zillion forms for us to fill out, so I'm thinking we're off the books."

A few nurses and people in white coats looked at them as they passed, but nobody objected or even questioned. In fact, most of them very studiously went back to whatever they'd been doing.

Hollis was silent and thoughtful until they were heading out through the emergency-room lobby, then said, "Bishop?"

"Probably. You know how he hates to leave records or a paper trail for the media or any other interested parties to follow. I can't decide if he's secretive or just stealthy."

"Both. Where's the— Oh, there." They were approaching what looked like their black SUV, parked off to the side barely out of the way of emergency vehicles. "Do you have the keys?"

Reese produced them. "I think I'll drive."

"You got shot today. Twice."

"Yeah, and you nearly died from the wounds." He lifted her hand to his lips briefly, then opened the passenger door for her, more or less helped her in, then closed the door and went around to slide behind the wheel.

"That's the first time you've ever done that," she said, interested.

"Not the first time I've wanted to," he confessed, starting up the vehicle and beginning to find his way out of the typically congested parking area around the small hospital. "My mama raised me to be a gentleman."

Hollis blinked. "Did I just hear a Southern drawl?"

"Possibly."

"How far Southern?"

"Just outside New Orleans."

Now *that* surprised her. "Wow. You have never said *anything* that sounded like it came from just outside New Orleans."

"I mostly lost the accent in the military," he explained. "I was in for eight years. Thought about making a career of it, but . . ."

"Bishop came calling?"

"How did you ever guess."

Hollis sighed. "You know, it's kind of spooky when you think about it. I mean, how Bishop just turns up at the right moment, and how he knows things he really shouldn't know, and—" She stopped herself, adding, "Spooky. And if you tell him I said that, I'll deny it. My relationship with Bishop is based entirely on my patent disbelief of his omniscience."

Reese chewed on that for a mile or two in silence, then said thoughtfully, "Not many of us question him, as a rule. So it's probably good that you do."

"Well, somebody has to. Because nobody's always right, even Bishop. We don't need a unit chief with a God complex."

"True enough." Reese glanced over to see that she was drumming her fingers against her knees. "Hollis?"

"Hmm?"

"Is the monster still hibernating?"

Staring straight ahead, she frowned slightly. "I'm not exactly sure. I think the thing with Joe, sending him after us, was planned before today. Maybe like a . . . post-hypnotic suggestion or something. And I don't know if he had to be out of hibernation to trigger that. Maybe something we did triggered it."

Before Reese could comment, she suddenly sat up straighter. "Damn. Remember where Joe was sitting in the Webbs' den? He was sitting on the end of the sectional that didn't face the TV. It faced that big window."

"Which," Reese remembered, "looked out the front of the house, which is at the end of a cul-de-sac, facing the main road through town. He could have seen us drive by before we pulled into the lookout."

"Bet he did."

"He had to move fast, if so. To get to the house, on foot, in time for that ambush."

"Yeah. But it wasn't really Joe, it was the monster controlling him. And we already know he can move fast."

Thinking of the late Reverend Pilate, his butchered body still dripping blood, Reese said, "Yeah, he's proved that."

"We'll have to figure out which murders he actually committed himself, instead of using tools. Obviously Reverend Pilate was one he did himself. Maybe he actually killed Perla, even though Joe helped set it up. Maybe the monster likes getting his hands bloody."

"Tools?"

"Hey, Joe was practically under house arrest, right? Keith Webb seemed like a more than capable guard."

Reese didn't repeat the question. "So he was. Until Joe apparently got up to use the bathroom, and then somehow managed to sneak up behind Webb and hit him over the head with a golf trophy."

"Is he okay?"

"He'll live. But he was pissed enough, according to Mal, not to look too terribly sad about Joe's death."

"I can see how he wouldn't be. He plays golf?" The question was almost absentminded, and she was frowning again and staring straight through the windshield.

"No. His wife, Carla, does."

Hollis's frown deepened. "So you found out all this stuff while I was out and you weren't?"

"Well, I only got shot. You nearly got dead. You had to heal me and then yourself. To say it used up a lot of your energy would be an understatement." He reached over and took one of her hands, his fingers twining with hers. "I was awake when EMS arrived. And Mal, and Cullen, and Kirby. And about half a dozen deputies. And the fire department. Just in case, apparently."

All looking at her unconscious self.

Hollis sighed.

"The deputies were impressed," Reese offered. "Not only did you shoot a bad guy who had shot—at—us, but you hit him with a head shot, and did it with my gun."

"At. He shot at us. That was your story?"

"Well, for everybody outside the team. Mal's probably still got deputies out at the Cross house looking for those bullets that missed us."

"That's mean."

"You want to tell him the truth?"

"Not really."

"Well, then."

A sound that wasn't quite a laugh but definitely held amusement escaped Hollis. "So . . . in this fairy tale, how did I end up shooting the bad guy with your gun and how did I end up unconscious?"

"Do we need to talk about this now?"

"One of us does."

It was Reese's turn to sigh. "I made myself look like a klutz," he offered. "Said I tripped over one of the roots of that damned tree and went down. I was dazed. You were bending over me when you saw Joe coming toward us with his rifle, saw him cock it, aim it—and your hand was practically on my gun anyway, so that's what you used. But the recoil knocked you back against the tree, you hit your head, and went out."

Since she actually had hit the ground with considerable force after firing his powerful gun, Hollis couldn't really argue with that point. Still . . .

"Who uses somebody else's gun when they're accustomed to drawing their own?"

"Listen, best I could do spur of the moment."

"And they bought it."

"Obviously there are some lingering questions. Like how Joe managed to kill Reverend Pilate when he had a cast-iron alibi—because nobody wants to think there are two killers. I didn't have an answer for that, so I didn't offer one."

"One killer," Hollis said. "Several tools."

"Several?"

"What are the other lingering questions?"

Allowing his own lingering question to stand, Reese said, "Like the holes in my jacket and shirt. Like how long you were out after a bump on the head. That, by the way, was what had all the medical people so concerned. Because you were out, all told, more than an hour."

Hollis nodded slowly. "Since my head doesn't hurt, I'm assuming I healed that along with the rest?"

"There were a number of confused medical personnel," Reese admitted.

"We'll be lucky to get out of town without Mal arresting us."

"Not if we can capture and cage or kill the real monster in Clarity. And can back it up with proof of his guilt. Can we do that, by the way?"

Hollis was silent for a moment, and her face was grave when she looked at her partner. "The phrase 'by the numbers.' That's military, isn't it?"

"Yeah. Originally from the American Revolution, actually. Battle plans. Positions of weapons, soldiers, timing. Why?"

"Well, if I'm right, we need to move very carefully tonight. We have to have a plan, and it has to be by the numbers. We have to get it right. No room for error."

"Or?"

"Or somebody besides the monster dies."

"WOW." CULLEN RUBBED his temples unconsciously, his gaze roving between Hollis and DeMarco. "He is . . . not the first person I would have thought of. Or even the hundredth."

Kirby just looked stunned.

"Do admit it's been an excellent cover," Hollis said. "We called Bishop from the car, and he had the analysts at Quantico do a quick check. They hadn't gotten to his name yet, but when they did, everything fit. He grew up in Clarity, went away for schooling and his first couple of jobs, returning here about five years ago. Right around the time those candlesticks were stolen."

Kirby blinked. "He needed them?"

"He believed he did. He'd been collecting antiquities

of that sort most of his life. It amused him to have them out in the open, where only another Satanist might recognize them."

"Okay, but . . . but . . ."

"He likes to travel and everyone knows it. He's been picking up . . . trinkets . . . like those candlesticks all over the world."

"I'm surprised he'd give them up," Cullen said slowly.

"He didn't give them up."

"But the expert guy, he finished for the day. When we got back here after tearing out to the Cross house to help you guys, Mal said the candlesticks were locked away in his safe."

"Did he?" Hollis asked quietly. "Did you hear him say that, Cullen?"

"I . . . Somebody said it. I thought it was Mal."

Hollis smiled slightly, her eyes locked with his. Without following that subject, she said instead, "It was an odd time frame, we thought. It seemed strange that the fake accidents only started last month. But he needed time to plan, and not only is he meticulous, but he had a fairly demanding job and other obligations. And he wasn't in a hurry."

Cullen murmured, "Revenge is a dish best served cold."

"Yes. It is. To the very, very dangerous and very, very patient, that's exactly what it is. Delayed gratification."

Kirby said, "I don't— What set him off? I mean, isn't there always a trigger for serial killers?"

"Yeah," DeMarco said. "His was a simple, senseless accident that caused the death of someone he loved."

"And he blamed someone here in Clarity for that?"

"Not exactly," Hollis said. "He just needed some people to die. First in seeming accidents, and then in obvious murders. Until a pattern began to emerge. Until outsiders needed to be called in to investigate."

"How did he pick the victims?" Cullen asked.

"We think we know," Hollis said. "There's bound to be evidence we can use against him, if we dig deeply enough. But . . . what we really need is a confession. That—or catching him on the verge of committing another murder."

Cullen rose to his feet slowly. "Wait a minute. You said tonight. So he already has a victim under his control?"

Hollis nodded.

"And we aren't going to break some land-speed record to get there in time to save them?"

"We'll save her," Hollis said. "We'll save her, and we'll cage or destroy the monster."

"But—"

Frowning, seemingly deep in thought, Hollis walked around the table toward him. Cullen had a sudden odd sense he couldn't quite put a finger on, but when he opened his mouth to say something, his eyes met De-Marco's, and the other man shook his head very slightly.

Cullen looked back at Hollis just as she walked behind his partner's chair, turned abruptly, and placed her hands on either side of her head, just above her ears.

"Kirby," Hollis said softly

————

"FIVE TO NINE," Reese said softly. "The others should be in position."

"They'd better be," Hollis said, equally quiet. "He's vicious and single-minded. We have to throw him off his game, and fast. We won't get a better chance."

"Almost time."

She glanced at the unaccustomed watch on her left wrist and muttered, "Damn, I hope this thing keeps working. Just long enough, that's all I ask."

"It will. Besides, you're with me."

The plan had been more than a little difficult because there were only two entrances to the room, not counting three small windows, very high up, windows that would hardly allow the passage of a determined child. But they had planned carefully, and everyone, please God, understood exactly what to do, and they functioned perfectly as a team. Perfectly executing their plan.

By the numbers.

Hollis knew how much her team had trusted her to have followed her like this, and without a whole lot of explanation on her part. To ignore their own instincts to rush in when a helpless victim's life was at stake.

But they trusted her.

Hollis hoped to God she was right. Her team would never forgive her if she wasn't. And she would never, ever forgive herself.

She wondered, for the first time, if every team leader had these doubts.

If their unit chief had these doubts.

Reese nodded to her and began moving, not making a sound. On his heels, she was just as quiet, just as careful. Through the exterior door whose alarm he had disabled only minutes before. Into a stairwell. Moving so quickly but quietly, quietly, because the stairs were hardly designed to muffle sound.

All the way to the bottom.

Through another door, precious seconds required to disable its alarm. Into a quiet hallway that wasn't brightly lit, but wasn't dark either. Probably a place very few people would think of as fun to visit.

"If he sees us," Hollis breathed.

"He won't unless he's moved the table," Reese responded in a whisper. "The angle is wrong."

"God, I hope so." Hollis looked at the watch on her wrist and wasn't surprised it had stopped. That was, after all, the reason she and Reese were both taking this entrance. Because he had a clock in his head, and she could never carry or wear any kind of timepiece.

Especially now.

"Good thing I'm not looking for spirits," she whispered. As always when she was enclosed within Reese's shield, everything around her looked oddly . . . washed out. Gray.

Almost lifeless.

For the first time, she wondered if this was the way he saw the world when his shields were up. Surely not.

"No, it isn't," he whispered. "And we'll talk about it later."

"Right. Right." There was a lot, she thought fleet-ingly, that they would have to talk about later.

Reese really was a very patient man.

They were nearly at the double doors at the end of the hallway. The doors with frosted glass windows etched with a single word most people found chilling.

Morgue.

Tonight, though, it was even more chilling, because behind the doors, the frosted glass, the chilling word, the light was red. He must have brought his own lights with red bulbs, turning off the normal overhead fluores-cents.

They looked at each other, then separated, each tak-ing one side of the hallway. Hollis spared a few seconds to wonder how he'd been so certain of having this space all to himself tonight, but answered the question in her mind almost before she could ask herself.

Because he believed in his power. In the power he summoned. And because he thought he had all his bases covered.

From his side of the hallway, Reese had the best angle. As they reached the doors, he moved just far enough to peer inside. When he went utterly still, Hollis felt a surge of almost wild anxiety, but then, in her head . . .

It's okay. You were right. He's waiting for nine o'clock. Ten seconds now. Ready? Three . . . two . . . one—

She didn't even have a moment to think about this new and both amazing and unsettling thing between them, something she had heard telepaths refer to as "mind talk."

No time. They had to do this.

They pushed open the doors in the same second, both of them leveling their weapons—at a man neither of them had actually met until this moment.

He had covered the metal autopsy table with rich scarlet material, draped all the way to the floor. On the peculiar altar, she was bound and gagged, her brown eyes more furious than afraid, which was undoubtedly not the reaction he'd expected. But Hollis knew that Jill had known rescue was just a few feet away, she knew they were very good at what they did, and it was obvious to Hollis that one of the first things she'd ask them when they eventually freed her—as Hollis was utterly determined they would—would be what the hell had taken them so long.

The time she had spent with this monster, no matter how strong and spirited she was, must have been a kind of hell.

He stood over her, wearing a long black robe with a scarlet lining, both hands holding high, almost above his head, an ornate dagger that looked old, very old. Like the candlesticks he had placed at Dr. Jill Easton's head and feet.

There was room. She wasn't very big.

Black candles burned in each of the candlesticks.

Hollis kept her eyes on him. "Hey, there, Reverend Webb," she said softly. "If your congregation only knew."

For a man who prided himself on control, who prized it, the moment was not one he had probably ever envisioned. He looked startled, if only for a moment. He was an unusually big man, and powerful, and Hollis expected his voice to thunder because so often a preacher had that skill.

In his day job, at least.

"You didn't know," he said, in a voice that did indeed rumble. "You couldn't know. I made sure."

"You mean your little spell? Your incantation to Satan? While you were crouched on the roof of the Cross house Friday night? Drawing symbols, the pentagram and whatever else you've perverted to justify torture and murder, and cutting yourself or maybe . . . maybe sacrificing some poor bird."

His eyes flickered, and his mouth began to twitch.

"What, you didn't think we'd know? Didn't think we'd figure out sooner rather than later that in your twisted mind you had convinced yourself that Satan was speaking to you? That his voice was more powerful than God's—no matter what you preach on Sundays?"

"Don't blaspheme," he said, still holding the dagger above Jill, his hands steady.

Hollis didn't bother to point out the irony.

"I'm not doing that, *Reverend*. You are. You pervert ancient pagan rites, twisting and using the power of earth and nature to suit your needs, the needs you *know*, deep down inside, are more sick and evil than any normal human could ever understand. But even with all that, even with the trappings of an old religion you used or tried to use, actually, you're just another serial killer. With a more than usually creative explanation for why you enjoy killing people."

He smiled, and on his wide, pleasant face it was an ugly thing. "I tricked you, didn't I, witch?"

"Did you? Did you really?" She made her voice lightly mocking, and it had just the effect she expected.

His smile twisted, and the darker-than-normal eyes narrowed as they stared at her. "I did. I got inside your head. I found your weakness, witch. And my Higher Power gave me the strength to turn it against you."

"Yeah? So you—what? Slowed me down for forty-eight hours? I guess you didn't know that most serial-killer investigations take months, even years, to solve. Our unit tends to be faster, but . . . forty-eight hours may be a record. I'll have to look it up when I get back to Quantico."

His face was reddening, and the hands above Jill began to tremble. Hollis didn't have to look at the big clock on the wall to know that nine o'clock had already come and gone. And that, having missed the time he had set for himself, this monster would either give up, betraying the absolute weakness of his soul—or try to "sacrifice" Jill anyway, knowing he would be doing what he had forced poor Joe to do. Commit suicide by cop.

It would be the quickest and easiest way for him. Dying in a blaze of glory, at least in his own mind, and convinced his Higher Power had promised him a place of honor in the afterlife, at his Master's side.

Hollis also didn't bother to point out that what she and other SCU team members knew of true evil, and what the mediums knew of limbo and the afterlife, would have sent him fleeing in terror.

She was tempted. But she had already made up her mind how this would end.

And didn't have to shift her gaze to know that behind Webb the walk-in freezer door was slowly, silently opening. And that off to her right at the middle of the three small windows that were high up down in this space, but at ground level outside, there was yet another gun leveled at the monster.

They had every angle covered. And none of them was in danger of being caught in the crossfire.

"My Master—" he began.

"Your *Master* is no more supernatural than the tricks you tried to use on us. The tricks you used on poor Joe, and probably others in Clarity. The trick you tried to use on one of my team."

"She isn't— I don't see—"

"You don't see Kirby? You poor bastard. You had no idea she knew immediately when you tried to trick her mind. She might *look* innocent and childlike, and she may even pretend she's weaker than she is sometimes, even needing an arm for support. She may appear to you and others as just a girl, afraid of things she really doesn't fear at all. And you fell for it, hook, line, and sinker. She knew, and I knew—and we let you believe you'd succeeded. Just long enough for us to be able to track you here. To know you'd be *here*.

"Waiting for us. See, what you probably don't know, because you never got deep enough inside any of us to find out, is that we manipulate energy all the time. And we don't have to shed our blood—or sacrifice any other living thing—to do it. It's a perfectly normal human ability. You only know how to tap into that—barely. How to use it to control weak minds. Young minds. But all of us? We know a hell of a lot more than that. It's a sick and twisted game for you, but for us it's just another day's work."

"No. You don't—you can't—"

She ignored him, still mocking, sarcastic. "For instance, the electromagnetic impulses in your brain have already told me your real secret. Your real sickness."

He shook his head just a little, the hectic color beginning to drain from his face. "No. She— This bitch has to die. She killed my sister."

"No, she tried to save your sister. A car accident is what really killed . . . Sharon. Three years ago."

"Don't . . . You don't . . . don't say her name. You aren't fit to say her name!"

His voice really did thunder.

"She was your priestess, huh? You perverted even your own sister? There's a word for that, you know. An ugly word. When did you first climb into your sister's bed, Martin? When she was six? Seven? Did you begin tormenting her that young, twisting her mind as yours was twisted?

"She was your partner in all these fun, pretend-satanic things, for so many years. Taking the sexual abuse from you at first because you'd half convinced her you were right. And you loved her . . . *so* much. But she had doubts. And the doubts tore at her, more and more. Until she needed drugs to help her through a day—and a night. Until crawling into a whiskey bottle was the only way she could cope. Until she'd had enough, or drank enough to give her the courage and the desperation to cut the unnatural tie between you the only way she knew how. By driving her car over a cliff. And *that* is what killed your sister, Martin. You killed her. You destroyed her. She was just another victim of your sickness."

"No. She—this bitch—"

"Dr. Easton did everything in her power to save your sister when her broken body was airlifted to the hospital in Asheville. But Sharon was beyond help. *You* had done that to her."

He opened and closed his mouth several times, his eyes darting around the room, looking at her and the gun she held steadily, at Reese and the big silver handgun that fit him so well, and Martin Webb began to look very afraid.

But Hollis didn't stop.

"And, of course, you never told your wife about all those things. About what you did with and to Sharon for so many years, even during your marriage. About black robes and ancient artifacts you were convinced held dark power, artifacts you told your wife were just . . . religious objects. She believed you. She's a God-fearing preacher's wife. And your kids, those two cute little blond kids, they don't know what Daddy gets up to when he's away from home, do they?"

"I am all-powerful!" he roared.

Hollis was unimpressed and really didn't have to fake her contempt. "Yeah, yeah. You'd be surprised how often we hear bullshit like that. And usually just like this, from some very ordinary guy in a Halloween costume holding a funny knife, pretending to be an evil badass. So tell me. Didn't your Higher Power ever warn you never to bring a knife to a gunfight?"

Reverend Martin Webb let out what really sounded like an animal roar, and would have ended the life of Dr. Jill Easton then and there.

Hollis didn't hesitate even a split second, and neither did her team. Bullets slammed into the Reverend from all four of the feds, Kirby's shattering the glass window, revealing her lying prone on the ground just outside, Cullen's possibly a little cold from the freezer where he'd waited, probably a bit longer than he'd expected—and Reese's very accurately piercing the heart of the monster.

Hollis's shot got him right between his infinitely surprised eyes.

EIGHTEEN

"What the hell took you so long?" Jill demanded when Hollis removed the tape over her mouth.

Hollis grinned at her. "Sorry."

"Seriously," Jill Easton said earnestly, "I thought you were going to talk him to death. You should teach a course at Quantico in advanced sarcasm."

"Just trying to get a confession," Hollis replied solemnly.

Jill stared at her. "You caught him standing over me holding a knife he was about to plunge into my bound and gagged body. We both know you didn't need a confession. You just wanted to make him good and mad so you could justifiably shoot him."

"Who, me? That would make me a bad person."

DeMarco murmured, "Or just a good monster hunter."

"Dammit," Jill muttered as she maneuvered herself

into a sitting position after Cullen, who'd produced a pocketknife, cut the tape binding her to the table. Cullen looked rather frosted after his wait in the freezer but appeared none the worse for wear. He cut through the duct tape wrapped around Jill's wrists and ankles.

"There you go," he said.

"Thanks. I couldn't get any leverage. Thought he might blow before you got here, and had decided to do my best to at least try to roll off this damned table."

"That's a fairly long drop onto tile," Hollis said. "And with your wrists taped to the table like that, you probably would have broken an arm. Or both of them."

"Who's the doctor here?" Jill glared briefly, then looked down at herself. She was not wearing her customary casual clothing but an odd little Greek goddess–type draping of virtually see-through white material. And was clearly naked beneath it. She was suddenly and obviously self-conscious about the results.

Studiously keeping his eyes on her face, Cullen said, "Do you want me to get your real clothes?"

"He cut them off me. Ruined them. Threw them into one of the biohazard bins. And then dressed me in this absurd thing. After hitting me on the head. Dammit."

Hollis shrugged out of her light jacket and handed it to the other woman.

Jill lost no time in putting it on. "Thank you," she said.

"Don't mention it." Hollis kept a hand on Jill's shoulder for no more than a moment, and when she allowed her hand to fall, Jill lifted both eyebrows at her.

"Well, I knew you healed Reese after he was shot, nearly killing yourself in the process. But that was . . . really fast."

"No headache?"

"Not anymore. Thank you."

"Don't mention it," Hollis repeated.

Jill looked at the others with a frown. "Where's Sam? The message I got was to meet *him* here. Don't tell me—he's having room service at his hotel."

Mildly, Hollis said, "Actually, our monster here visited Sam before he sent you that message from Sam's phone. Don't worry—Sam's okay. He also got hit over the head, but just has a mild concussion. I've had them, so I think I can speak with authority there. Anyway, Mal got a tip just a few minutes ago that a guest of Solomon House had been left bound and gagged in his room. Possibly robbed."

"That actually happened?" Jill asked cautiously.

"Well, the bound and gagged part. And the concussion. I imagine Sam told them exactly who he admitted to his room, baffled but curious. And who hit him over the head." She looked thoughtful. "I think Mal decided to come straight here. You know, I wonder if he's a latent. He's picked up on a few things most nonpsychics just don't."

Before anyone could venture an answer to that, the double doors to the morgue burst open, and Kirby came in, gun holstered now, smiling but also with raised brows.

"Heads up," she warned them.

She had barely gotten inside when Sheriff Malachi

Gordon and two of his deputies also pushed their way in, their guns drawn.

"What the hell?" Mal demanded after one sweeping glance around the room. He saw DeMarco just holstering his big gun, and the other three feds, their weapons already holstered, regarding him calmly. Jill was sitting on the table, bare legs dangling, wearing an odd toga thing that was sheer as hell and probably showed a lot more than she wanted it to, which was why Hollis had clearly sacrificed her Windbreaker to a good cause.

"Hey, Mal," Hollis said cheerfully. "We had a little bit of a situation here. But all's under control now."

The sheriff came forward a few steps until he could see Reverend Martin Webb crumpled on the floor. His clothing, including the strange floor-length robe, was mostly black and so didn't immediately show signs of bullet holes.

The blood pooled around his body, some of it making its way to the drain under the table, was mute testimony to the fact that he had been shot more than once. And killed.

Normally careful with protocol with the feds, at least at the station and around his own deputies, Mal clearly didn't care about protocol or rules right now—which seemed to be going around.

"That's Preacher Webb," he told them in total confusion. "He's my pastor!"

"Funny how that happens sometimes," Hollis murmured.

"Wait—*he's* the unsub? But I thought Joe—"

"Joe was just a tool," DeMarco explained. "Webb liked to use tools. Especially weak or young minds."

"Young?"

Hollis said, "Yeah, you need to meet Sean Brenner. He's eight. And he's what caused Clara Adams to swerve her car—and then lose control. Well, sort of. Sean was playing with a toy in the middle of the street, and Clara swerved to avoid him. After that, the carefully sabotaged electrical system caused the accident."

Mal stared at her. "Eight?"

"He was one of Webb's tools," Hollis explained. "He really doesn't remember much but . . . there's some missing time. And he has the same automatic response Joe had to being asked if he was okay."

"Which is?"

"'I'm fine. I'm absolutely fine.'"

"Well, wouldn't he say—"

"Not an eight-year-old. Or, at least, not Sean. Anyway, I think he was practice as much as anything else. Face-to-face, Webb was a fair hand at a form of hypnosis." She didn't mention the more inexplicable "tricks" to attempt to control her or Kirby. That really wasn't a conversation she wanted to have with the sheriff.

And it wasn't necessary, after all.

Since it was obvious the sheriff needed time to process, Hollis said, "You know, I think maybe it'd be best if we—most of us, anyway—went back to the station to talk."

"I," Jill said definitely, "am not doing the post on this guy. And tonight I really, *really* want to take a couple of hot showers and drink some wine. Mal, I'll give you my statement later."

"But what about—" He gestured somewhat helplessly toward the body on the floor.

"My suggestion? Open the freezer door and seal off this room until you can get another ME here. I couldn't do the post officially anyway, since I was a potential victim." She glanced to either side, then slipped off the autopsy table. "I want to get away from these candlesticks too. I don't like them."

"Cursed," Mal offered rather absently.

"Yeah? Well, I'd say sell 'em to a museum. And don't handle them very much in the meantime. They sure don't need to belong to a preacher. Any preacher."

"Stolen. From a museum in France."

Jill eyed the sheriff, trying not to smile. "Well, in that case, I bet there's a finder's fee. And I'll bet it'll keep the Widow Webb and her kids in comfort, probably for the rest of their lives."

Hollis nodded. "Especially if she wants to sell the other artifacts he collected. I'm betting some were stolen, some bought legitimately, and most all will be worth a lot more to a museum or a collector than they will be to her."

"I'll have to make notification," Mal said. "Jesus, what am I supposed to tell her? This—all this—"

"Probably needs to stay inside this room," Hollis said. "Jill can talk to Sam, but I doubt he'll want to advertise that he got knocked out by a preacher. Even an evil one."

"Got that right," Jill said.

To the sheriff, Hollis said seriously, "Mal, I really don't think Clarity needs to deal with the fact that one of their pastors murdered people, including another pastor, and worshiped Satan on the side."

"I wouldn't even know how to start explaining that," he admitted.

"Look, I know it goes against the grain, but right now everybody believes Joe Cross was the killer. He doesn't have blood family here, nobody who might object or demand further investigation to learn more or to remove a stain from the family name. And from all we can tell he didn't even have many casual friends. His world was Perla. Everybody knew that. Everybody. And when she threatened to leave him again, this time for good, he . . . snapped."

Mal shifted uncomfortably, conscious of the two silent deputies behind him. "And the others? The . . . accidents?"

"They were . . . accidents. Horrible, and inexplicable, like so many bad things that happen in life. You called in FBI agents because you wanted to be sure, and they did what we call an equivocal death investigation and concluded that the first four deaths were just accidents. Nobody to blame, including the victims. And that they have no connection to what happened later to Perla Cross and Reverend Pilate, both murdered by Joe Cross, who couldn't bear to lose Perla when she wanted to leave him for good. And who maybe hated the Reverend Marcus Pilate for trivializing the death of his wife by wanting her personal things to sell to raise money for his church."

"But . . . how Pilate was left in his church . . ."

DeMarco shrugged. "Gossip has already added elaborate details to what was believed to be a strange and gruesome murder. Only law enforcement, Jill, and her assistant actually saw the body. You can close that case by announcing that Joe Cross killed him, and why—and how Cross was later killed by a federal agent. And why. We were on his land, at his home. And he had already snapped. He didn't think twice about shooting at federal agents." He shrugged again. "Nobody's going to question you, Mal. Especially when all of us give statements to verify that's what happened."

Mal gestured, this time silently, toward the late Reverend Webb.

Hollis shrugged. "As I see it, you have two viable options to explain this death. One: Reverend Webb, after confronting your temporary ME's assistant in his own hotel room, knocking him out, and leaving him bound and gagged, lured Jill here to kill her because he blamed her for the death of his sister three years ago in Asheville. There's plenty of documented evidence about Sharon Webb's death, and how upset her brother was at the time."

"I never even saw him," Jill murmured. "A whole team worked on her, and still we lost her. The chief of surgery is the one who notified her family. Him, Webb."

"But he blamed you, for whatever reason," Hollis said matter-of-factly. "People do irrational things in grief. And when you came here to help us investigate all the accidents, and then the murders, Webb lost it. He blamed you, and he wanted to kill you here, in exactly the sort of place where he had to identify his sister's body. She was carrying ID, but the police needed a family member to verify it was her. So that's where he saw her broken body. On a stainless steel table in a morgue. And that's what broke him. It just took three years for him to realize he was broken."

DeMarco pointed out quietly, "There won't be a trial. Whatever evidence was collected here won't be used, because this man was killed by four federal agents, the justified shootings witnessed by the medical examiner he was about to murder. The Bureau will want statements from all of us, and from Jill, but our unit chief will make sure it doesn't go any further than that."

After a long moment, Mal said, "Or?"

Hollis said, "Or . . . maybe the devil told one of your most respected pastors to kill some of his fellow citizens. Including another pastor. Brutally. Maybe he practiced Satanism, and sacrificed people because he was trying to summon unnatural power. Hell, maybe he was a member of a coven, and neighbor looks at neighbor, wondering, asking questions or, worse, not asking them."

Mal held up a hand to stop her. "No, you're right. A whiff of devil worship in Clarity, and this whole town could be destroyed."

Behind him, Deputy Brent Cannon, with a degree in criminal justice under his belt, said, "I don't see how justice could be served any other way, Mal. For the good of the town. And because, in the end, we'll be the only ones who know the truth. Pieces of the truth, at least."

Beside him, Deputy Ray Marx nodded, his own face as grave. And for the first time, Hollis realized these were the two detectives who had been with the sheriff and agents when Pilate's mutilated body had been found.

Deputy Cannon said, "I can live with that."

"I can live with it too," Deputy Marx agreed. "We say what we saw, what we know, and Clarity will never be the same. I want my kids to grow up in the Clarity I grew up in."

Mal had turned to listen to them, and their stolid support and understanding made the decision for him. "Okay." He turned back to the others. "Jill, as long as I have a statement from you and from Sam before you leave, we're good. I'll probably just ask one of our doctors here to do the autopsy on Webb. There isn't, after all, anything mysterious about his death.

"The rest of you, if you don't mind, go back to the station and write up your statements, give me whatever reports I need to have on hand of your findings. I'll follow a bit later—after Brent, Ray, and I get rid of that cloak thing, and everything else that makes this death look like . . . something it wasn't."

Hollis said, "Burn all the material, including the black candles. As for the candlesticks, they *are* valuable, and selling them can help provide for his family. But if I were you, I'd cover them with something and stuff them in that freezer until your expert, or whoever he recommends, can come fetch them."

Remembering the pentagram on the base of each

candlestick, Mal didn't argue. He merely said, "I had nightmares about those things last night. Happy to leave them here."

"Good idea," DeMarco murmured. "And you might want to very quietly look around Webb's home, when his wife and kids aren't there, just in case he kept other . . . tools . . . of a Satanist's beliefs."

"Oh, shit," Mal said.

CULLEN PUSHED THE legal pad in front of him farther away and yawned hugely. "'Scuse me. I don't know about the rest of you, but I am beat. I think I still have questions, but I'm too tired to remember them. Except one."

Hollis, expecting it, said, "Kirby."

"Well, yeah. Kirby—and you. Am I right in thinking that you and Kirby both managed to share information *and* hide it from a clairvoyant and a telepath?"

Kirby gave her partner an innocent look. "Look at this face. How could this face hide anything?" Then she grinned, and innocent suddenly looked more elfin and more than a little sly.

"Damn," he said, but not as if the revelation of a core of steel underneath Kirby's childlike exterior disturbed him.

In fact, Hollis thought it pleased him. And she had a hunch that theirs was a partnership that would last.

"I'm tired too," Kirby told the room at large, then looked at her partner. "I finished my statement. Anything else Mal needs, we can give him in the morning. Walk me to the hotel?"

Cullen sent the other two agents a glance but was already rising to his feet. "Sure. Will we be leaving early tomorrow?"

Hollis shook her head. "No real reason to. Unless you get a message to the contrary, just plan on checking out of the hotel at their standard time and coming back here to make sure Mal has everything he needs."

"Gotcha. Come on, partner."

When the door closed behind the two of them, Hollis looked down at the legal pad and frowned when she realized she'd been doodling. Her statement was written and had been torn from the pad minutes earlier.

She had "doodled" a rather comical sketch of Mal and his new canine buddy, Felix. The Yorkie was tucked inside his half-open jacket, peering out at the world from his perch with bright eyes.

"It's good," Reese said.

"Is it?"

"Yeah." Reese leaned forward and held out a stack of pages that had been piling up, without Hollis paying any attention, at his end of the table. "And so are these."

More than a little surprised, Hollis flipped through page after page of sketches she didn't even remember drawing. There were faces, buildings, mountain views. There were cattle and horses in distant pastures. There was a little girl with an ice cream cone bending down to the very attentive Sheltie at her feet. A man in a sports car leaned out the window to gesture to someone not shown, his exaggerated patience very evident.

"I don't even remember seeing half these things," Hollis said slowly, looking through the sketches again one by one. "And I certainly don't remember drawing them."

"You've been drawing pretty much every time we've been in this room. Not paying attention. Autopilot."

"What?"

"You were on autopilot," Reese said. "Beau Rafferty, Maggie Garrett's artist brother, says sometimes an artist's best work is done on autopilot. Because the artist gets out of his—or her—own way. Have you met him?"

"Yes." Hollis was still frowning. "Reese, I'm not an artist anymore."

"Aren't you?"

"This isn't— I haven't drawn anything in years."

"Not since the attack."

"No. Not since the attack."

"Until now."

Hollis dropped her gaze to the sketches, going through them again, more slowly this time. And it dawned on her only gradually as she looked at work she *knew* was very, very good that this was what had been stolen from her soul by the animal that had brutalized her and left her to die.

He had stolen her drive to create beauty.

If she had not been able to see again, then perhaps she would have grieved most that loss of sight. That inability to see the world as she had seen it, with an artist's clear, fascinated gaze. It had been, ironically, that drive to become a better artist that had prompted her move to Seattle. Where the monster had found her.

And destroyed that other Hollis.

Very quiet, still looking at the sketches, Hollis said, "In the back of my mind, or maybe buried deep with all the memories, there was a . . . fear . . . of even trying to sketch again."

"You were afraid you'd draw monsters. Violence."

She looked at Reese, into eyes she had known the first time they had met were sharp enough to probe far more deeply than some people would ever be able to bear. Maybe most people. But she knew she could.

"Yeah. I was afraid I'd draw . . . dark, horrible things. Things I had felt. Things I'd seen. The attack that took so much and left me psychic—and everything else I've seen in the years since. I didn't want to draw most of those things. That wasn't why I became an artist. I didn't want to create . . . ugly things."

Reese reached out and tapped the sketch closest to him, which happened to be the little girl with her ice cream and her dog. "There's nothing ugly here. There's nothing ugly in any of these. Do you know why?"

Hollis was afraid to ask—literally afraid.

"Because," Reese answered anyway, "there's nothing ugly in you."

"Monsters," she murmured.

"There are no monsters in you, Hollis. You've faced and fought so many of them since the first monster, the one who really did change your life. But no matter what you believed then, no matter what you've believed since, he didn't destroy what was most important to you. Your creativity. You've held it and protected it all these years. Kept it safe."

"I buried it," she realized slowly. "The way I buried the ugly things. The ugly memories. The ugly night-mares." She was reaching out a hand before she realized it, and watched, felt, as his fingers twined with hers. "But now . . ."

He was smiling, that faintly crooked smile that was rare, and all the more valuable because it was. "Now, like the memories and the nightmares, it's something you can accept. Because you're ready to let that happen. You're ready to find out how *this* Hollis, how the woman you've become, will tap into that creativity. Ready to find out what she can create . . . now."

"I'm still . . . a little bit afraid," she confessed.

"I know. But it'll pass. Look at what you could create when you weren't even trying, Hollis. Just imagine what you'll be able to create when you do."

Hollis felt herself smiling, even felt the fear almost melting away. "What I can create when I try."

Reese nodded. "You've fought monsters, Hollis. Not the storybook kind, but real evil. Fought and won. Fought and never let the evil stain your soul. *Of course* you can create beauty. You've always been able to, even when you didn't think so. You'll create beauty the way you create humor. The way you create spirit. The way you heal, and can see the colors of someone's feelings, and know things most artists will never know."

"I like the sound of that," she said.

"Good." His fingers tightened slightly, but before he could say anything else, a voice spoke dryly from the doorway.

"Don't let me interrupt."

Hollis turned her head slowly, not very surprised because she had known he was coming tonight, that he had been on his way almost from the moment the bullets had struck Reese.

"Bishop, your timing sucks," she told him.

"Really? It looks pretty good to me." He came into the room a few steps and reached over to place something in front of Hollis. "In fact, I'd say it was perfect."

It was a large sketch pad. And charcoal pencils.

Hollis looked at the gift, still smiling, then glanced at her partner before looking back at their unit chief.

"Thank you. Do me a favor?"

"Sure. What?"

"Stay out of my head. For good. There's someone else in there now." She was getting to her feet because Reese was getting to his, but she kept her gaze on Bishop. "You and Miranda can stop worrying about me now."

"Can we?"

"Yeah. I'm okay now. In fact, I've never been better in my life." With her free hand, she picked up the sketch pad and pencils, because she knew exactly what Reese was going to say.

"Bishop, Hollis and I are now officially taking our annual leave. Which neither of us has taken in years. We're going to find an island somewhere, or maybe a cave, where there's no cell service, and where even if you retask a satellite you won't be able to find us."

"Understood," Bishop murmured, smiling. "I'll expect you when I see you."

"Good. Give our regards to Sheriff Gordon, will you? And anybody else who notices we're gone." He didn't let go of her hand even when Hollis paused in the doorway to look back at their unit chief.

"Bishop?"

"Yeah?"

"Forty-eight hours?"

She didn't have to clarify the question. Bishop smiled slowly, something few people ever saw. "A new record for the unit," he confirmed.

She grinned at him. "Good. See you later, Bishop."

"Much later," DeMarco said, and led her from the room.

Bishop looked down at the remarkable sketches on the big table, and heard his wife's voice in his head, their mind talk one of his greatest joys, laughing now.

Told you so.

SPECIAL CRIMES UNIT AGENT BIOS

HOLLIS TEMPLETON—FBI SPECIAL CRIMES UNIT

Job: Special Agent, profiler.

Adept: Medium. Perhaps because of the extreme trauma of Hollis's psychic awakening (see *Touching Evil*) her abilities tend to evolve and change much more rapidly than those of many other agents and operatives. Even as she struggles to cope with her mediumistic abilities, each investigation in which she's involved seems to bring about another "fun new toy" for the agent, such as seeing auras, healing herself and others, and possessing the ability to sense, define, channel, and use sheer energy. She also consistently tests at the higher, more powerful end of the scale the SCU has developed to measure psychic abilities—with virtually every new ability gained.

Appearances: *Touching Evil, Sense of Evil, Blood Dreams, Blood Sins, Blood Ties, Haven, Hostage, Haunted, Wait for Dark*

REESE DEMARCO—FBI SPECIAL CRIMES UNIT

Job: Special Agent, pilot, military-trained sniper; has specialized in the past in deep-cover assignments, some long-term.

Adept: An "open" telepath, he is able to read a wide range of people. He possesses an apparently unique double shield, which sometimes contains the unusually high amount of sheer energy he produces. He also possesses something Bishop has dubbed a "primal ability": he always knows when a gun is pointed at or near him, or if other imminent danger threatens.

Appearances: *Blood Sins, Blood Ties, Haven, Hostage, Haunted, Wait for Dark*

NOAH BISHOP—FBI SPECIAL CRIMES UNIT

Job: Unit chief, profiler, pilot, sharpshooter; highly trained and skilled in several martial arts.

Adept: An exceptionally powerful touch-telepath, he also shares with his wife, Miranda, a strong precognitive ability, the deep emotional link between them making them, together, far exceed the limits of the scale developed by the FBI to measure psychic talents. Also possesses an "ancillary" ability of enhanced senses (hearing, sight, scent), which he has trained other agents to use as well, something they informally refer to as "spider senses." Whether present in the flesh or not, Bishop virtually always knows what's going on with his agents in the field, somehow maintaining what seem to be psychic links with almost all of his agents without in any way being intrusive.

Appearances: *Stealing Shadows, Hiding in the Shadows, Out of the Shadows, Touching Evil, Whisper of Evil, Sense of Evil, Hunting Fear, Chill of Fear, Sleeping with Fear, Blood Dreams, Blood Sins, Blood Ties, Haven, Hostage, Haunted, Fear the Dark, Wait for Dark*

KIRBY BELL—FBI SPECIAL CRIMES UNIT

Job: Special Agent.

Adept: Eighth-degree empath, which puts her at the more powerful end of the scale the SCU has developed to measure the strength of psychic abilities. But Kirby is young, her abilities largely untried in the field, and she can become overwhelmed by the emotions of the people around her. She also *looks* like a teenager, which is a bit of a trial to her since she always gets carded and no one ever believes she's a real FBI agent.

Appearances: *Wait for Dark*

CULLEN SHERIDAN—FBI SPECIAL CRIMES UNIT

Job: Special Agent.

Adept: Seventh-degree clairvoyant, which puts him also at the higher end of the scale of power. Unlike many of the newer agents, Cullen has very good control when he uses his abilities, as well as a solid shield, so he seldom gets blindsided with unwanted information. He does, however, suffer a common side effect many of the more powerful psychics share: occasional "wall-banging" headaches, especially when he's pushed himself and his abilities to their limits.

Appearances: *Wait for Dark*

MIRANDA BISHOP—FBI SPECIAL CRIMES UNIT

Job: Special Agent, investigator, profiler, black belt in karate, sharpshooter.

Adept: Touch-telepath, seer, remarkably powerful, and possesses unusual control, particularly in a highly developed shield capable of protecting herself psychically, a shield she's able to extend beyond herself to protect others. Shares abilities with her husband, due to their intense emotional connection, and together they far exceed the scale developed by the SCU to measure psychic abilities.

Appearances: *Out of the Shadows, Touching Evil, Whisper of Evil, Sense of Evil, Hunting Fear, Chill of Fear, Blood Dreams, Blood Sins, Blood Ties, Hostage, Haunted, Fear the Dark, Wait for Dark*

PSYCHIC TERMS AND ABILITIES

(As Classified/Defined
by Bishop's Special Crimes Unit and by Haven)

Absolute Empath: The rarest of all abilities. An absolute empath can literally absorb the pain of another, to the point that she physically takes on the same injuries, healing the injured person and then healing herself.

Adept: The general term used to label any functional psychic; the specific ability is much more specialized.

Clairvoyance: The ability to know things, to pick up bits of information, seemingly out of thin air.

Dream-projecting: The ability to enter another's dreams.

Dream-walking: The ability to invite/draw others into one's own dreams.

Empath: A person who experiences the emotions of others, often up to and including physical pain and injuries.

Healing: The ability to heal injuries to self or others, often but not always ancillary to mediumistic abilities.

Healing Empathy: The ability to not only feel but also heal the pain/injury of another. It can be extremely dangerous for the healing empath, depending on how serious the pain or injury they attempt to heal, since it always depletes their own life energy.

Latent: The term used to describe unawakened or inactive abilities, as well as to describe a psychic not yet aware of being psychic.

Mediumistic: Having the ability to communicate with the dead; some see the dead, some hear the dead, but most mediums in the unit are able to do both.

Precognition: The ability to correctly predict future events. The SCU differentiates between predictions and prophesies: A prediction can sometimes be changed, even avoided, but a prophesy will happen no matter what anyone does to try to change the outcome.

Psychometric: The term used to describe the ability to pick up impressions or information from touching objects.

Regenerative: The term used to describe the ability to heal one's own injuries/illnesses, even those considered by medical experts to be lethal or fatal. (A classification unique to one SCU operative and considered separate from a healer's abilities.)

Spider Sense: The ability to enhance one's normal senses (sight, hearing, smell, etc.) through concentration and the focusing of one's own mental and physical energy.

Telekinesis: The ability to move objects with the mind. A very rare ability.

Telepathic mind control: The ability to influence/control others through mental focus and effort; an *extremely* rare ability.

Telepathy (touch and non-touch or open): The ability to pick up thoughts from others. Some telepaths only receive, while others have the ability to send thoughts. A few are capable of both, usually due to an emotional connection with the other person.

UNNAMED ABILITIES:

The ability to see into time, to view events in the past, present, and future without being or having been there physically while the events transpired. Another rare ability, it seems to be a combination of clairvoyance, precognition, and, sometimes, mediumistic traits, though the ability is so rare it hasn't been studied in depth.

The ability to see the aura or another person's energy field, and to interpret those colors and energies.

   White = healing
   Blue/lavenders = calm
   Red/rich yellows = energy/power

Green = unusual, tends to mix with other colors,
   peaceful

Metallic = repelling energy from another source

Black = extremely negative, even evil, especially if it
   has red streaks of energy and power

More than one color in an aura is common, reflecting the outward sign of human complexities of emotion.

The ability to absorb and/or channel energy usefully as a defensive or offensive tool or weapon. Extremely rare due to the level of power and control needed, and highly dangerous, especially if the energy being channeled is dark or negative energy.

AUTHOR'S NOTE

The first books in the Bishop/SCU series were published back in 2000, and readers have asked me whether these stories are taking place in "real" time and if, at this point, more than sixteen years have passed in the series. The answer is no. I chose to use "story time" in order to avoid having my characters age too quickly. Roughly speaking, each trilogy takes place within the same year, with some overlaps.

So, from an arbitrary start date, the timeline looks something like this:

Stealing Shadows—February

Hiding in the Shadows—October/November

YEAR ONE:

Out of the Shadows—January (SCU formally introduced)

Touching Evil—November

YEAR TWO:

Whisper of Evil—March

Sense of Evil—June

Hunting Fear—September

YEAR THREE:

Chill of Fear—April

Sleeping with Fear—July

Blood Dreams—October

YEAR FOUR:

Blood Sins—January

Blood Ties—April

Haven—July

Hostage—October

YEAR FIVE:

Haunted—February

Fear the Dark—May

Wait for Dark—August

So, with the publication of *Wait for Dark*, the Special Crimes Unit has been a functional (and growing) unit of agents for about five years: time to have grown from being known within the FBI as the "Spooky Crimes Unit" to becoming a well-respected unit with an excellent record of solved cases— a unit that has, moreover, earned respect in various law enforcement agencies, with word quietly passed from this sheriff to that chief of police that they excel at solving crimes that are anything but normal using methods and abilities that are unique to each agent, and that they neither seek nor want media attention.

An asset to any level of law enforcement, they do their jobs with little fanfare and never ride roughshod over locals, both traits very much appreciated, especially by small-town cops and citizens wary of outsiders. They regard both skepticism and interest with equal calm, treating their abilities as merely tools with which to do their jobs, and their very matter-of-factness helps normally hard-nosed cops accept, if not understand, at least something of the paranormal.

Olivia Castle had experienced some monster headaches in her time, but this one, she felt sure, was about to make her head quite literally explode. It had come out of nowhere, as if something had just yanked her head into an invisible, tightening vise without warning. A vise with teeth. In pain, queasy, and shaking, she managed to lever herself up from the couch, holding one hand against the head she was sure was about to fall off, and hardly spared a moment to wonder why she'd been on the couch.

Work. She should have been at work.

Shouldn't she be at work?

Had she come home for lunch? She didn't remember.

Her head hurt too much to keep thinking about that.

She made it to the kitchen by holding on to various pieces of furniture as she passed, fighting nausea and accidentally grabbing Rex's tail when she gripped the edge of the sink.

"*Waaaurr!*"

"Sorry, sorry," she muttered, the headache so bad by then that her cat's cry sounded like a dozen angry crows, her own quiet voice sounded like booming thunder in her head, and even her vision was affected in some way she didn't understand; she couldn't see the pleasant Vermont view normally visible from this window. She couldn't see any real view at all.

She was seeing colors she was reasonably sure didn't exist in nature. Or anywhere else, for that matter. Moving, swirling, like colorful smoke driven by a capricious breeze, opaque and translucent by turn. And everything was so damned *bright*. "Shouldn't sit on the counter. How many times have I told you? Didn't see you, pal. Oh, *damn*, what is going on?"

There was a large economy-sized bottle of an OTC painkiller near the sink (just as there was one in just about every room of her small house, and in her purse, with a box of extra bottles in the storage closet, in case the zombie apocalypse came without warning and all the pharmacies got looted before she could get to them). Olivia closed her eyes against the unnatural brightness, fumbling the bottle open while bitterly cursing childproof caps foisted upon people who had no children, fumbled just as blindly for a glass and the faucet, and managed, finally, to swallow about eight pills, hoping she could keep them down long enough to do some good.

"*Prrupp,*" Rex said.

"I know it's too many, you don't have to tell me that." She stood there, eyes still closed, still hanging on to the edge of the sink with one hand and her head with the other, trying to breathe normally despite the pain keeping all her muscles rigid and snatching at her ability to breathe at all, her stomach churning, the weird colors still swirling even though her eyes were closed, wishing pain meds took effect faster. Like immediately. It would have been nice, she thought, to just take a shot of morphine and become unconscious for the duration. But she'd discovered the hard way that both the law and doctors frowned on patients self-medicating, far less walking out the door of any hospital, clinic, or pharmacy with their own supply of morphine or any other industrial-strength painkiller. And besides, they said it was only migraines.

Only migraines. *Only migraines. Jesus.* Even though no migraine remedy known to medical science and quite a few exotic possibilities Olivia had experimented with herself had so much as touched her periodic killer headaches.

She fumbled blindly for the bottle again.

"Waaauurr!"

"All right, all right. I know there hasn't been enough time. But if the pain doesn't stop soon, I'm gonna take more. *Shit.*"

A moment later, Rex hissed.

Olivia managed to pry her eyes open no matter how much the ungodly brightness all around her hurt, and squinted at her cat in surprise. Because Rex didn't hiss, or at least never had. But as she focused on her rather odd-looking cat, his brindle/tortie coat at odds with the brilliant blue eyes of a Siamese, she realized even through the bright, swirling colors she was still seeing that Rex was scared.

Really scared.

And Rex didn't scare easily. Or . . . at all.

He was staring past her into the space behind her, the kitchen and den, and his pupils were so narrow that his eyes looked incredibly creepy, like the unnaturally blue eyes of a snake. The fur along his back was standing straight up, and his tail was about three times its natural size.

At the same time, Olivia began hearing a strange rustling sound. At first it sounded like dry leaves skittering along pavement, which was weird enough to hear inside her house with no pavement around. But then she realized it was . . . whispering. Lots of voices. Lots and lots of voices. Whispering.

It was coming from behind her.

Olivia did *not* want to turn around. Her mouth was dry despite the nausea, her skin was crawling unpleasantly, the pain in her head was getting impossibly worse rather than better, and she was afraid if she turned to confront an axe murderer, she'd beg him to just cut off her head and be quick about it.

Axe murderer. Idiot.

Not an axe murderer, of course. Not anyone.

Not any one . . . thing. Because she heard more than one whisper, many whispers, countless whispers. And she didn't know what they were saying, but she had the eerie feeling they were all whispering the same thing. The same words.

Still holding the edge of the sink with one hand, Olivia turned slowly to see what so frightened her cat and was making her own skin crawl in a sensation she'd never felt before.

"Oh, shit," she whispered.

The headache that was still hellishly painful didn't seem such a big deal now. Because despite all the swirling colors nearly blinding her, she could see, very clearly, why Rex was afraid. Every sharp object in her kitchen and den—every single one from every kitchen knife and fork she owned to three letter openers, two pairs of scissors, two box cutters with razor blades visible, the iron fireplace poker, and half a dozen pens and twice that many sharpened pencils—floated in midair. Different levels, some low, some as high as eye level.

With their pointy ends aimed right at her.

And they were all whispering.

"*Waaurr,*" Rex muttered, his voice unusually quiet, questioning.

"I'm not doing it. I'd know if I were doing it, right? I always know. I have to concentrate to do it. I mean, unless I'm mad. Angry, not crazy. Though maybe crazy too. Because this has never . . . And, anyway, even if I'm mad, I don't . . . know how . . . to make anything . . . whisper."

Or how to stop it when she instinctively tried, an effort that was definitely not rewarded.

Unconsciously, both her hands lifted to her head, pressing as if to hold something in, because the headache suddenly grew horribly worse, impossibly worse, dragging a guttural groan from somewhere deep inside her, and through the bright swirl of colors that was beginning to truly blind her, she could still see all the scary-sharp weapons floating inexorably toward her.

Whispering.

What was whispering? Inanimate objects couldn't communicate, right? Not like this, at least.

The pain edged into agony, but even so she heard as if from a great distance her own shaking, pleading question.

"What? What are you saying? What do you want of me?"

And from the same great distance, she heard the whispered demand that made no sense to her.

Prosperity. Go to Prosperity.

They were still floating eerily toward her, all the pointy things that promised even more pain if they came much closer, and hard as she tried, Olivia couldn't do anything about it, couldn't stop it, couldn't see anything but them or hear anything except for that whispered demand.

Go to Prosperity.

Go to Prosperity.

Olivia heard one last thing: A moan of agony escaped her, and then everything went black.

Ready to find
your next great read?

Let us help.

Visit prh.com/nextread

Penguin
Random
House